ACCLAIM FOR Haruki Murakami

"[*A Wild Sheep Chase* is] a bold new advance in international fiction. . . . Youthful, slangy, political, and allegorical."

—*The New York Times*

"Murakami's writing injects the rock 'n' roll of everyday language into the exquisite silences of Japanese literary prose."

—*Harper's Bazaar*

"[Murakami belongs] in the topmost rank of writers of international stature."

—*Newsday*

"Greatly entertaining. . . . Will remind readers of the first time they read Tom Robbins or . . . Thomas Pynchon."

—*Chicago Tribune*

"Murakami captures a kind of isolation that is special in its beauty, and particular to our time. . . . His language speaks so directly to the mind that one remembers with gratitude what words are for."

—*Elle*

"[*A Wild Sheep Chase*] begins as a detective novel, dips before long into screwball comedy, and at its close—when the dead speak—becomes a tale of possession. That such unruly, disjunctive elements mingle harmoniously within it is perhaps the signal feat in this highly accomplished piece of craftsmanship."

—Brad Leithauser, *The New Yorker*

"A world-class writer who has both eyes open and takes big risks. . . . If Murakami is the voice of a generation, then it is the generation of Thomas Pynchon and Don DeLillo."

—*The Washington Post Book World*

Haruki Murakami

A WILD SHEEP CHASE

Haruki Murakami was born in Kyoto in 1949 and now lives near Tokyo. His work has been translated into thirty-eight languages, and the most recent of his many honors is the Yomiuri Literary Prize, whose previous recipients include Yukio Mishima, Kenzaburo Oe, and Kobo Abe.

INTERNATIONAL

BOOKS BY Haruki Murakami

Fiction

Blind Willow, Sleeping Woman

Kafka on the Shore

After the Quake

Dance Dance Dance

The Elephant Vanishes

Hard-Boiled Wonderland and the End of the World

Norwegian Wood

South of the Border, West of the Sun

Sputnik Sweetheart

Vintage Murakami

A Wild Sheep Chase

The Wind-Up Bird Chronicle

Nonfiction

Underground: The Tokyo Gas Attack and the Japanese Psyche

A WILD SHEEP CHASE

A WILD SHEEP CHASE

Haruki Murakami

Translated from the Japanese by

Alfred Birnbaum

VINTAGE INTERNATIONAL

Vintage Books

A Division of Random House, Inc.

New York

FIRST VINTAGE INTERNATIONAL EDITION, APRIL 2002

Published in the United States by Vintage Books, a division of Random House, Inc., New York. Originally published in Japanese under the title *Hitsuji o meguru bōken,* by Kodansha Ltd., Tokyo, in 1982. This translation first published in the United States by Kodansha International Ltd., New York, in 1989.

Library of Congress Cataloging-in-Publication Data
Murakami, Haruki, 1949–
[Hitsuji o meguru bōken, English]
A wild sheep chase : a novel by Haruki Murakami ;
translated by Alfred Birnbaum.
p. cm.
ISBN 0-375-71894-X (trade paper)
I. Birnbaum, Alfred. II. Title.
PL856.U673 H5713 2002
895.6'35—dc21
2001045516

www.vintagebooks.com

Printed in the United States of America
20 19 18 17 16 15 14 13

Part One

November 25, 1970

1

Wednesday Afternoon Picnic

It was a short one-paragraph item in the morning edition. A friend rang me up and read it to me. Nothing special. Something a rookie reporter fresh out of college might've written for practice.

The date, a street corner, a person driving a truck, a pedestrian, a casualty, an investigation of possible negligence.

Sounded like one of those poems on the inner flap of a magazine.

"Where's the funeral?" I asked.

"You got me," he said. "Did she even have family?"

Of course she had a family.

I called the police department to track down her family's address and telephone number, after which I gave them a call to get details of the funeral.

Her family lived in an old quarter of Tokyo. I got out my map and marked the block in red. There were subway and train and bus lines everywhere, overlapping like some misshapen spiderweb, the whole area a maze of narrow streets and drainage canals.

The day of the funeral, I took a streetcar from Waseda. I got off near the end of the line. The map proved about as helpful as a globe would have been. I ended up buying pack after pack of cigarettes, asking directions each time.

It was a wood-frame house with a brown board fence around it. A small yard, with an abandoned ceramic brazier filled with standing rainwater. The ground was dark and damp.

She'd left home when she was sixteen. Which may have been the reason why the funeral was so somber. Only family present, nearly everyone older. It was presided over by her older brother, barely thirty, or maybe it was her brother-in-law.

Her father, a shortish man in his mid-fifties, wore a black armband of mourning. He stood by the entrance and scarcely moved. Reminded me of a street washed clean after a downpour.

On leaving, I lowered my head in silence, and he lowered his head in return, without a word.

I met her in autumn nine years ago, when I was twenty and she was seventeen.

There was a small coffee shop near the university where I hung out with friends. It wasn't much of anything, but it offered certain constants: hard rock and bad coffee.

She'd always be sitting in the same spot, elbows planted on the table, reading. With her glasses—which resembled orthodontia—and skinny hands, she seemed somehow endearing. Always her coffee would be cold, always her ashtray full of cigarette butts.

The only thing that changed was the book. One time it'd be Mickey Spillane, another time Kenzaburo Oe, another time Allen Ginsberg. Didn't matter what it was, as long as it was a book. The students who drifted in and out of the place would lend her books, and she'd read them clean through, cover to cover. Devour them, like so many ears of corn. In those days, people lent out books as a matter of course, so she never wanted for anything to read.

Those were the days of the Doors, the Stones, the Byrds, Deep Purple, and the Moody Blues. The air was alive, even as everything seemed poised on the verge of collapse, waiting for a push.

She and I would trade books, talk endlessly, drink cheap whiskey, engage in unremarkable sex. You know, the stuff of everyday. Meanwhile, the curtain was creaking down on the shambles of the sixties.

I forget her name.

I could pull out the obituary, but what difference would it make now. I've forgotten her name.

Suppose I meet up with old friends and mid-swing the conversation turns to her. No one ever remembers her name either. Say, back then there was this girl who'd sleep with anyone, you know, what's-her-face, the name escapes me, but I slept with her lots of times, wonder what she's doing now, be funny to run into her on the street.

"Back then, there was this girl who'd sleep with anyone." That's her name.

Of course, strictly speaking, she didn't sleep with just anyone. She had standards.

Still, the fact of the matter is, as any cursory examination of the evidence would suffice to show, that she was quite willing to sleep with almost any guy.

Once, and only once, I asked her about these standards of hers.

"Well, if you must know . . . ," she began. A pensive thirty seconds went by. "It's not like anybody will do. Sometimes the whole idea turns me off. But you know, maybe I want to find out about a lot of different people. Or maybe that's how my world comes together for me."

"By sleeping with someone?"

"Uh-huh."

It was my turn to think things over.

"So tell me, has it helped you make sense of things?"

"A little," she said.

From the winter through the summer I hardly saw her. The university was blockaded and shut down on several occasions, and in any case, I was going through some personal problems of my own.

When I visited the coffee shop again the next autumn, the clientele had completely changed, and she was the only face I recognized. Hard rock was playing as before, but the excitement in the air had vanished. Only she and the bad coffee were the same. I plunked down in the chair opposite her, and we talked about the old crowd.

Most of the guys had dropped out, one had committed suicide, one had buried his tracks. Talk like that.

"What've you been up to this past year?" she asked me.

"Different things," I said.

"Wiser for it?"

"A little."

That night, I slept with her for the first time.

About her background I know almost nothing. What I do know, someone may have told me; maybe it was she herself when we were in bed together. Her first year of high school she had a big falling out with her father and flew the coop (and high school too). I'm pretty sure that's the story. Exactly where she lived, what she did to get by, nobody knew.

She would sit in some rock-music café all day long, drink cup after cup of coffee, chain-smoke, and leaf through books, waiting for someone to come along to foot her coffee and cigarette bills (no mean sum for us types in those days), then typically end up sleeping with the guy.

There. That's everything I know about her.

From the autumn of that year on into the spring of the next, once a week on Tuesday nights, she'd drop in at my apartment outside Mitaka. She'd put away whatever simple dinner I cooked, fill my ashtrays, and have sex with me with the radio tuned full blast to an FEN rock program. Waking up Wednesday mornings, we'd go for a walk through the woods to the ICU campus and have lunch in the dining hall. In the afternoon, we'd have a weak cup of coffee in the student lounge, and if the weather was good, we'd stretch out on the grass and gaze up at the sky.

Our Wednesday afternoon picnic, she called it.

"Everytime we come here, I feel like we're on a picnic."

"Really? A picnic?"

"Well, the grounds go on and on, everyone looks so happy . . ."

She sat up and fumbled through a few matches before lighting a cigarette.

"The sun climbs high in the sky, then starts down. People come, then go. The time breezes by. That's like a picnic, isn't it?"

I was twenty-one at the time, about to turn twenty-two. No prospect of graduating soon, and yet no reason to quit school. Caught in the most curiously depressing circumstances. For months I'd been stuck, unable to take one step in any new direction. The world kept moving on; I alone was at a standstill. In the autumn, everything took on a desolate cast, the colors swiftly fading before my eyes. The sunlight, the smell of the grass, the faintest patter of rain, everything got on my nerves.

How many times did I dream of catching a train at night? Always the same dream. A nightliner stuffy with cigarette smoke and toilet stink. So crowded there was hardly standing room. The seats all caked with vomit. It was all I could do to get up and leave the train at the station. But it was not a station at all. Only an open field, with not a house light anywhere. No stationmaster, no clock, no timetable, no nothing—so went the dream.

I still remember that eerie afternoon. The twenty-fifth of November. Gingko leaves brought down by heavy rains had turned the footpaths into dry riverbeds of gold. She and I were out for a walk, hands in our pockets. Not a sound to be heard except for the crunch of the leaves under our feet and the piercing cries of the birds.

"Just what is it you're brooding over?" she blurted out all of a sudden.

"Nothing really," I said.

She kept walking a bit before sitting down by the side of the path and taking a drag on her cigarette.

"You always have bad dreams?"

"I *often* have bad dreams. Generally, trauma about vending machines eating my change."

She laughed and put her hand on my knee, but then took it away again.

"You don't want to talk about it, do you?"

"Not today. I'm having trouble talking."

She flicked her half-smoked cigarette to the dirt and carefully ground it out with her shoe. "You can't bring yourself to say what you'd really like to say, isn't that what you mean?"

"I don't know," I said.

Two birds flew off from nearby and were swallowed up into the cloudless sky. We watched them until they were out of sight. Then she began drawing indecipherable patterns in the dirt with a twig.

"Sometimes I get real lonely sleeping with you."

"I'm sorry I make you feel that way," I said.

"It's not your fault. It's not like you're thinking of some other girl when we're having sex. What difference would that make anyway? It's just that—" She stopped mid-sentence and slowly drew three straight lines on the ground. "Oh, I don't know."

"You know, I never meant to shut you out," I broke in after a moment. "I don't understand what gets into me. I'm trying my damnedest to figure it out. I don't want to blow things out of proportion, but I don't want to pretend they're not there. It takes time."

"How much time?"

"Who knows? Maybe a year, maybe ten."

She tossed the twig to the ground and stood up, brushing the dry bits of grass from her coat. "Ten years? C'mon, isn't that like forever?"

"Maybe," I said.

We walked through the woods to the ICU campus, sat down in the student lounge, and munched on hot dogs. It was two in the afternoon, and Yukio Mishima's picture kept flashing on the lounge TV. The volume control was broken so we could hardly make out what was being said, but it didn't matter to us one way or the other. A student got up on a chair and tried fooling with the volume, but eventually he gave up and wandered off.

"I want you," I said.

"Okay," she said.

So we thrust our hands back into our coat pockets and slowly walked back to the apartment.

I woke up to find her sobbing softly, her slender body trembling under the covers. I turned on the heater and checked the clock. Two in the morning. A startlingly white moon shone in the middle of the sky.

I waited for her to stop crying before putting the kettle on for tea. One teabag for the both of us. No sugar, no lemon, just plain hot tea. Then lighting up two cigarettes, I handed one to her. She inhaled and spat out the smoke, three times in rapid succession, before she broke down coughing.

"Tell me, have you ever thought of killing me?" she asked.

"You?"

"Yeah."

"Why're you asking me such a thing?"

Her cigarette still at her lips, she rubbed her eyelid with her fingertip.

"No special reason."

"No, never," I said.

"Honest?"

"Honest. Why would I want to kill you?"

"Oh, I guess you're right," she said. "I thought for a second there that maybe it wouldn't be so bad to get murdered by someone. Like when I'm sound asleep."

"I'm afraid I'm not the killer type."

"Oh?"

"As far as I know."

She laughed. She put her cigarette out, drank down the rest of her tea, then lit up again.

"I'm going to live to be twenty-five," she said, "then die."

July, eight years later, she was dead at twenty-six.

Part Two

July, Eight Years Later

2

Sixteen Steps

I waited for the compressed-air hiss of the elevator doors shutting behind me before closing my eyes. Then, gathering up the pieces of my mind, I started off on the sixteen steps down the hall to my apartment door. Eyes closed, exactly sixteen steps. No more, no less. My head blank from the whiskey, my mouth reeking from cigarettes.

Drunk as I get, I can walk those sixteen steps straight as a ruled line. The fruit of many years of pointless self-discipline. Whenever drunk, I'd throw back my shoulders, straighten my spine, hold my head up, and draw a deep lungful of the cool morning air in the concrete hallway. Then I'd close my eyes and walk sixteen steps straight through the whiskey fog.

Within the bounds of that sixteen-step world, I bear the title of "Most Courteous of Drunks." A simple achievement. One has only to accept the fact of being drunk at face value.

No ifs, ands, or buts. Only the statement "I am drunk," plain and simple.

That's all it takes for me to become the Most Courteous Drunk. The Earliest to Rise, the Last Boxcar over the Bridge.

Five, six, seven, . . .

Stopping on the eighth step, I opened my eyes and took a deep breath. A slight humming in my ears. Like a sea breeze whistling through a rusty wire screen. Come to think of it, when was the last time I was at the beach?

Let's see. July 24, 6:30 A.M. Ideal time of year for the beach, ideal time of day. The beach still unspoiled by people. Seabird tracks scattered about the surf's edge like pine needles after a brisk wind.

The beach, hmm . . .

I began walking again. Forget the beach. All that's ages past.

On the sixteenth step, I halted, opened my eyes, and found myself planted square in front of my doorknob, as always. Taking two days' worth of newspapers and two envelopes from the mailbox, I tucked the lot under my arm. Then I fished my keys out of the recesses of my pocket and leaned forward, forehead against the icy iron door. From somewhere behind my ears, a click. Me, a wad of cotton soaked through with alcohol. With only a modicum of control of my senses.

Just great.

The door maybe one-third open, I slid my body in, shutting the door behind me. The entryway was dead silent. More silent than it ought to be.

That's when I noticed the red pumps at my feet. Red pumps I've seen before. Parked in between my mud-caked tennis shoes and a pair of cheap beach sandals, like some out-of-season Christmas present. A silence hovered about them, fine as dust.

She was slumped over the kitchen table, forehead on her arms, profile hidden by straight black hair. A patch of untanned white neckline showed between the strands of hair, through the open sleeve of her print dress—one I'd never seen before—a glimpse of a brassiere strap.

I removed my jacket, undid my black tie, took off my watch, with not a flinch from her the whole while. Looking at her back called up memories. Memories of times before I'd met her.

"Well then," I spoke up in a voice not quite my own, the sound piped in.

As expected, there was no reply. She could have been asleep, could have been crying, could have been dead.

I sat down opposite her and rubbed my eyes. A short ray of sunlight divided the table, me in light, her in shadow. Colorless shadow. A withered potted geranium sat on the table. Outside, someone was watering down the street. Splash on the pavement, smell of wet asphalt.

"Want some coffee?"

No reply.

So I got up and went over to grind coffee for two cups. It occurred to me after I ground the coffee that what I really wanted was ice tea. I'm forever realizing things too late.

The transistor radio played a succession of innocuous pop songs. A perfect morning sound track. The world had barely changed in ten years. Only the singers and song titles. And my age.

The water came to a boil. I shut off the gas, let the water cool thirty seconds, poured it over the coffee. The grounds absorbed all they could and slowly swelled, filling the room with aroma.

"Been here since last night?" I asked, kettle in hand.

An ever so slight nod of her head.

"You've been waiting all this time?"

No answer.

The room had steamed up from the boiling water and strong sun. I shut the window and switched on the air conditioner, then set the two mugs of coffee on the table.

"Drink," I said, reclaiming my own voice.

Silence.

"Be better if you drank something."

It was thirty seconds before she raised her head slowly, evenly, and gazed absently at the potted plant. A few fine strands of hair lay plastered against her dampened cheeks, an aura of wetness about her.

"Don't mind me," she said. "I didn't mean to cry."

I held out a box of tissues to her. She quietly blew her nose, then brushed the hair from her cheek.

"Actually, I planned on being gone by the time you returned. I didn't want to see you."

"But you changed your mind, I see."

"Not at all. I didn't have anywhere else I wanted to go. But I'm going now, don't worry."

"Well, have some coffee anyway."

I tuned in to the radio traffic report as I sipped my coffee and slit open the two pieces of mail. One was an announcement from a furniture store where everything was twenty percent off. The second was a letter from someone I didn't want to think about, much less read a letter from. I crumpled them up and tossed them into the wastebasket, then nibbled on leftover cheese crackers. She cupped her hands around the coffee cup as if to warm herself and fixed her eyes on me, her lip lightly riding the rim of the mug.

"There's salad in the fridge," she said.

"Salad?"

"Tomatoes and string beans. There wasn't anything else. The cucumbers had gone bad, so I threw them out."

"Oh."

I went to the refrigerator and took out the blue Okinawa glass salad bowl and sprinkled on the last drops from the bottle of dressing. The tomatoes and string beans were but chilled shadows. Tasteless shadows. Nor was there any taste to the coffee or crackers. Maybe because of the morning sun? The light of morning decomposes everything. I gave up on the coffee midway, dug a bent cigarette out of my pocket, and lit up with matches that I'd never seen before. The tip of the cigarette crackled dryly as its lavender smoke formed a tracery in the morning light.

"I went to a funeral. When it was over, I went to Shinjuku, by myself."

The cat appeared out of nowhere, yawned at length, then sprang into her lap. She scratched him behind the ears.

"You don't need to explain anything to me," she said. "I'm out of the picture already."

"I'm not explaining. I'm just making conversation."

She shrugged and pushed her brassiere strap back inside her dress. Her face had no expression, like a photograph of a sunken city on the ocean floor.

"An acquaintance of sorts from years back. No one you knew."

"Oh really?"

The cat gave his legs a good stretch, topped it off with a puff of a breath.

I glanced at the burning tip of the cigarette in my mouth.

"How did this acquaintance die?"

"Hit by a truck. Thirteen bones fractured."

"Female?"

"Uh-huh."

The seven o'clock news and traffic report came to an end, and light rock returned to the airwaves. She set her coffee back down and looked me in the face.

"Tell me, if I died, would you go out drinking like that?"

"The funeral had nothing to do with my drinking. Only the first one or two rounds, if that."

A new day was beginning. Another hot one. A cluster of skyscrapers glared through the window.

"How about something cool to drink?"

She shook her head.

I got a can of cola out of the refrigerator and downed it in one go.

"She was the kind of girl who'd sleep with anyone." What an obituary: the deceased was the kind of girl who would sleep with anyone.

"Why are you telling me this?"

Why indeed? I had no idea.

"Very well," she picked up where I trailed off, "she was the kind of girl who'd sleep with anyone, right?"

"Right."

"But not with you, right?"

There was an edge to her voice. I glanced up from the salad bowl.

"You think not?"

"Somehow, no," she said quietly. "You, you're not the type."

"What type?"

"I don't know, there's something about you. Say there's an hourglass: the sand's about to run out. Someone like you can always be counted on to turn the thing over."

"That so?"

She pursed her lips, then relaxed.

"I came to get the rest of my things. My winter coat, hats, things I left behind. I packed them up in boxes. When you have time, could you take them to the parcel service?"

"I can drop them by."

She shook her head. "That's all right. I don't want you to come. You understand, don't you?"

Of course I did. I talk too much, without thinking.

"You have the address?"

"Yes."

"That's all that's left to do. Sorry for staying so long."

"And the paperwork, was that it?"

"Uh-huh. All done."

"I can't believe it's that easy. I thought there'd be a lot more to it."

"People who don't know anything about it all think so, but it really is simple. Once it's over and done with." Saying that, she went back to scratching the cat's head. "Get divorced twice, and you're a veteran."

The cat did a back stretch, eyes closed, then quickly nestled his head into the crook of her arm. I tossed the coffee mugs and salad bowl into the sink, then swept up the cracker crumbs with a bill. My eyes were throbbing from the glare of the sun.

"I made out a list of details. Where papers are filed, trash days, things like that. Anything you can't figure out, give me a call."

"Thanks."

"Had you wanted children?" she suddenly asked.

"Nah, can't say I ever wanted kids."

"I wondered about that for a while there. But seeing how it

ended up like this, I guess it was just as well. Or maybe if we'd had a child it wouldn't have come to this, what do you think?"

"There're lots of couples with kids who get divorced."

"You're probably right," she said, toying with my lighter. "I still love you. But I guess that's not the point now, is it? I know that well enough myself."

3

The Slip

Once she was gone, I downed another cola, then took a hot shower and shaved. I was down to the bottom on just about everything—soap, shampoo, shaving cream.

I stepped out of the shower and dried my hair, rubbed on body lotion, cleaned my ears. Then to the kitchen to heat up the last of the coffee. Only to discover: no one sitting at the opposite side of the table. Staring at that chair where no one sat, I felt like a tiny child in a De Chirico painting, left behind all alone in a foreign country. Of course, a tiny child I was not. I decided I wouldn't think about it and took my time with my coffee and cigarette.

For not having slept in twenty-four hours, I felt surprisingly awake. My body was hazed to the core, but my mind kept swimming swiftly around through the convoluted waterways of my consciousness, like a restless aquatic organism.

The vacant chair in front of me made me think of an American novel I'd read a while back. After the wife walks out, the husband keeps her slip draped over the chair. It made sense, now that I thought about it. True, it wouldn't really help things, but it beat having that dying geranium staring at me. Besides, probably even the cat would feel more comfortable having her things around.

I checked the bedroom, opening all of her drawers, all empty. Only a moth-eaten scarf, three coat hangers, and a packet of mothballs. Her cosmetics, toiletries, and curlers, her toothbrush, hair dryer, assortment of pills, boots, sandals, slippers, hat boxes, accessories, handbags, shoulder bags, suitcases, purses, her ever-tidy stock of underwear, stockings, and socks, letters, everything with the least womanly scent was gone. She probably even wiped off her fingerprints. A third of the books and records was gone too—anything she'd bought herself or I'd given her.

From the photo albums, every single print of her had been peeled away. Shots of the both of us together had been cut, the parts with her neatly trimmed away, leaving my image behind. Photos of me alone or of mountains and rivers and deer and cats were left intact. Three albums rendered into a revised past. It was as if I'd been alone at birth, alone all my days, and would continue alone.

A slip! She could have at least left a slip!

It was her choice, and her choice was to leave not a single trace. I could either accept it or, as I imagined was her intention, I could talk myself into believing that she never existed all along. If she never existed, then neither did her slip.

I doused the ashtray, thought more about her slip, then gave up and hit the sack.

A month had passed since I agreed to the divorce and she moved out. A non-month. Unfocused and unfelt, a lukewarm protoplasm of a month.

Nothing changed from day to day, not one thing. I woke up at seven, made toast and coffee, headed out to work, ate dinner out, had one or two drinks, went home, read in bed for an hour, turned off the lights, and slept. Saturdays and Sundays, instead of work, I was out killing time from morning on, making the rounds of movie theaters. Then I had dinner and a couple of drinks, read, and went to sleep, alone. So it went: I passed through the month the way people X out days on a calendar, one after the one.

In one sense, her disappearance was due to circumstances beyond my control. What's done is done, that sort of thing. How we got on the last four years was of no consequence. Any more than the photos peeled out of the albums.

Nor did it matter that she'd been sleeping with a friend of mine for a long time and one day upped and moved in with him. All this was within the realm of possibility. Such things happened often enough, so how could I think her leaving me was anything out of the ordinary? The long and the short of it was, it was up to her.

"The long and short of it is, it's up to you," I said.

It was a Sunday afternoon, as I dawdled with a pull-ring from a beer can, that she came out with it. Said she wanted a divorce.

"Either way is fine with you then?" she asked, releasing her words slowly.

"No, either way is not fine with me," I said. "I'm only saying it's up to you."

"If you want to know the truth, I don't want to leave you," she said after a moment.

"All right, then don't leave me," I said.

"But I'm going nowhere staying with you."

She wouldn't say any more, but I knew what she meant. I would be thirty in a few months; she would be twenty-six. And if you considered the vastness of the rest of our lives, the foundations we'd laid barely scraped zero. All we'd done our four years together was to eat through our savings.

Mostly my fault, I guess. Probably I never should have gotten married. At least never to her.

In the beginning, she thought she was the one unfit for society and made me out to be the socially functioning one. In our respective roles, we got along relatively well. Yet no sooner had we thought we'd reached a lasting arrangement than something crumbled. The tiniest hint of something, but it was never to be recovered. We had been walking ever so peacefully down a long blind alley. That was our end.

To her, I was already lost. Even if she still loved me, it didn't matter. We'd gotten too used to each other's role. She understood it instinctively; I knew it from experience. There was no hope.

So it was that she and her slip vanished forever. Some things are forgotten, some things disappear, some things die. But all in all, this was hardly what you could call a tragedy.

July 24, 8:25 A.M.

I checked the numerals of the digital clock, closed my eyes, and fell asleep.

Part Three

September, Two Months Later

4

The Whale's Penis and the Woman with Three Occupations

To sleep with a woman: it can seem of the utmost importance in your mind, or then again it can seem like nothing much at all. Which only goes to say that there's sex as therapy (self-therapy, that is) and there's sex as pastime.

There's sex for self-improvement start to finish and there's sex for killing time straight through; sex that is therapeutic at first only to end up as nothing-better-to-do, and vice versa. Our human sex life—how shall I put it?—differs fundamentally from the sex life of the whale.

We are not whales—and this constitutes one great theme underscoring our sex life.

When I was a kid, there was an aquarium thirty minutes by bicycle from where I lived. A chill aquarium-like silence always pervaded the place, with only an occasional splash to be heard. I could almost feel the Creature from the Black Lagoon breathing in some dim corner.

Schools of tuna circled 'round and 'round the enormous pool. Sturgeon plied their own narrow watercourse, piranha set their razor-sharp teeth into chunks of meat, and electric eels sputtered and sparked like shorted-out lightbulbs.

The aquarium was filled with countless other fish as well, all with different names and scales and fins. I couldn't figure out why on earth there had to be so many kinds of fish.

There were, of course, no whales in the aquarium. One whale would have been too big, even if you knocked out all the walls and made the entire aquarium into one tank. Instead, the aquarium kept a whale penis on display. As a token, if you will.

So it was that my most impressionable years of boyhood were spent gazing at not a whale but a whale's penis. Whenever I tired of strolling through the chill aisles of the aquarium, I'd steal off to my place on the bench in the hushed, high-ceilinged stillness of the exhibition room and spend hours on end there contemplating this whale's penis.

At times it would remind me of a tiny shriveled palm tree; at other times, a giant ear of corn. In fact, if not for the plaque—WHALE GENITAL: MALE—no one would have taken it to be a whale's penis. More likely an artifact unearthed from the Central Asian desert than a product of the Antarctic Ocean. It bore no resemblance to my penis, nor to any penis I'd ever seen. What was worse, the severed penis exuded a singular, somehow unspeakable aura of sadness.

It came back to me, that giant whale's penis, after having intercourse with a girl for the very first time. What twists of fate, what tortuous circumnavigations, had brought it to that cavernous exhibition room? My heart ached, thinking about it. I felt as if I didn't have a hope in the world. But I was only seventeen and clearly too young to give up on everything. It was then and there I came to the realization I have borne in mind ever since.

Which is, that I am not a whale.

In bed now with my new girlfriend, running my fingers through her hair, I thought about whales for the longest time.

In the aquarium of my memory, it is always late autumn. The glass of the tanks is cold. I'm wearing a heavy sweater. Through the large picture window of the exhibition room, the sea is dark as lead, the countless whitecaps reminiscent of lace collars on girls' dresses.

"What're you thinking about?" she asked.

"Something long ago," I said.

She was twenty-one, with an attractive slender body and a pair of the most bewitching, perfectly formed ears. She was a part-time proofreader for a small publishing house, a commercial model specializing in ear shots, and a call girl in a discreet intimate-friends-only club. Which of the three she considered her main occupation, I had no idea. Neither did she.

Nonetheless, sizing up her essential attributes, I would have to say her natural gifts ran to ear modeling. She agreed. Which was well and good until you considered how extremely limited are the opportunities for a commercial ear model, how abysmal the status and pay. To your typical P.R. man or makeup artist or cameraman, she was just an "earholder," someone with ears. Her mind and body, apart from the ears, were completely out of the picture, disregarded, nonexistent.

"But you know, that's not the real me," she'd say. "*I* am my ears, my ears are me."

Neither her proofreader self nor her call girl self ever, not for one second, showed her ears to others.

"That's because they're not really me," she explained.

The office of her call girl club, registered as a "talent club" for appearances, was located in Akasaka and run by a gray-haired Englishwoman whom everyone called Mrs. X. She'd been living in Japan for thirty years, spoke fluent Japanese, and read most of the basic Chinese characters.

Mrs. X had opened an English-language tutorial school for women not five hundred yards from the call girl office and used the place to scout promising faces for the latter. Conversely, several of the call girls were also going to her English school. At reduced tuition, of course.

Mrs. X called all her call girls "dear." Soft as a spring afternoon, her "dears."

"Make sure to wear frilly undies, dear. And no pantyhose." Or "You take your tea with cream, don't you, dear?" She had a firm understanding of her market. Her clientele were wealthy businessmen in their forties and fifties. Two-thirds foreigners, the rest Japanese. Mrs. X expressed a dislike for politicians, old men, perverts, and the poor.

A dozen long-stemmed beauties she kept on call, but out of the whole bouquet my new girlfriend was the least attractive bloom. As a call girl, she seemed no more than ordinary. In fact, with her ears hidden, she was plain. I couldn't figure out how Mrs. X had singled her out. Maybe she'd detected in her plainness some special glimmer, or maybe she thought one plain girl would be an asset. Either way, Mrs. X's sights had been right on target, and my girlfriend quickly had a number of regular customers. She wore ordinary clothes, ordinary makeup, ordinary underwear, and an ordinary scent as she'd head out to the Hilton or Okura or Prince to sleep with one or two men a week, thereby making enough to live on for a month.

Half the other nights she slept with me for free. The other half I have no idea how she spent.

Her life as a part-time proofreader for the publishing house was more normal. Three days a week she'd commute to Kanda, to the third floor of a small office building, and from nine to five she'd proofread, make tea, run downstairs (no elevator in the building) and buy erasers. She'd be the one sent out, not because anyone held anything against her, but because she was the only unmarried woman in the company. Like a chameleon, she would change with place and circumstance, able, at will, to summon or control that glimmer of hers.

I first became acquainted with her (or rather, her ears) right after I broke up with my wife. It was the beginning of August. I was doing a subcontracted copywriting job for a computer software company, which brought me face-to-face, so to speak, with her ears.

The director of the advertising firm placed a campaign proposal and three large black-and-white photos on my desk, telling me to prepare three head copy options for them within the week. All three photos were giant close-ups of an ear.

An ear?

"Why an ear?" I asked.

"Who knows? What's the difference? An ear it is. You've got a week to think about ears."

So for one whole week I ear-gazed. I taped the three giant ears to the wall in front of my desk, and all day, while smoking cigarettes, drinking coffee, clipping my nails, I immersed myself in those ears.

The job I finished in a week, but the ear shots stayed taped up on my wall. Partly it was too much trouble to take them down, partly I'd grown accustomed to those ears. But the real reason I didn't take the photos down was that those ears had me in their thrall. They were the dream image of an ear. The quintessence, the paragon of ears. Never had any enlarged part of the human body (genitals included, of course) held such strong attraction for me. They were like some great whirlpool of fate sucking me in.

One astonishingly bold curve cut clear across the picture plane, others curled into delicate filigrees of subtle shadow, while still others traced, like an ancient mural, the legends of a past age. But the supple flesh of the earlobe surpassed them all, transcending all beauty and desire.

A few days later, I rang up the photographer for the name and number of those ears.

"What's this now?" asked the photographer.

"Just curious, that's all. They're such striking ears."

"Well, I guess as far as the ears go, okay, but the girl herself is nothing special. If it's a young piece you want, I can introduce you to this bathing-suit model I shot the other day."

I refused, took down the name and number of the ears, thanked him, and hung up.

Two o'clock, six o'clock, ten o'clock, I kept trying her number, but got no answer. Apparently she was going about her own life.

It was ten the next morning before I finally got ahold of her. I introduced myself briefly, then added that I had to talk to her about some business related to the advertisement and could she see clear to having dinner with me.

"But I was told the job was finished," she said.

"The job is finished," I said.

She seemed a bit taken aback, but didn't inquire further. We set a date for the following evening.

I called for a reservation at the fanciest French restaurant I knew. On Aoyama Boulevard. Then I got out a brand-new shirt, took my time selecting a tie, and put on a jacket I'd only worn twice before.

True to the photographer's warning, the girl was nothing special. Plain clothes, plain looks. She seemed like a member of the chorus of a second-rate women's college. But that was beside the point as far as I was concerned. What disappointed me was that she hid her ears under a straight fall of hair.

"You're hiding your ears," said I, nonchalantly.

"Yes," said she, nonchalantly.

We had arrived ahead of schedule and were the first dinner customers at the restaurant. The lights were dimmed, a waiter came around with a long match to light the red taper on our table, and the maître d'hôtel cast fishy eyes over the napkins and dinnerware to be sure all was in place. The herringbone lay of the oak floorboards gleamed to a high polish, and the waiter walked about with a click of his heels. His shoes looked loads more expensive than mine. Fresh bud roses in vases, and modern oils, originals, on white walls.

I glanced over the wine list and chose a crisp white wine, and for hors d'oeuvres *pâté de canard, terrine de dorade,* and *foie de baudroie à crème fraîche*. After an intensive study of the menu she ordered *potage tortue, salade verte,* and *mousse de sole,* while I ordered *potage d'oursin, rôti de veau avec garnie persil,* and a *salade de tomate*. There went half a month's salary.

"What a lovely place," she said. "Do you come here often?"

"Only occasionally on business," I answered. "The truth of the matter is, I don't usually go to restaurants when I'm alone. Mostly I go to bars where I eat and drink whatever they've got. Easier that way. No unnecessary decisions."

"And what do you usually eat at a bar?"

"All sorts of things. Omelettes and sandwiches often enough."

"Omelettes and sandwiches," she repeated. "You eat omelettes and sandwiches every day at bars?"

"Not every day. I cook for myself every three days or so."

"So you eat omelettes and sandwiches two days out of three."

"I guess so," I said.

"Why omelettes and sandwiches?"

"A halfway decent bar can make a pretty good omelette and sandwich."

"Hmm," she said. "Pretty strange."

"Not at all."

I couldn't figure how to get out of that, so I sat there quietly admiring the ashes in the ashtray.

She turned on the juice. "Let's talk business."

"As I told you yesterday, the job is finished. No problems. So I have nothing to say."

She fished a slender clove cigarette out of her handbag, lit up with the restaurant matches, and gave me a look that said "So?"

I was about to speak when the maître d'hôtel advanced on our table. He showed me the wine label, all smiles as if showing me a photo of his only son. I nodded. He unscrewed the cork with a pleasant pop, then poured out a small mouthful in my glass. It tasted like the price of the entire dinner.

The maître d'hôtel withdrew and in his place appeared a waiter who set out the three hors d'oeuvres and a small plate before each of us. When the waiter departed, leaving us alone again, I blurted out, "I had to see your ears."

Speaking not a word, she proceeded to help herself to the *pâté* and *foie de baudroie*. She took a sip of wine.

"Sorry to have imposed," I hedged.

She smiled ever so slightly. "Fine French cuisine is no imposition at all."

"Does it bother you to have your ears discussed?"

"Not really. It depends on the angle of discussion." She shook her head as she lifted her fork to her mouth. "Tell me straight, because that's my favorite angle."

We silently sipped our wine and continued our meal.

"I turn a corner," I offered, "just as someone ahead of me turns the next corner. I can't see what that person looks like. All I can make out is a flash of white coattails. But the whiteness of the coattails is indelibly etched in my consciousness. Ever get that feeling?"

"I suppose so."

"Well, that's the feeling I get from your ears."

Again, we ate in silence. I poured wine for her, then for myself.

"It's not the scene that comes into your head," she asked, "but the feeling, right?"

"Right."

"Ever have that feeling before?"

I gave it some thought, then shook my head. "No, I guess not."

"Which means it's all on account of my ears."

"I couldn't swear to it. There's no way I could be that sure. I've never heard of the shape of someone's ears arousing anyone this way."

"I know someone who sneezed every time he saw Farrah Fawcett's nose. There's a big psychological element to sneezing, you know. Once cause and effect link up, there's no escape."

"I'm no expert on Farrah Fawcett's nose," I said, taking a sip of wine. Then I forgot what I was about to say.

"That's not quite what you meant, is it?" she said.

"No, not quite," I said. "The feeling I get is terribly unfocused, yet very solid." I demonstrated, holding my hands a yard apart, then compressing the span to two inches. "I'm not explaining this well, I'm afraid."

"A concentrated phenomenon based on vague motives."

"Exactly," I said. "You're seven times smarter than I am."

"I take correspondence courses."

"Correspondence courses?"

"That's right, psychology by mail."

We split the last of the *pâté*. Now I was completely lost.

"You still haven't gotten it? The relationship between my ears and your feelings?"

"In a word, no," said I. "That is, I have no firm grasp on whether your ears appeal to me directly, or whether something else in you appeals to me through your ears."

She placed both her hands on the table and shook her head gently. "Is this feeling of yours of the good variety or the bad variety?"

"Neither. Or both. I can't tell."

She pinioned her wineglass between her palms and looked me straight in the face. "It seems you need more study in the means of expressing emotions."

"Can't say I'm too good at describing them either," I said.

At that she smiled. "Never mind. I think I have a good idea of what you mean."

"Well then, what should I do?"

She said nothing for the longest while. She seemed to be thinking of something else entirely. Five dishes lay empty on the table, a constellation of five extinct planets.

"Listen," she ended the silence. "I think we ought to become friends. That is, of course, if it's all right with you."

"Of course it's all right with me," I said.

"And I mean very close friends," she said.

I nodded.

So it was we became very close friends. Not thirty minutes after we'd first met.

"As a close friend, there're a couple things I want to ask you," I said.

"Go right ahead."

"First of all, why is it you don't show your ears? Second, have your ears ever exerted any special power over anyone besides me?"

Without a word, she trained her eyes on her hands resting on the table.

"Some, yes," she said quietly.

"Some?"

"Sure. But to put it another way, I'm more accustomed to the self who doesn't show her ears."

"Which is to say that the you when you show your ears is different from the you when you don't show your ears."

"Right enough."

Two waiters cleared away our dishes and brought the soup.

"Would you mind telling me about the you who shows her ears."

"That's so long ago I doubt I can tell it very well. The truth is, I haven't shown my ears once since I was twelve."

"But when you did that modeling job, you showed your ears, didn't you?"

"Yes," she said, "but not my real ears."

"Not your real ears?"

"Those were blocked ears."

I had two spoonfuls of soup and looked up at her.

"Tell me more about your 'blocked ears.'"

"Blocked ears are dead ears. I killed my own ears. That is, I consciously cut off the passageway. . . . Do you follow me?"

No, I didn't follow her.

"Ask me, then," she said.

"By killing your ears, do you mean you made yourself deaf?"

"No, I can hear quite fine. But even so, my ears are dead. You can probably do it too."

She set her soupspoon back down, straightened her back, raised her shoulders two inches, thrust her jaw full out, held that posture for all of ten seconds, and suddenly dropped her shoulders.

"There. My ears are dead. Now you try."

Three times I repeated the movements she'd made. Slowly, carefully, but nothing left me with the impression that my ears had died. The wine was rapidly circulating through my system.

"I do believe that my ears aren't dying properly," I said, disappointed.

She shook her head. "That's okay. If your ears don't need to die, there's nothing wrong with them not dying."

"May I ask you something else?"

"Go right ahead."

"If I add up everything you've told me, it seems to come down to this: that up to age twelve you showed your ears. Then one day you hid your ears. And from that day on, not once have you shown your ears. But at such times that you must show your ears, you block off the passageway between your ears and your consciousness. Is that correct?"

A winsome smile came to her face. "That is correct."

"What happened to your ears at age twelve?"

"Don't rush things," she said, reaching her right hand across the table, lightly touching the fingers of my left hand. "Please."

I poured out the rest of the wine into our glasses and slowly drank mine.

"First, I want to know more about you," she started.

"What about me?"

"Everything. How you were brought up, how old you are, what you do for a living, stuff like that."

"It's your ordinary story. So utterly ordinary, you'd probably doze off in the middle of it."

"I like ordinary stories."

"Mine is the kind of ordinary story no one could possibly enjoy."

"That's okay, give me ten minutes' worth."

"I was born in 1948, on December twenty-fourth, Christmas Eve. Now Christmas Eve doesn't make a very good birthday. I mean, you don't get separate birthday and Christmas presents. Everyone figures they save money that way. My sign is Capricorn and my blood type is A—a perfect combination for bank tellers and civil servants. I'm not supposed to get along well with Sagittarians and Libras and Aquarians. A boring life, don't you think?"

"I'm fascinated."

"I grew up in an ordinary little town, went to an ordinary school. I was a quiet child, but grew into a bored kid. I met this ordinary girl, had an ordinary first romance. When I was eighteen, I came to Tokyo to go to college. When I got out of college, a friend and I set up a small translation service, and somehow we scraped by. Three years ago, we branched out into P.R. newsletters and advertising-related work, and that's going fairly well. I got involved with one of the women who worked at the firm. We got married four years back and got divorced two months ago. No one reason I can put it all down to. I have an old tomcat for a pet. Smoke forty cigarettes a day. Can't seem to quit. I own three suits, six neckties, plus a collection of five hundred records that are hopelessly out of style. I've memorized all the murderers' names in every Ellery Queen mystery ever written. I own the complete *A la recherche du temps perdus,* but have only read half. I drink beer in summer, whiskey in winter."

"And two days out of three you eat omelettes and sandwiches in bars, right?"

"Uh-huh," I said.

"What an interesting life."

"It's been boring so far. It'll probably be the same from here on. Not that that bothers me. I mean, I take what I get."

I looked at my watch. Nine minutes, twenty seconds.

"But what you've just told me isn't everything, no?"

I gazed at my hands on the table. "Of course that's not everything. There's no telling every last thing about someone's life, no matter how boring."

"May I comment?"

"Certainly."

"Whenever I meet people for the first time, I get them to talk for ten minutes. Then I size them up from the exact opposite perspective of all they've told me. Do you think that's crazy?"

"No," I said, shaking my head, "I'd guess your method works quite well."

A waiter came, set the table with new plates, onto which another waiter served the entrée, topped with sauce by still another waiter. A quick double play, shortstop to second, second to first.

"Applying this method to you, I've learned one thing," she said, putting the knife to her sole mousse. "That your life is not boring. You wish your life was boring. Am I off base?"

"Maybe not. Maybe my life isn't boring, maybe I don't really seek a boring life. But effectively it's the same thing. Either way I've already got what's coming. Most people, they're trying to escape from boredom, but I'm trying to get into the thick of boredom. That's why I'm not complaining when I say my life is boring. It was enough to make my wife bail out, though."

"Is that why you and your wife split up?"

"Like I said before, there's no one thing I can put it all down to. But as Nietzsche said, 'The gods furl their flags at boredom.' Or something like that."

We took our time eating. She had seconds on the sauce, and I had extra bread. Then our plates were cleared away, we had blueberry sorbet, and about the time they came out with espresso I lit up a cigarette. The smoke drifted about only a short while before it was discreetly whisked away by the noiseless ventilation system.

People had begun to take their places at other tables. A Mozart concerto played from the overhead speakers.

"I'd like to ask you more about your ears, if I may," I said.

"You want to ask whether or not my ears possess some special power?"

I nodded.

"That is something you'd have to check for yourself," she said. "If I were to tell you anything, it might not be of any interest to you. Might even cramp your style."

I nodded once more.

"For you, I'll show my ears," she said, after finishing her espresso. "But I don't know if it will really be to your benefit. You might end up regretting it."

"How's that?"

"Your boredom might not be as hard-core as you think."

"That's a chance I'll have to take," I said.

She reached out across the table and put her hand on mine. "One more thing: for the time being—say, the next few months—don't leave my side. Okay?"

"Sure."

With that, she pulled a black hairband out of her handbag. Holding it between her lips, she pulled her hair back with both hands, gave it one full twist, and swiftly tied it back.

"Well?"

I swallowed my breath and gazed at her, transfixed. My mouth went dry. From no part of me could I summon a voice. For an instant, the white plaster wall seemed to ripple. The voices of the other diners and the clinking of their dinnerware grew faint, then once again returned to normal. I heard the sound of waves, recalled the scent of a long-forgotten evening. Yet all this was but a mere fragment of the sensations passing through me in those few hundredths of a second.

"Exquisite," I managed to squeeze out. "I can't believe you're the same human being."

"See what I mean?" she said.

5

Unblocked Ears

"See what I mean?" she said.

She'd become so beautiful, it defied understanding. Never had I feasted my eyes on such beauty. Beauty of a variety I'd never imagined existed. As expansive as the entire universe, yet as dense as a glacier. Unabashedly excessive, yet at the same time pared down to an essence. It transcended all concepts within the boundaries of my awareness. She was at one with her ears, gliding down the oblique face of time like a protean beam of light.

"You're extraordinary," I said, after catching my breath.

"I know," she said. "These are my ears in their unblocked state."

Several of the other customers were now turned our way, staring agape at her. The waiter who came over with more coffee couldn't pour properly. Not a soul uttered a word. Only the reels on the tape deck kept slowly spinning.

She retrieved a clove cigarette from her purse and put it to her lips. I hurriedly offered her a light with my lighter.

"I want to sleep with you," she said.

So we slept together.

6

The Further Adventures of Unblocked Ears

The manifestation of her full splendor, though, I had yet to await. For the next two or three days, she exposed her ears only intermittently, then hid those marvels of creation behind her hair again and returned to ordinariness.

To her, it was as if she'd tried taking off her coat at the beginning of March. "I guess it's still not time to show my ears," she said. "I'm not entirely comfortable with them yet."

"Really, I don't mind," I said. Even with her ears covered she wasn't bad.

She'd show me her ears on occasion; mostly on sexual occasions. Sex with her with her ears exposed was an experience I'd never known. When it was raining, the smell of the rain came through crystal clear. When birds were singing, their song was a thing of sheer clarity. I'm at a loss for words, but that's what it was like.

"You don't show your ears when you sleep with other men?" I once asked her.

"Of course not," she said. "They probably don't even know I have ears."

"What's sex like for you without your ears showing?"

"A duty. Dry and tasteless, like chewing newsprint. But that's okay. Nothing bad about fulfilling a duty, you know."

"But with your ears out it's a thousand times better, isn't it?"

"Sure."

"Then you ought to show them," I said. "No need to go out of your way to put up with such dull times."

Dead serious, she stared at me and said, "You don't understand anything."

For sure, there were a lot of things I didn't understand at all.

For instance, the reason why she treated me special. I couldn't for the life of me believe I might be any better or different in any way than anyone else.

But when I told her that, she only laughed.

"It's really very simple," she said. "You sought me out. That's the biggest reason."

"And supposing somebody else had sought you out?"

"At least for the present, it's you who wants me. What's more, you're loads better than you think you are."

"So why is it I get to thinking that way?" I puzzled.

"That's because you're only half-living," she said briskly. "The other half is still untapped somewhere."

"Hmm."

"In that sense, you're not unlike me. I'm sitting on my ears, and you've got only half of you that's really living. Sure seems that way, doesn't it?"

"Even if that were the case, my remaining half couldn't possibly compare to your ears."

"Maybe not," she smiled. "You wouldn't have any idea, would you?"

And with that smile in place, she lifted back her hair and unbuttoned her blouse.

That September afternoon toward summer's end, I took the day off and was lying in bed with her, stroking her hair and thinking about the whale's penis. The sea, a dark lead-gray. A brisk wind beating against the aquarium window. The lofty ceiling, the empty exhibition room. The penis severed forever from the whale, its meaning as a whale's penis irretrievably lost.

Then I gave my wife's slip one more spin-around in my thoughts. There was no real slip. Only, stuck in my head, a vague image of a slip draped over a kitchen chair. I couldn't remember what it had meant to me. Had somebody else been living my life all this time?

"Tell me, you don't wear slips, do you?" I asked my girlfriend.

She lifted her head from my shoulder and stared at me blankly.

"I don't have any."

"Umm," I said.

"But if you think you'd have a better time if I did . . ."

"No, it's not that," I quickly interjected. "That wasn't why I was asking."

"No, really, there's no need to be shy. I'm quite used to that kind of stuff from work. I wouldn't be the least bit embarrassed."

"I'm not asking for anything," I said. "Honestly, all I need is you and your ears, nothing more."

She gave a pouting shake of her head and pressed her forehead against my shoulder. Not fifteen seconds later, she looked up again.

"Listen, an important phone call is going to come through in ten minutes."

"A phone call?" I glanced over at the bedside telephone.

"That's right, the phone's going to ring."

"You can tell?"

"I can tell."

She had herself a cigarette, head resting on my chest. A moment later, her ash fell beside my navel and she pursed her lips to blow it off. I felt her ear between my fingers. It was a wonderful sensation. My head was empty with shapeless images drifting and diffusing.

"Something about sheep," she said. "Lots of sheep and one sheep in particular."

"Sheep?"

"Uh-huh," she said, handing her half-smoked cigarette to me. I took one drag, then crushed it out in an ashtray. "And that'll be the beginning of a wild adventure."

Shortly thereafter, the telephone rang. I shot her a look, but she had dozed off on my chest. I let the phone ring four times before picking up the receiver.

It was my partner. "Could you come here right away?" he said. There was an edge to his voice. "I have a terribly urgent matter to discuss with you."

"Just how urgent is it?"

"Come in and you'll find out," said he.

"Heaven knows it's got to be about sheep," I said, letting go a trial balloon. It was something I shouldn't have said. The receiver grew cold as ice.

"How did you know?" my partner asked.

The wild sheep chase had begun.

Part Four

A Wild Sheep Chase, I

7

Before the Strange Man

There are various reasons why an individual might habitually consume large quantities of alcohol, but they all effectively boil down to the same thing.

Five years ago, my business partner was a happy drunk. Three years later, he had become a moody drunk. And by last summer, he was fumbling at the knob of the door to alcoholism. As with most habitual drinkers, he was a nice-enough, regular-if-not-exactly-sharp kind of guy when sober. Everyone thought of him as a nice-enough, regular-if-not-exactly-sharp kind of guy. He thought so too. That's why he drank. Because it seemed that with alcohol in his system, he could more fully embody this idea of being that kind of guy.

Things were fine at first. But as time went on and the quantity of alcohol increased, subtle changes occurred, and these subtle changes gradually wore into a deep rut. His regularity and nice-enoughness got ahead of him, excessively so. A typical case. Typically, however, people don't think of themselves as typical cases. And not-exactly-sharp types even less so. The attempt to regain sight of what he'd lost sent him wandering in an even thicker alcoholic fog.

Still, at least for the time being, he was a regular guy until the sun went down. And since for years now I had made a conscious effort not to meet up with him after sunset, as far as I was concerned he was regular enough. Even so, I knew full well that after sunset he became not quite regular, and he himself knew it too. As neither of us would ever broach the subject, we got along the same as always. We just weren't the friends we had once been.

While I can't say I understood him one hundred percent (even seventy percent would have been doing well), for what it was worth, he had been my only friend in college, and it wasn't easy watching him deteriorate from close up. Ultimately, I guess, that's what age does.

By the time I'd get to the office he'd already had one shot of whiskey. As long as it was one shot, he could be mister regular, but there was no telling when he'd up his regular to two. When that happened, I knew we'd have to go our separate ways.

I was standing in the gust of the air conditioner, letting my sweat dry as I sipped a cool glass of barley tea. I wasn't saying anything. He wasn't saying anything. The harsh afternoon sun spilled across the linoleum floor in hallucinatory sprays. Below, on the park's expanse of greenery, people lay on the grass sunning themselves. My partner tapped at the palm of his right hand with the tip of a ballpoint pen.

"I hear you got divorced," he started.

"That was news two weeks ago," I said, still staring out the window. I took off my sunglasses, and my eyes hurt.

"So why'd you get divorced?"

"Personal reasons."

"I know that," he said. "Never heard of a divorce for other than personal reasons."

I said nothing. Didn't we have a long-standing unspoken agreement never to touch upon each other's private affairs?

"I don't mean to pry," he said, "but she was a friend of mine too. It came as a shock. I thought you two were always so close."

"We always were close. It's not like we parted on bad terms."

My partner smirked, continuing to tap the palm of his hand with the pen. He was wearing a deep-blue shirt with a black tie, hair neatly combed, cologne. While I was in a T-shirt with Snoopy carrying a surfboard, old Levi's that had been washed colorless, and dirty tennis shoes. To anyone else, he clearly was the regular one.

"You remember when she and the two of us worked together?"

"I remember very well," I said.

"Those were happy times," my partner said.

I moved away from the air conditioner, walked over to the center of the room, and dropped myself down on the plush sky-blue Swedish sofa. I extracted a filter-tip Pall Mall from the special visitors' cigarette case and lit up with the heavy tabletop lighter.

"So?" I said.

"So what I'm saying is maybe we've overextended ourselves."

"You talking about the ads and magazine work?"

My partner nodded, though it must have been hard for him to admit it. I weighed the lighter in my hand, turned the screw to adjust the flame, and felt sorry for him.

"Okay, I know what you're trying to say," I said, returning the lighter to the table, "but remember, I wasn't the one who brought in the business, and it wasn't my idea to do this work. You walked in with it. You're the one who wanted to give it a go."

"There were pressing circumstances. We had nothing . . ."

"It made money."

"Sure it made money. Let us move to a larger office and take on more staff. I got a new car, bought a condo, sent two kids to an expensive private school. Not bad for thirty years old, I suppose."

"You earned it. Nothing to be ashamed of."

"Who's ashamed?" said my partner, retrieving the ballpoint pen that had flown across his desk and taking another few pokes at the middle of his palm. "But you know, it doesn't seem real. There we were, the two of us with nothing but debts, trying to scrounge up translation work, passing out handbills down by the station."

"What's to stop us from passing out handbills now if we wanted?"

My partner looked up at me. "Hey, I'm not joking."

"Neither am I."

A silence fell between us.

"A lot of things have changed," my partner said. "The pace of our lives, our thinking. Above all, we don't even know ourselves how much we really make. A tax accountant comes in and does all that awful paperwork, with exemptions and depreciations and write-offs and what not."

"The same as everywhere else."

"I know, I know. That's what we've got to do and that's what we're doing. But it was more fun in the old days."

"For lo the shadows of a gaol untold, Do grow about our days now many fold." Lines from a poem suddenly popped out of my mouth.

"How's that again?"

"Nothing, sorry. You were saying?"

"I just feel like we're engaged in some kind of exploitation."

"Exploitation?" I looked up in surprise.

There were two yards between us, and with the different heights of our seats his head rose ten inches above mine. A lithograph hung behind him. A new lithograph I'd not seen before, of a fish with wings. The fish didn't look too happy about its wings. Probably wasn't sure how to use them either.

"Exploitation?" I muttered to myself.

"Exploitation."

"And who, pray tell, is doing the exploiting?"

"Different interests, little by little."

I crossed my legs on the sky-blue sofa and fixed my gaze at the drama of his hand and ballpoint pen, now exactly at eye level.

"In any case, don't you think we've changed?" asked my partner.

"We're still the same. Not anyone or anything has changed."

"You really think so?"

"I really do. Exploitation doesn't exist. It's a fairy tale. Even you don't believe that Salvation Army trumpets can actually save the world, do you? I think you think too much."

"Well all right, maybe I do think too much," my partner said. "Last week you—I mean we—wrote the copy for that magazine ad. And it wasn't bad copy. It went over real well. But tell me, have you eaten margarine even once in the past couple years?"

"No, I hate margarine."

"Same here. That's what I mean. At the very least, in the old days we did work we believed in, and we took pride in it. There's none of that now. We're just tossing out fluff."

"Margarine is good for you. It's vegetable fat, low in cholesterol. It guards against heart problems, and lately it doesn't taste bad. It's cheap and keeps well too."

"So eat the stuff."

I sank back into the sofa, stretching out my arms and legs.

"It doesn't matter," I said. "It's the same whether we eat margarine or don't. Dull translation jobs or fraudulent copy, it's basically the same. Sure we're tossing out fluff, but tell me, where does anyone deal in words with substance? C'mon now, there's no honest work anywhere. Just like there's no honest breathing or honest pissing."

"You were more innocent in the old days."

"Maybe so," I said, crushing out a cigarette in the ashtray. "And no doubt there's an innocent town somewhere where an innocent butcher slices innocent ham. So if you think that drinking whiskey from the middle of the morning is innocent, go ahead and drink as much as you want."

The room was treated to an extended pen-on-desktop staccato solo.

"Sorry, I didn't mean to say that."

"That's okay," said my partner. "I certainly can't deny it."

The air conditioner thermostat made a funny noise. This was a terribly quiet afternoon.

"Have some confidence in yourself," I said. "Haven't we made it this far on our own? With just the two of us. The only thing that separates us from all those precious success stories is they have backers and titles."

"And to think we used to be friends," said my partner.

"We're still friends," I said. "We've come all this way together."

"I didn't want to see you get divorced."

"I know," I said. "But what do you say we start talking about sheep?"

He nodded. He placed the ballpoint pen back in its tray and rubbed his eyes.

"It was eleven o'clock this morning when the man came," my partner began.

8

Now the Strange Man

It was eleven o'clock in the morning when the man came. Now there are two types of eleven-in-the-mornings for a small-scale company like ours. That is, either absolutely busy or absolutely unbusy. Nothing in between. So at eleven A.M. we are either mindlessly working up a flurry or we are mindlessly daydreaming. In-between tasks, should there be such an animal, we set aside for the afternoon.

It was the latter sort of eleven A.M. when the man came. And a monumentally unbusy one at that. The first half of September had been insane, and then work fell flat off. Three of us took a month-delayed summer vacation, but even so the rest of the crew had been consigned to an agenda of pencil sharpening and other exciting tasks. My partner himself had stepped out to the bank to get a money draft, while someone else had repaired to the neighboring audio-equipment showroom to listen to new record releases. The secretary was left to answer the telephone as she thumbed through the "Autumn Hairstyles" pages of a women's magazine.

The man opened the door to the office without a sound, and he closed it without a sound. Not that he made any conscious effort to move quietly. It was second nature to him. So much so the secretary had no awareness whatsoever of him. The man was all the way to her desk and peering down at her before she noticed him.

"There is a matter I would like to take up with your employer," said the man. He spoke as if running a white-gloved hand over a tabletop.

What could have happened to bring him here? She looked up at the man. His eyes were too piercing for a business client, his attire too fastidious for a tax inspector, his air too intellectual for a policeman. Yet she could think of nothing else he could be. This man, a refined piece of bad news now hovering over her, had materialized out of nowhere.

"I'm afraid he's stepped out at the moment," she said, slapping her magazine shut. "He said he'd be back in another thirty minutes."

"I'll wait," pronounced the man without a moment's hesitation. A foregone conclusion, it seemed.

She wondered whether to ask his name. She decided against it and simply conducted him to the reception area. The man took a seat on the sky-blue sofa, crossed his legs, peered up at the electric wall clock directly before him, and froze in position. He moved not an iota. When she brought him a glass of barley tea a bit later, he was in the exact same pose.

"Right where you're sitting now," my partner said. "He sat there staring at the clock in the same position for a full thirty minutes."

I looked at the sofa where I was sitting, then looked up at the wall clock, then I looked back at my partner.

Despite the unusually hot late-September weather outside, the man was rather formally dressed. Impeccably. His white shirt cuffs protruded precisely two-thirds of an inch from the sleeves of his well-tailored gray suit. His subtly toned striped tie, accented with a hint of asymmetry, was positioned with the utmost care. His black shoes were buffed to a fine gloss.

Mid-thirties to forty in age, five foot ten plus in height, trimmed of every last ounce of fat, slender hands without telltale wrinkles. His long fingers suggested nothing so much as a troop of animals that had retained deep primal memories despite long years of training and control. His fingernails were meticulously manicured, a clean, perfect arc at the end of each fingertip. Truly beautiful hands, if somehow unsettling. They bespoke a high degree of specialization in some rarefied field—but what that field might be was anyone's guess.

His face was even harder to figure. It was a straightforward face, but expressionless, a blank slate. His nose and eyes were angular, as if scored with a paper knife in afterthought, his lips bloodless and thin. He was lightly tanned, though clearly not from the pleasures of the beach or the tennis court. That tan could only have been the result of some unknown sun shining in some unknown sky.

The thirty minutes passed very slowly. Coldly, solidly, rigidly. By the time my partner returned from the bank, the atmosphere in the room had grown noticeably heavy. You might even say everything in the room seemed practically nailed down to the floor.

"Of course, it only seemed that way," said my partner.

"Of course," said I.

The lone secretary was worn out from nervousness. Bewildered, my partner went over to the reception area and introduced himself as the manager. Only then did the man unfreeze, whereupon he pulled a thin cigarette out of his pocket, lit it, and with a pained expression blew out a puff of smoke. The atmosphere lightened ever so slightly.

"We don't have much time, so let's keep this short," said the man in a hush. Out of his wallet he flicked a name card sharp enough to cut your fingers with and placed it on the table. The name card was hermetically laminated, unnaturally white, and printed with tiny, intensely black type. No title or affiliation, no address, no telephone number. Only the name. It was enough to hurt your eyes just looking at it. My partner turned it over, saw that the back was entirely blank, glanced at the front side again, then looked back at the man.

"You are familiar with the party's name, I trust?" said the man.

"I am."

The man advanced his chin a few hundredths of an inch and nodded curtly. His line of vision did not shift in the least. "Burn it, please."

"Burn it?" My partner stared dumbfounded at the man.

"That name card. Burn it. Now," the man spoke sharply.

My partner hurriedly picked up the tabletop lighter and set fire to a corner of the name card. He held it by its edge until half of it had burned, then laid it in the large crystal ashtray. The two of them watched it as it burned. By the time the name card was white ash, the room was shrouded in a ponderous silence such as follows a massacre.

"I come here bearing the total authority of that party," said the man, breaking the silence at length. "Which is to say that everything I say from this point on represents that party's total volition and wishes."

"Wishes . . . ," mouthed my partner.

" 'To wish,' an elegant word to express a basic position toward a specified objective. Of course," said the man, "there are other methods of expressing the same thing. You understand, do you not?"

My partner did a quick mental translation. "I understand."

"Notwithstanding, this is neither a conceptual issue nor a political deal; this is strictly a business proposition." *Biz*ness, the man enunciated, which marked him as a foreign-born Japanese; most Japanese Japanese will say *biji*ness.

"You are a *biz*nessman and I am a *biz*nessman," he went on. "Realistically, there should be nothing between us to discuss but *biz*ness. Let us leave discussions regarding the unrealistic to others. Are we agreed?"

"Certainly," said my partner.

"It is rather our role to take what unrealistic factors that exist and to work them into a more sophisticated form that might be grounded in the grand scheme of reality. The doings of men run to unrealities. Why is that?" the man asked, rhetorically. He fingered the green stone ring on the middle finger of his left hand. "Because it appears simpler. Added to which, there are circumstances whereby unreality contrives to create an impression that overwhelms reality. Nevertheless, business has no place in the world of unreality. In other words," the man said, continuing to finger his ring, "we are a breed whose very existence consists in the rechanneling of difficulties. Therefore, should anything I say from this point forward demand difficult labors or decisions of you, I ask your forbearance. Such is the nature of things."

My partner was utterly lost now, but he nodded anyway.

"Very well then, I shall state the wishes of the party concerned. Number one, it is wished that you cease publication of the public relations bulletin you produce for the 'P' Life Insurance Company."

"But—"

"Number two," the man interrupted, "it is wished that an interview be arranged with the person actually responsible for the production of this page."

Pulling a white envelope from his pocket, the man extracted a sheet of paper neatly folded in quarters and handed it to my partner. My partner unfolded the sheet of paper. Sure enough, it was a copy of a photograph for a P.R. bulletin that our office had done. An ordinary photograph of an idyllic Hokkaido landscape—clouds and mountains and grassy pastures and sheep, superimposed with lines of an undistinguished pastoral verse. That was all.

"While our wishes are herewith two, as regards the first of these, it is less a wish than a fait accompli. To be more precise, a decision has already been reached in accordance with our wishes. Should you have any doubts, please call the public relations head of the life insurance company."

"I see," said my partner.

"Nonetheless, we can easily imagine that for a company the size of yours, damages incurred by inconvenience such as this could be sizable. Fortunately, we are in a position—as you are no doubt aware—to wield no small degree of influence in this arena. Therefore, upon compliance with our second wish, granted that the person responsible gives us a report complete to our satisfaction, we are prepared to recompense you fully for your loss. Probably more than recompense, I would think."

Silence prevailed.

"If you should fail to comply with our wishes," said the man, "you will have no occupation in this or any other field, and henceforth, the world will hold no place for you, ever."

Again silence.

"Have you any questions?"

"So, uh, it's the photo that's the problem?" my partner stammered.

"Yes," said the man, choosing his words carefully, as if sorting through options on an outstretched palm. "Such is indeed the case. However, I am not at liberty to discuss the matter any further with you. I have not that authority."

"I will phone the man you want to see. He should be here by three o'clock," said my partner.

"Excellent," said the man, glancing at his wristwatch. "I shall send a car here for him at four o'clock. Now this is important: you must speak of this to absolutely no one. Is that understood?"

Whereupon the two of them parted in a most *biz*nesslike manner.

9

"The Boss"

"That's the size of it," said my partner.

"I can't make head or tail of it," said I, an unlit cigarette at my lips. "First of all, I have no idea who the person on the name card is. Second, I can't imagine why he would get so upset about a photo of sheep. And last, I don't understand how he could put a stop to a publication of ours."

"The person on the name card is a major right-wing figure. His name and face are almost never publicized, so he's not widely known, but you're probably the only one in our line of work who doesn't know who he is."

"Dumb to the world, that's me," was my feeble excuse.

"He's right wing, but not the so-called right wing. Or you could say, not even right wing."

"You're losing me."

"The truth of the matter is no one knows what he thinks. He has no writings to his name, doesn't make speeches in public. He never gives interviews, is never photographed. It's not even certain he's alive. Five years back, a magazine reporter got a scoop implicating him in some shady investment deals, but the story never saw the light of day."

"Been doing your homework, I see."

"I knew the reporter personally."

I picked up the lighter and lit my cigarette. "What's the reporter doing nowadays?"

"Got transferred to administration. Files forms morning to night. Mass media is a surprising small world, and he made a fine example. Like a skull posted at the entrance to an African village."

"Gotcha," I said.

"But we do know something of the man's prewar background. He was born in Hokkaido in 1913, came to Tokyo after graduating from normal school, changed jobs repeatedly, and drifted to the right. He was imprisoned once, I believe. Upon his release, he went to Manchuria, where he fell in with the upper echelons of the Kanto Army and became party to some plot. Not much is known about the organization behind it, but he suddenly becomes a mysterious figure around this time. Rumor has it he was dealing in drugs, which may well have been true. He plundered his way all over the Chinese mainland only to board a destroyer two weeks before the Soviet troops arrived, beating a quick retreat back to Japan. In his booty—a huge, nearly inexhaustible stash of gold and silver."

"He had, you might say, uncanny timing," I threw in.

"For a fact. Our man had a real knack for seizing the moment. He'd learned instinctively when to go on the attack and when to withdraw. Plus his eyes were always trained on the right thing. Even when he was incarcerated by the Occupation forces as a Class A war criminal, his trial was cut short midway and never reconvened. For reasons of health, ostensibly, but the facts get a little fuzzy here. More likely, a deal was worked out with the Americans, what with MacArthur looking toward the Chinese mainland."

My partner pulled another ballpoint pen out of the pencil tray and twirled it between his fingers.

"When he was released from Sugamo Prison, he took half his stash and put an entire faction of the conservative party on his payroll. The other half went to buying up the advertising industry. Note that this was back when advertising wasn't anything but cheap handbills."

"The gift of foresight. But weren't there claims about concealment of funds?"

"Nothing of the kind. Remember he'd bought out an entire faction of the conservatives."

"Ah."

"In any case, he used his money to corner the market on both politics *and* advertising, setting up a power base that thrives to this day. He never surfaces because he doesn't need to. So long as he keeps a grip on certain centers of political authority and on the core sectors of the public relations industry, there's nothing he can't do. Do you have any idea what it means to hold down advertising?"

"I guess not."

"To hold down advertising is to have nearly the entire publishing and broadcasting industries under your thumb. There's not a branch of publishing or broadcasting that doesn't depend in some way on advertising. It'd be like an aquarium without water. Why, ninety-five percent of the information that reaches you has already been preselected and paid for."

"There's something I still don't understand," I said. "I follow you as far as our man having the information industries in the palm of his hand, but how does that extend to his putting the clamps on a life insurance company's P.R. bulletin? That didn't even pass through the hands of any major rep. That was a direct contract."

My partner coughed, then drank down the last of his now-lukewarm barley tea. "Stocks. They're his principal source of revenue. Manipulating the market, forcing hands, takeovers, the works. His newsboys gather all the necessary information, and he picks and chooses according to his fancy. Only a minuscule slice of what really goes on ever hits the wires. All the other news is set aside for the Boss. No overt pressuring, of course, but things do get awfully close to blackmail at times. And if blackmail doesn't work, he sends word around to his politicos to go prime a few pumps."

"Every company's got to have a weak point or two."

"Every company's got a secret it doesn't want exploded right in the middle of the annual shareholders' meeting. In most cases, they'll listen to the word handed down. In sum, the Boss sits squarely on top of a trilateral power base of politicians, information services, and the stock market. So as you can probably surmise, it's as easy for him to rub out one P.R. bulletin and put us out of business as it is to shell a hardboiled egg."

"Hmm, then tell me why should such a major fixture get so heated up over one landscape photo of Hokkaido?"

"A very good question," said my partner. "I was just about to ask you the same thing."

I could only shrug.

"So tell me, how did you know all this had to do with sheep?" my partner asked. "Is something funny going on behind my back?"

"Nameless elves out in the woods have been busy at the spinning wheel."

"Care to run that by me again?"

"Sixth sense."

"Give me a break," my partner sighed. "Well anyway, let me fill you in on the latest two developments. Just to snoop around a bit, I phoned that ex-reporter at the monthly. Word has it that the Boss is down for the count with a brain hemorrhage, but it hasn't been officially confirmed yet. The other piece of news concerns the man who came in here. He turns out to be the Boss's personal secretary, his number two, the guy he entrusts with actually running the organization. Japanese-American, Stanford graduate, been working for the Boss for twelve years. He's something of a mystery man himself. Undoubtedly got a head on his shoulders. That's about all I could find out."

"Thanks," I said, meaning it.

"You're welcome," said my partner without even glancing my way.

Any way you looked at it, when my partner wasn't drinking he was far more of a regular guy than I was. He was more innocent and more considerate and more organized in his thinking. But sooner or later he'd get himself drunk. Not a comforting thought: that my betters could fall to pieces before me.

As soon as my partner left the room, I pulled the whiskey bottle out of his drawer and had myself a drink.

10

Counting Sheep

We can, if we so choose, wander aimlessly over the continent of the arbitrary. Rootless as some winged seed blown about on a serendipitous spring breeze.

Nonetheless, we can in the same breath deny that there is any such thing as coincidence. What's done is done, what's yet to be is clearly yet to be, and so on. In other words, sandwiched as we are between the "everything" that is behind us and the "zero" beyond us, ours is an ephemeral existence in which there is neither coincidence nor possibility.

In actual practice, however, distinctions between the two interpretations amount to precious little. A state of affairs (as with most face-offs between interpretations) not unlike calling the same food by two different names.

So much for metaphors.

My placing a photo of sheep in the life insurance company's P.R. bulletin can be seen from one perspective, (a) as coincidence, but from another perspective, (b) as no coincidence at all.

(a) I was looking for a suitable photo for the P.R. bulletin. By coincidence, I happened to have a photo of sheep in my drawer. I decided to use that photograph. An innocent photograph in an innocent world.

(b) The photo of the sheep in my desk drawer had been waiting for me all this time. If not for use in that bulletin, then for something else at some later date.

Come to think of it, these formulas apply across the board to everything I've experienced thus far in life. With a little practice, I'm sure I'd be able to conduct, (a) a life with my right hand and, (b) a life with my left. Not that it matters much. It's like doughnut holes. Whether you take a doughnut hole as blank space or as an entity unto itself is a purely metaphysical question and does not affect the taste of the doughnut one bit.

Sitting on the sofa drinking whiskey, blown on softly by the air conditioner like a dandelion seed wafted along on a pleasant breeze, I stared at the electric wall clock. As long as I stared at the clock, at least the world remained in motion. Not a very consequential world, but in motion nonetheless. And as long as I knew the world was still in motion, I knew I existed. Not a very consequential existence, but an existence nonetheless. It struck me as wanting that someone should confirm his own existence only by the hands of an electric wall clock. There had to be a more cognitive means of confirmation. But try as I might, nothing less facile came to mind.

I gave up and had another sip of whiskey. A burning sensation passed through my throat, traveled down the wall of my esophagus and into the pit of my stomach. Outside the window, a bright blue summer sky and billowing white clouds. A beautiful if secondhand sky showing telltale signs of wear. I took another sip of whiskey to toast the brand-new sky it once was. Not bad Scotch. Not a bad sky either, once you got used to it. A jumbo jet traversed the sky from left to right like some gleaming beetle.

I had polished off my second whiskey when it came to me: what the hell was I doing here?

What the hell was I thinking about?

Sheep.

I got up from the sofa, picked up the copy of the photo from my partner's desk, and returned to the sofa. For twenty seconds, I stared at it, sucking on the whiskey-tinged ice cubes, racking my brain to figure out what was going on in it.

The photo showed a flock of sheep on a grassy meadow. On one edge, the meadow adjoined a birch wood. Huge birch trees of the kind you find up in Hokkaido, not the puny stunted variety that flank the entrance to your neighborhood dentist's office. These were birches that four bears could have sharpened their claws on simultaneously. Given the foliage, the season was probably spring. Snow lingered on the mountain peaks in the background, in the folds of the mountainside as well. April or May. When the ground is slushy with melting snow. The sky was blue (or rather what I took for blue from the monochrome photo-gray—it could have been salmon pink for all I knew), with light white clouds drawn across the mountaintops. All things considered, the flock of sheep could only be taken for a flock of sheep, the birch wood only for a birch wood, the white clouds only for white clouds. Simply that and nothing more.

I tossed the photograph on the table, smoked a cigarette, and yawned. Then picking the photo up again, I tried counting the sheep. The meadow was so vast, the sheep scattered in patches like picnickers, that it was hard to tell whether those white specks off in the distance were sheep or just white specks. And the closer I looked, the harder it was to tell whether the white specks were actually white specks or my eyes playing tricks with me, until finally I could be sure of nothing. I took a ballpoint pen in hand and marked everything I could be sure was a sheep. The count came to thirty-two. Thirty-two sheep. A perfectly straightforward photograph. Nothing unusual about the composition, nothing particular in the way of style.

Yet there was something there. Something funny. I suppose I sensed it the first time I saw the photo three months before, and I had been feeling it ever since.

I rolled over on the sofa and, holding the photo above my head, I went through the count once more.

Thirty-three.

Thirty-three?

I shut my eyes and shook my head. My mind was a blank. I tried counting sheep one last time, then drifted into a deep two-whiskey-afternoon sleep. The last thing I remember thinking about was my girlfriend's ears.

11

The Limo and Its Driver

The car came at four, as promised. Exactly on the dot, like a cuckoo clock. The secretary shook me awake from my deep slumber. Whereupon I went to the washroom and splashed water on my face. My drowsiness wasn't budging in the least. I yawned three times in the elevator on the way down. Yawns you could have built a lawsuit on. But who was there to do the suing? Who was there to be sued but myself?

Looming there in front of the entrance to our building was a giant submarine of a limousine. An impoverished family could have lived under the hood of that car, it was so big. The windows were opaque blue, reflective glass so you couldn't see in. The body was an awesome black, with not a smudge, not on the bumper, not on the hubcaps.

Standing alertly by the limo was a middle-aged chauffeur wearing a spotless white shirt and orange tie. A real chauffeur. I had but to approach him, and without a word he opened the car door. His eyes followed me until I was properly seated, then he closed the door. He climbed into the driver's seat and closed the door after himself. All without any more sound than flipping over a playing card. And sitting in this limo, compared to my fifteen-year-old Volkswagen Beetle I'd bought off a friend, was as quiet as sitting at the bottom of a lake wearing earplugs.

The car interior was fitted out to the hilt. You might expect this in a limousine, as the taste of most so-called luxury accessories is questionable, and this one was no exception. Still, I couldn't help being impressed. In the middle of my sofa-like seat was a chic push-button telephone, next to which were arranged a silver cigarette case, a lighter, an ashtray. Molded into the back of the driver's seat was a small folding desk. The air conditioning was unobtrusive and natural, the carpeting sumptuous.

Before I knew it, the limo was in motion, like a washtub gliding over a sea of mercury. The sum of money sunk into this baby must have been staggering.

"Shall I put on some music?" asked the chauffeur.

"Something relaxing, maybe."

"Very good, sir."

The chauffeur reached down below his seat, selected a cassette tape, and touched a switch in the dashboard. A peaceful cello sonata seemed to flow out of nowhere. An unobjectionable score, unobjectionable fidelity.

"They always send you to meet people in this car?" I asked.

"That is correct," answered the chauffeur cautiously. "Lately, that is all I do."

"I see."

"Originally this limousine was reserved exclusively for the Boss," said the chauffeur shortly after, his previous reserve wearing off. "However, his condition being what it is this spring, he does not venture out much. Yet what point could there be to letting this car sit there? As I am sure you realize, an automobile must be driven regularly or its performance drops off."

"Of course," I said. Apparently, then, it was no organizational secret that the Boss was in ill health. I took a cigarette out of the cigarette case, examined it, held it up to my nose. A specially made plain-cut cigarette without a brand, an aroma akin to that of Russian tobacco. I debated whether to smoke it or slip it into my pocket, but in the end merely put it back. Engraved in the center of the lighter and cigarette case was an intricately patterned emblem. A sheep emblem.

A sheep?

I shook my head and closed my eyes. All this was beyond me. It seemed that ever since the ear photo came into my life, things had begun to escape me.

"How much longer till we get there?" I asked.

"Thirty or forty minutes, depending on the traffic."

"Then maybe you could turn down the air conditioning a bit? I'd like to catch the end of an afternoon nap."

"Most certainly, sir."

The chauffeur adjusted the air conditioning, then flicked a switch on the dashboard. A thick panel of glass slid up, sealing the passenger compartment off from the driver's seat. I was enveloped in near total silence, save for the quiet strains of Bach, but by this point, hardly anything surprised me. I buried my cheek in the backseat and dozed off.

I dreamed about a dairy cow. Rather nice and small this cow, the type that looked like she'd been through a lot. We passed each other on a big bridge. It was a pleasant spring afternoon. The cow was carrying an old electric fan in one hoof, and she asked whether I wouldn't buy it from her cheap.

"I don't have much money," I said. Really, I didn't.

"Well then," said the cow, "I might trade it to you for a pair of pliers."

Not a bad deal. So the cow and I went home together, and I turned the house upside down looking for the pliers. But they were nowhere to be found.

"Odd," I said, "they were here just yesterday."

I had just brought a chair over so I could get up and look on top of the cabinet when the chauffeur tapped me on the shoulder. "We're here," he said succinctly.

The car door opened and the waning light of a summer afternoon fell across my face. Thousands of cicadas were singing at a high pitch like the winding of a clockspring. There was the rich smell of earth.

I got out of the limo, stretched, and took a deep breath. I prayed that there wasn't some kind of symbolism to the dream.

12

Wherefore the Worm Universe

There are symbolic dreams—dreams that symbolize some reality. Then there are symbolic realities—realities that symbolize a dream. Symbols are what you might call the honorary town councillors of the worm universe. In the worm universe, there is nothing unusual about a dairy cow seeking a pair of pliers. A cow is bound to get her pliers sometime. It has nothing to do with me.

Yet the fact that the cow chose me to obtain her pliers changes everything. This plunges me into a whole universe of alternative considerations. And in this universe of alternative considerations, the major problem is that everything becomes protracted and complex. I ask the cow, "Why do you want pliers?" And the cow answers, "I'm really hungry." So I ask, "Why do you need pliers if you're hungry?" The cow answers, "To attach them to branches of the peach tree." I ask, "Why a peach tree?" To which the cow replies, "Well, that's why I traded away my fan, isn't it?" And so on and so forth. The thing is never resolved, I begin to resent the cow, and the cow begins to resent me. That's a worm's eye view of its universe. The only way to get out of that worm universe is to dream another symbolic dream.

The place where that enormous four-wheeled vehicle transported me this September afternoon was surely the epicenter of the worm universe. In other words, my prayer had been denied.

I took a look around me and held my breath. Here was the stuff of breath taking.

The limo was parked on a high hill. Behind us was the gravel road which we'd come on, trailing away in an all-too-picturesque course of twists and turns to the front gate off in the distance. Probably, at a leisurely pace, a solid fifteen minutes' walk away. Lining either side of the road stood cedars and mercury-vapor lights, stationed like pencil holders at equal intervals. Clinging to each cedar trunk were innumerable cicadas screeching feverishly, as if the end of the world were at hand.

Each row of cedars bordered on neatly mowed turf, which sloped down in banks dotted with azaleas and hydrangeas and other plants beyond my powers of identification. A flock of starlings rushed, en masse, left and right across the lawn, like the aimless migration of a sand dune.

Stone steps led down both sides of the hill: the steps to the left descended to a Japanese garden with a stone lantern and a pond, the steps to the right opened onto a small golf course. At the edge of the golf course was a gazebo the color of rum raisin, and across from it stood a classical Greek statue in stone. Beyond was an enormous garage where a different chauffeur was hosing down a different limousine. I couldn't tell the make, but it wasn't a used Volkswagen.

I folded my arms and took another look around me. An impeccable garden vista, to be sure, but oh, what a sight.

"And where is the mailbox?" I asked impertinently. I mean somebody had to go to fetch the paper every morning and evening.

"The mailbox is by the back gate," said the chauffeur. A sudden revelation. Of course there had to be a back gate.

Having concluded my viewing of the grounds, I turned straight ahead and found myself facing a massive, towering structure.

It was—how shall I put it?—a painfully solitary building. Let me explain. Say we have a concept. It goes without saying that there will be slight exceptions to that norm. Now, over time these exceptions spread like stains until finally they form a separate concept. To which other exceptions crop up. It was that kind of building, some ancient life-form that had evolved blindly, toward who knows what end.

In its first incarnation, it seems to have been a Meiji-era Western-style manor. A high-ceilinged portico offered entrance to a two-story cream-colored house. The windows tall and double-hung in the true old style, the paint redone time and again. The roof was, as expected, copper-shingled, and the rain gutters as solid as a Roman aqueduct. A fine house in itself, exuding a period charm.

But then some joker of an architect came along to attach another wing of the same style and color scheme onto the right side of the original structure. The intention wasn't bad, but the effect was unpalatable. Like serving sherbet and broccoli on the same silver platter.

This unhappy combination stood untouched for several decades until someone added a stone tower off to one side. At the pinnacle of this tower was affixed a decorative lightning rod. A mistake. Lightning was meant to strike the building and burn it down.

Now a walkway covered by a solemn roof linked the tower directly to yet another wing. This wing was a separate entity once again, though it at least carried through a unified theme. The "mutual opposition of ideologies," shall we call it. It bespoke a certain pathos, rather like the mule who, placed between two identical buckets of fodder, dies of starvation trying to decide which to eat first.

To the left of the original structure, no less antithetical to the multiple elements already there, sprawled a traditional one-story Japanese-style villa. With marvelous hallways planked straight out like bowling lanes, surrounded with hedges and well-trained pines.

This triple-feature-plus-coming-attractions mélange of a house perched atop the hill was not a common sight. Had it been someone's grand scheme constructed over many years in an effort to shake off a stupor or chase away sleep, then it was an admirable success. Needless to say, an unlikely supposition. The monstrosity stood simply for money, piles of it, to which a long line of second-rate talents, era after era, had availed themselves.

I must have been staring at this apparition a while before I noticed the chauffeur next to me, looking at his watch. A pose he looked somehow accustomed to. He'd probably stood in that same spot with any number of persons he'd driven there. All of whom had gawked at the surroundings in exactly the same way.

"View all you care to, sir. Please do take your time," he said. "We still have eight minutes free."

"It sure is big," I said, for want of anything less inappropriate to say.

"Ninety-six thousand six hundred seventy-one square feet," said the chauffeur.

"Wouldn't surprise me if you had an active volcano in the place," I laughed, trying to inject some levity. But the joke didn't register. No one joked here.

Thus passed eight minutes.

I was conducted through the entryway to a large Western-style room on the immediate right. The ceiling, framed with elaborately carved moldings, was extraordinarily high. There was a handsome antique sofa and tea table, and on the wall a still life, the epitome of realism. Apples and a flower vase and a paper knife. Maybe the idea was to crack open the apples with the vase, then peel them with the paper knife. Seeds and cores could go in the vase.

The windows were appointed with thick curtains over lace curtains, pulled to the side with sashes of the same material. Through the opening between the curtains, a relatively sedate section of the gardens could be seen. The oak flooring was polished to a fine luster. A carpet, with a full pile despite its faded colors, covered half the floor.

Not a bad room. Not a bad room at all.

An elderly maid in kimono entered the room, set down a glass of grape juice, and left without a word. The door closed with a click. Then everything was dead quiet.

On the tea table were a silver cigarette case and lighter and ashtray identical to what was in the limo. Engraved with the same sheep emblem. I pulled one of my own filter tips out of my pocket, lit it with the silver lighter, and blew a puff of smoke up at the high ceiling. Then I took a sip of grape juice.

Ten minutes later, the door opened and in walked a tall man in a black suit. The man offered no "Welcome" or "Sorry to keep you waiting." I didn't say anything either. He took a seat opposite me, cocked his head slightly, and looked me over.

Time was surely passing.

Part Five

Letters from the Rat and Assorted Reminiscences

13

The Rat's First Letter

(Postmarked December 21st, One Year Ago)

So how's everything?

Seems like an awful long time since I saw you last. How many years is it now? What year was it?

I think I've gradually lost my sense of time. It's like there's this impossible flat blackbird flapping about over my head and I can't count above three. You'll have to excuse me, but why don't you do the counting?

I skipped town without telling anybody and maybe you had your share of troubles because of it. Or maybe you were upset at me for leaving without a word to you. You know, I meant to set things straight with you any number of times, but I just couldn't. I wrote a lot of letters and tore them all up. It should've been obvious, but there was no way I could explain to others what I couldn't even explain to myself.

I guess.

I've never been good at writing letters. Everything comes out backwards. I use exactly the wrong words. If that isn't bad enough, writing letters makes me more confused. And because I have no sense of humor, I get all discouraged with myself.

Generally, people who are good at writing letters have no need to write letters. They've got plenty of life to lead inside their own context. This, of course, is only my opinion. Maybe it's impossible to live out a life in context.

It's terribly cold now and my hands are numb. It's like they aren't my own hands. My brains, they aren't like my own brains either. Right now it's snowing. Snow like flakes of someone else's brains. And it'll pile up deeper and deeper like someone else's brains too. (What is this bullshit all about anyway?)

Other than the cold, though, I'm doing fine. How about you? I won't tell you my address, but don't take it personally. It's not like I'm trying to hide anything from you. I want you to know that. This is, you see, a delicate question for me. It's just this feeling I've got that, if I told you my address, in that instant something inside me would change. I can't put it very well.

It seems to me, though, that you always understand very well what I can't say very well. Trouble is I end up being even worse at saying things well. It's got to be an inborn fault.

Naturally everyone's got faults.

My biggest fault is that the faults I was born with grow bigger each year. It's like I was raising chickens inside me. The chickens lay eggs and the eggs hatch into other chickens, which then lay eggs. Is this any way to live a life? What with all these faults I've got going, I have to wonder. Sure, I get by. But in the end, that's not the question, is it?

In any case, I've decided I'm not giving you my address. I'm sure things'll be better that way. For me and for you.

Probably we'd have been better off born in nineteenth-century

Russia. I'd have been Prince So-and-so and you Count Such-and-such. We'd go hunting together, fight, be rivals in love, have our metaphysical complaints, drink beer watching the sunset from the shores of the Black Sea. In our later years, the two of us would be implicated in the Something-or-other Rebellion and exiled to Siberia, where we'd die. Brilliant, don't you think? Me, if I'd been born in the nineteenth century, I'm sure I could have written better novels. Maybe not your Dostoyevsky, but a known second-rate novelist. And what would you have been doing? Maybe you'd only have been Count Such-and-such straight through. That wouldn't be so bad, just being Count Such-and-such. That'd be nice and nineteenth century.

But well, enough of this. To return to the twentieth century.

Let me tell you about the towns I've seen.

Not the town where I was born, but different other towns.

There really are a lot of different other towns in the world. Each with its own specific features, incomprehensible things that attract me. Which is why I've passed through my share of towns these past few years.

Wherever I end up, I just get off at, and there's a small rotary where a map of the town is posted and a street of shops. That much is the same everywhere. Even the dogs look the same. First thing I do is a quick once-around the place before heading to a real estate agent to see about cheap room and board. Sure I'm an outsider and nobody in a small town will trust me right off, but as you know I can be decent enough if I put half a mind to it. Give me fifteen minutes, and I can generally get on good terms with most people. That much accomplished, I've found out where I can fit in and all sorts of information about the town.

Next, I look for work. This also begins with getting on good terms with a lot of different people. I'm sure this'd be a comedown for someone like you (and believe me, I've seen enough comedowns to last me) because you know you're only going to stick around for four months anyway. But there's nothing hard about getting on good terms with people. You find the local watering hole where all the kids hang out (every town has one—it's like the town navel), you become a regular customer, meet people, get an introduction for some work. Of course, you come up with some likely name and life story. So that by now I've got a string of names and identities like you wouldn't believe. At times I forget what I was like originally.

In the work department, I've done all kinds of jobs. Most have been boring, but still I enjoy the work. Most often it's been at a gasoline station. Next is tending some rinky-dink bar. I've minded shop at bookstores, even worked at a radio station. I've hired out as a day laborer. Been a cosmetics salesman. I had quite a reputation as a salesman, let me tell you. And I've slept with my share of women. Sleeping with women each time with a different name and identity isn't half bad.

You get the picture, in all its variations.

So now I'm twenty-nine, turning thirty in another nine months.

I still don't know whether I'm cut out for this kind of life or not. I don't know if there's something universal about wanting to be a drifter. But as somebody once wrote somewhere, you need one of three things for a long life of wandering—a religious temperament, or an artistic temperament, or a psychic temperament. If you have one but only on the short side, an extended drifter's existence is out of the question. In my case, I can't see myself with any of them. In a pinch, I might say . . . no, better not.

Otherwise, I might end up opening the wrong door some day, only to find I can't back out. Whatever, if the door's been opened,

I better make a go of it. I mean I can't keep buying my kicks for the rest of my life, can I?

That's about the size of it.

Like I said at the beginning (or did I?), when I think of you, I get a little uneasy. Because you remind me of when I was a comparatively regular guy.

Your friend,
The Rat

P.S.: *I enclose a novel I wrote. It doesn't mean anything to me anymore, so do whatever you want with it. I'm sending this special delivery to make sure it reaches you by December 24. Hope it gets there on time.*

Anyway, Happy Birthday.

And by the way, Merry Christmas.

The Rat's package was shoved all crumpled up into my apartment mailbox on December 29. Attached was a forwarding slip. It had been sent to my previous address. There'd been no way to tell him I'd moved.

Four pages of pale-green stationery packed solid with writing. I read the letter through three times before I brought out the envelope to check the blurred postmark. It was a place I'd never heard of. I got the atlas down from my bookshelf and looked the place up.

The Rat's words had reached me from a small town on the northern tip of Honshu, smack in the middle of Aomori Prefecture. According to my book of train schedules, about an hour from the city of Aomori. Five trains stopped every day, two in the morning, one at noon, two in the evening.

I'd been to Aomori several times in December. Frigid. The traffic signals freeze.

I showed the letter to my wife, wife at the time, that is. All she could say was "poor guy." What she probably meant was *you poor guys*. Hell, it makes no difference now.

I tossed the novel, around two hundred pages, into my desk drawer without bothering to read the title. I don't know why, I just didn't feel like reading it. The letter was enough.

I pulled a chair up in front of the heater and smoked three cigarettes.

The Rat's next letter came in May the following year.

14

The Rat's Second Letter

(Postmarked May, This Year)

Last letter I think maybe I was a little too chatty. Even so, I've forgotten completely what I said.

I changed addresses again. Some place totally different from any place I've been up to now. It's really quiet here. Maybe a little too quiet.

In a sense, I've reached what is for me a final destination. I feel like I've come to where I was meant to come. What's more, I feel I've had to swim against the current to get here. But that's nothing I can pass judgment on.

What lousy writing! It's so vague you probably have no idea what I'm talking about. Or maybe you think I'm reading too much meaning into my fate. If that's the case, then the blame is all mine.

I want you to know that the more I try to explain to you what's going on with me, the more I start to digress like this. Still, I'm in good shape. Maybe better shape than I've ever been.

Let me put things more concretely.

Hereabouts, as I said earlier, it's incredibly quiet. There's noth-

ing to do around here, so I read books (I've got enough books here to last me a decade) or listen to FM music or to records (got a whole lot here too). It's been ten years since I listened to so much music. To my surprise, the Rolling Stones and Beach Boys are still going strong. Time really is one big continuous cloth, no? We habitually cut out pieces of time to fit us, so we tend to fool ourselves into thinking that time is our size, but it really goes on and on.

Here, there is nothing my size. There's nobody around here to make himself the measure of everything, to praise or condemn others for their size.

Time keeps on flowing unchanged like a clear river too. Sometimes just being here I feel my slate has been cleaned, and I'm all the way back to my primal state. For example, if I catch sight of a car, it takes me a few seconds before I realize it's a car. Sure, I must have some kind of fundamental awareness that it's a car, but it doesn't quite get across to my immediate waking consciousness. These experiences have been happening to me more and more lately. Maybe it's because for a long time now I've been living by myself.

The nearest town is an hour and a half away by car. No, it's not even a town. Imagine your smallest town, then reduce it to a skeleton. I doubt you can picture it. I guess you'd have to call it a town anyway. You can buy clothes and groceries and gasoline. And if you get an urge to see other human beings, they're there to be seen.

All winter long the roads are frozen and almost no cars come through. Off the roads, it's damp, so the ground is frosted over like sherbet. When there's snowfall, it's impossible to tell what's road and what's not. It's a landscape that might as well be the end of the world.

I came here at the beginning of March. Driving through the thick of it, chains on the tires of the jeep. Just like being exiled to Siberia. But now it's May and the snow has all melted. From April on, the mountains were rumbling with snowslides. Ever hear a snowslide? Right after a snowslide comes the most perfect silence. Complete, total silence. You lose almost all sense of where you are. It's that quiet.

Sealed off in the mountains all this time, I haven't slept with a woman for the last three months. Which isn't bad, as far as that goes. All the same, if I stayed up here like this much longer, I know I'd lose all interest in people, and that's not something I want to do. So I'm thinking that when the weather gets a little warmer I'll stretch my legs and find myself a woman. I don't want to brag, but finding women has never been much of a problem for me. So long as I don't care—and staying here is living proof that I don't care—then sex appeal's easy, not a problem. It's not a big deal for me to put the moves on. The problem is, I myself am not at ease with this ability of mine. That is to say, when things get to a certain point, I lose track of where I myself stop and where my sex appeal begins. It's like where does Olivier stop and Othello begin? So midway when I find I'm not getting a return on all I'm putting into the situation, I toss everything overboard. Which makes problems for everyone all the way around. My whole life up to now has been nothing but one big repetition of this after another.

But this time I can be grateful (really, I am) that I don't have anything to throw overboard. A great feeling. The only thing I could possibly throw overboard would be myself. Not such a bad idea, throwing myself overboard. No, this is getting to sound pathetic. The idea itself, though, isn't pathetic in the least. I'm not feeling sorry for myself. It only sounds that way when I write it down.

Moan and groan.

What the hell was I talking about?

Women, that's right.

Each woman has a drawer marked "beautiful," stuffed full of all sorts of meaningless junk. That's my specialty. I pull out those pieces of junk one by one, dust them off, and find some kind of meaning in them. That's all that sex appeal really is, I think. But so what? What's that good for? There's nowhere to go from there short of stopping being myself.

So now I'm thinking about sex pure and simple. If I focus purely on sex, there's no need to get all bent out of shape whether I'm feeling sorry for myself or not.

It's like drinking beer on the shores of the Black Sea.

I just went back over what I've written so far. A few inconsistencies here and there, but pretty honest writing by my standards. All the more so because it's boring.

I don't even seem to be writing this letter to you. Probably the postbox is as far as my thinking goes. But don't get on my case for that. It's an hour and a half by jeep to the nearest postbox.

From here on, this letter is addressed to you.

I've got two favors to ask of you. Neither is in the particularly urgent category, so whenever you get around to taking care of them is fine. I'd really appreciate it. Three months ago I probably couldn't have brought myself to ask anything of you. But now I can. That's progress, I guess.

The first is a sort of sentimental request. Meaning it has to do with "the past." Five years ago when I skipped town, I was in such a confused hurry, I forgot to say goodbye to a number of people. Specifically, you and J and this woman you don't know. I guess I could probably see you again to tell you goodbye face-to-face, but with the other two I know I'll never have the chance. So if you're ever back there, can you say goodbye to them for me.

I know it's a selfish request. I ought to write them myself. But honestly, I'd rather have you go back there and see them for me. I know my feelings will get across better that way. I'm including her address and phone number separately. If she's moved or married by now, then it's okay, you don't have to see her. Leave things at that. But if she's still at the same address, give her my best.

And be sure to give J my best too. Have a beer for me.

That's one.

The other favor is maybe a bit odd.

I'm enclosing a photo. A picture of sheep. I'd like you to put it somewhere, I don't care where, but someplace people can see it. I realize I'm making this request out of the blue, but I've got no one else I can ask. I'll let you have every last ounce of my sex appeal if you do me this favor. I can't tell you the reason why, though. This photo is important to me. Sometime, at some later date, I'll explain everything to you.

I'm enclosing a check. Use it for whatever expenses you have. There's no need for you to have to worry about money. I'm hard put even to find a way to use money here, and anyway at the moment it's about the extent of what I can do for you.

Make sure you don't forget to have a beer for me.

Your friend,
The Rat

I found the letter in my mailbox as I was leaving my apartment and read it at my desk at the office.

The postmark was obliterated beyond legibility. I tore open the flap. Inside the envelope was a check for one hundred thousand yen, a piece of paper with a woman's name and address, and a black-and-white photograph of sheep. The letter was written on the same pale-green stationery as before and the check was drawn on a bank in Sapporo. Which would mean that the Rat had crossed further north to Hokkaido.

The bit about snowslides didn't register with me, but it did strike me, as the Rat himself had said, as an honest letter. Besides, nobody sends a check for one hundred thousand yen as a joke. I opened my desk drawer and tossed in the whole lot, envelope and all.

Maybe it was because my marriage was falling apart at the time, but spring that year had no joy for me. My wife hadn't come home in four days. Her toothbrush by the washbasin was caked and cracked like a fossil. The milk in the refrigerator smelled sour, and the cat was always hungry. A lazy spring sun poured in on this state of affairs. At least sunlight is always free.

A long, drawn-out dead-end street—probably just what she meant.

15

The Song Is Over

It was June before I returned to the town.

I cooked up some reason to take three days off and took the Bullet Train early one Tuesday. A white short-sleeved sports shirt, green cotton pants worn through at the knees, white tennis shoes, no luggage. I'd even forgotten to shave after getting up that morning. It was the first time I'd put on tennis shoes in ages and the heels were worn through crooked. I'd been walking off-center without knowing it.

Boarding a long-distance train without any luggage gave me a feeling of exhilaration. It was as if while out taking a leisurely stroll, I was suddenly like a dive-bomber caught in a space-time warp. In which there is nothing: no dentist's appointments, no pending issues in desk drawers, no inextricably complicated human involvements, no favors demanded. I'd left that behind, temporarily. All I had with me were my tennis shoes with their misshapen rubber soles. They held fast to my feet like vague memories of another space-time. But that hardly mattered. Nothing that some canned beer and dried-out ham sandwiches couldn't put out of mind.

It had been four years. Four years ago, the return home had been to take care of paperwork related to the family registry when I got married. When I thought back on it, what a pointless trip! I thought it was all paperwork. The problem was that nobody else thought it. It comes down to the different ways in which minds work. What's over for one person isn't over for another. But the path splits in two different directions, and so you end up apart.

From that point on there was no hometown for me. Nowhere to return to. What a relief! No one to want me, no one to want anything from me.

I had a second can of beer and caught thirty minutes of shut-eye. When I woke up, that initial carefree sense of release was gone. The train moved on, and as it did, the sky turned a rain-gray. Beneath which stretched the same boring scenery. No matter how much speed we put on, there was no escaping boredom. On the contrary, the faster the speed, the more headway into boredom. Ah, the nature of boredom.

Next to me sat a business type in his mid-twenties, engrossed in a newspaper, hardly moving the whole time. Navy-blue summer suit, not a wrinkle. Starched white shirt, just back from the cleaners. Shiny black shoes.

I looked up at the ceiling of the car and puffed on a cigarette. I made mental lists of all the songs the Beatles ever recorded. Seventy-three titles before I ran out. I wonder how many numbers Paul McCartney himself would remember? I stared out the window awhile, then shifted my eyes back to the ceiling.

I was twenty-nine years old. In six months my twenties would be over. A whole decade since living here. One big blank. Not one thing of value had I gotten out of it, not one meaningful thing had I done. Boredom was all there was.

How were things before? Surely there had to have been something positive. Had there been anything that really moved me, anything that really moved anyone? Maybe, but it was all gone now. Lost, perhaps meant to be lost. Nothing I can do about it, got to let it go.

At least I was still around. If the only good Indian is a dead Indian, it was my fate to go on living.

What for?

To tell tales to a stone wall?

Really, now.

"Why stay in a hotel?" J asked when I wrote my hotel number on the back of a matchbook and handed it to him. "You've got a home, haven't you? Why not stay there?"

"It's not my home anymore," I said.

J didn't say anything to that.

With three plates of snacks lined up in front of me, I drank half my beer, then pulled out the Rat's letters and handed them to J. He wiped his hands on a towel, read the two letters through quickly before going over them again carefully, word by word.

"Hmm, alive and kicking, is he?"

"He's alive, all right," I said, taking another sip of beer. "But you know, before I do anything else, I've got to shave. You have a razor and some shaving cream you could lend me?"

"I do," said J, bringing out a travel kit from behind the counter. "You can use the washroom, but there's no hot water."

"Cold water's fine," I said. "As long as there's no drunk woman sprawled out on the floor. Makes it hard to shave."

J's Bar had completely changed.

The old J's Bar had been a dank place in the basement of an old building by the highway. On summer nights with the air conditioner going, a fine mist would form. After a long bout of drinking, even your shirt would be damp.

J's real name was some unpronounceable Chinese polysyllable. The nickname J was given to him by some GIs on the base where he worked after the war. His real name was soon forgotten.

In 1954, J quit his job on the base and opened a small bar. The very first J's Bar. The bar proved quite successful. A large part of the clientele was from the air force officer candidate school, and the atmosphere wasn't bad. After the bar got its start, J got married, but five years later his wife died. J never talked about the cause of her death.

In 1963, as the Vietnam War was beginning to go great guns, J sold the bar and moved far away to my hometown. There he opened the second J's Bar.

He had a cat, smoked a pack of cigarettes a day, never touched a drop of alcohol. That's the sum of everything I know about J.

Up until the time I met the Rat, I always went to J's Bar alone. I'd sip a beer slowly, smoke cigarettes, and feed coins into the jukebox. This was when J's Bar was usually empty, so I'd sit at the counter talking about all kinds of things with J, though about what exactly I don't remember. What could a shy seventeen-year-old high school student and a Chinese widower have to talk about?

When I turned eighteen and left town, the Rat came along and took my place at the bar drinking beer. Five years ago, when the Rat left town, there was no one to take his place. Six months later, when the road was widened, J had to change shops again, and the second J's Bar was relegated to legend.

The third J's Bar was a quarter of a mile away, by the river. It wasn't much bigger than the old place, but it was on the third floor of a new four-story building with an elevator. Taking an elevator to J's Bar made me feel like I had the address wrong. The same with looking out over the lights of town from the counter.

This new place had big windows facing west and south, out onto the line of hills and the area where the ocean used to be. The oceanfront had been filled in a few years back, and the whole mile there was packed with gravestone rows of tall buildings.

"Used to be water over there," I said.

"Right," said J.

"Went swimming there a lot."

"Yeah," said J, bringing a generic lighter up to the cigarette at his lips, "they bulldoze the hills to put up houses, haul the dirt to the sea for landfill, then go and build there too. And they think it's all fine and proper."

I drank my beer. The ceiling speakers were playing the latest Boz Scaggs hit. There wasn't a jukebox in sight. Almost all the customers in the place were university student couples, neatly dressed and politely sipping their highballs. No girls on the verge of passing out drunk, no hot fights brewing. You could tell that when they went home, they put on pajamas, brushed their teeth, and went straight to bed. There was nothing wrong with that. Nice and neat is fine and dandy. There's nothing in a bar or in the world at large that says things have to be a certain way.

J kept his eyes on me the whole while.

"So, everything's different and you feel out of place?"

"Not really," I said. "It's just that the chaos has changed shape. The giraffe and the bear have traded hats, and the bear's switched scarves with the zebra."

"Same as ever," J laughed.

"Times have changed," I said. "A lot of things have changed. But the bottom line is, that's fine. Everyone trades places. No complaints."

J didn't say anything.

I had myself another beer, J had another cigarette.

"How's your life going?" asked J.

"Not bad."

"How's the wife?"

"Don't really know. You know how things are between two people. There are times when I think everything's working out fine and times I don't. Maybe that's what marriage is all about."

"Well maybe," said J, scratching the tip of his nose with his little finger. "I forget what married life is like. It's been so long."

"How's the cat?"

"Died four years ago. Right after you got married. Something intestinal. . . . But really, it had a good, long life. Lived twelve years. That's longer than my wife was with me. Twelve years isn't a bad little life, is it?"

"Guess not."

"There's this animal cemetery up on the hill, so I buried it there. Overlooking the tall buildings. Anywhere around here those buildings are all you can see. Not that it makes much difference to a cat."

"Sad?"

"Sure. Even if a person had died, I wouldn't have been as sad. Does that sound funny?"

I shook my head.

vodka lime instead of after-shave. J claimed it was just as effective, but now my whole face smelled like vodka.

The night was unexpectedly warm, though the sky was its usual heavy overcast. A moist breeze was blowing in slow and easy from the south. Same as it used to. A sea scent mingled with a hint of rain. Insects calling from the clumps of grass along the river. Everything brimming with a languid nostalgia. It seemed that it would rain any minute. When it did, it came in so fine a drizzle that you couldn't tell if it was raining or not, but I got completely drenched anyway.

I could just make out the river flowing in the white light of the mercury-vapor streetlamp. The water was as clear as ever. It came straight out of the hills with nothing to pollute it along the way. The river had silted up with the small rocks and gravel washed down from the hills, creating little falls here and there. Beneath each fall, a deep pool had formed where small fish gathered.

During dry spells, the whole river used to dry up into a sandy bed, leaving only a faintly damp white trail. Years ago, on my walks, I'd trace that trail upstream, searching for where the river had gone.

The road by the river had been one of my favorites. I could walk at the same speed as the river. I could feel it breathing. It was alive. More than anything, it was the river we had to thank for creating the town. For grinding down the hills over how many hundreds of thousands of years, for hauling the dirt, filling the sea, and making the trees grow. The town belonged to the river from the very beginning, and it would always be that way.

Because this was the rainy season, the river flowed uninterrupted to the sea. The trees planted along the banks were fragrant with new leaves. There was a greenness in the air. Couples strolled arm in arm, old folks walked their dogs, high school kids hung

J set to making some fancy cocktail and a Caesar salad for a customer. Meanwhile, I played with a Scandinavian puzzle on the counter. You were supposed to put together this picture of three butterflies midair over a field of clover, all inside a glass case. I gave up after ten minutes and put the thing aside.

"No kids?" J came back over to ask. "You're getting on the right age to have kids, you know."

"Don't want kids."

"Oh?"

"I mean I would be at a loss if I had a kid like me."

J chuckled and poured more beer into my glass. "You're always thinking too far ahead."

"No, that's not it. What I mean is, I don't really know if it's the right thing to do, making new life. Kids grow up, generations take their place. What does it all come to? More hills bulldozed and more oceanfront filled in? Faster cars and more cats run over? Who needs it?"

"That's only the dark side of things. Good things happen too, good people can make things worthwhile."

"Yeah? Name three," I said.

J gave it a thought, then laughed. "That's for your children's generation to decide, not you. Your generation . . ."

"Is already over and done with?"

"In a sense," said J.

"The song is over. But the melody lingers on."

"You always had a way of putting things."

"Just showing off," I said.

At nine o'clock, J's Bar was starting to get crowded, so I said good night to J and left. My face still tingled in the spots where I'd shaved, having only cold water. Maybe because I'd splashed on around their motorbikes, smoking cigarettes. Your typical early summer evening.

I stopped into a liquor store, bought two cans of beer, and carried them in a paper bag down to the sea. Where the river met the sea, it turned into an inlet, or rather into a half-filled-in canal. Here was the only untouched stretch of oceanfront left, fifty yards of it. There was even something of the old beach. Small waves rolled in, leaving smooth pieces of driftwood. On the concrete jetty, bits of old nails and spray-paint graffiti remained.

Fifty yards of honest-to-goodness shoreline. If you overlooked the fact that it was hemmed in by thirty-foot-high concrete walls. And that the walls kept going straight out for several miles, channeling the sea narrowly in between. And that tall buildings lined either side. Fifty yards of sea. The rest was history.

I left the river and walked east along what had been the coastline road. Bewilderingly enough, the old jetty was still there. Now a jetty without an ocean is an odd creature indeed. I stopped at the exact spot where I used to park to look at the sea, went over to sit down on the jetty, and drank a beer. What a view! Instead of ocean, a vast expanse of reclaimed land and housing developments met my eyes. Faceless blocks of apartments, the miserable foundations of an attempt to build a neighborhood.

Asphalt roads threaded through the building complexes, here a parking lot, there a bus terminal. A gasoline station and a large park and a wonderful community center. Everything brand new, everything unnatural. On one side, the piles of soil hauled down from the hills for landfill loomed harsh and gray next to the areas which, not a part of the grand scheme, had been overtaken by quick-rooting weeds.

But what was there to say? Already it was a whole new game played by new rules. No one could stop it now.

I polished off my two beers and hurled the empty cans across the reclaimed land, toward where the sea used to be. I watched them disappear into the sea of windblown weeds. Then I smoked a cigarette.

I was taking my last drag when I saw a man, flashlight in hand, heading my way. Fortyish, gray shirt, gray trousers, and a gray cap. Probably a security guard for the area.

"You just threw something, didn't you?" said the man.

"Yeah, I threw something."

"What did you throw?"

"Round, metallic, lidded objects."

The security guard put on a sour face. "Why'd you throw them?"

"No particular reason. Been throwing things from twelve years back. At times, I've thrown half a dozen things at once and nobody said a word."

"That was back then," said the security guard. "This is city property now and it's against the law to discard rubbish on city property."

I swallowed. For a moment something inside me trembled, then stopped. "The real problem here," I said, "is that what you say makes sense."

"It's the law," he said.

I sighed and took the pack of cigarettes out of my pocket.

"So what should I do?"

"Well, I can't ask you go pick them up. It's too dark and it's about to rain. So do me a favor and don't throw things again."

"I won't," I said. "Good night."

"Good night," said the security guard as he walked away.

I stretched out on the jetty and looked up at the sky. As the man said, it was starting to rain. I smoked another cigarette and thought over the encounter with the guard. Ten years ago I would have come on tougher. Well, maybe not. What difference would it make anyway?

I went back to the riverside road, and by the time I'd managed to catch a taxi the rain was coming down in a drizzle. To the hotel, I said.

"Here on a trip?" asked the old driver.

"Uh-huh."

"First time in these parts?"

"Second time," I said.

16

She Drinks Her Salty Dog, Talking about the Sound of the Waves

"I have a letter for you," I said.

"For me?" she said.

The connection was bad, so we practically had to shout, which was not very conducive to communicating delicate shades of feeling. It was like talking on a windswept hill through upturned collars.

"Actually, the letter's addressed to me, but somehow it seems to be meant more for you."

"It does, does it?"

"Yes, it does," I said. As soon as I'd said it, I knew this whole idiotic conversation was going nowhere fast.

She said nothing for a moment. Meanwhile, the connection cleared up.

"I have no idea what went on between you and the Rat. But he did ask me to see you, and that's why I'm calling. Besides, I think it'd be better if you read his letters."

"And that's why you came out all the way from Tokyo?"

"That's right."

She coughed, excused herself, then said, "Because he's your friend?"

"I suppose."

"Why do you suppose he didn't write to me directly?"

She did have a point.

"I don't know," I said, honestly.

"I don't know either. I mean, I thought everything was over. Or isn't it?"

I had no idea and I told her so. I lay back on the hotel bed, phone receiver in hand, and looked at the ceiling. I could be lying on the ocean floor counting fish, I thought. How many would I have to count before I could say I was done?

"It was five years ago when he disappeared. I was twenty-seven at the time," she said, distant voice sounding like an echo from the bottom of a well. "A lot of things can change in five years."

"True," I said.

"And really, even if nothing had changed, I wouldn't see it that way. I wouldn't want to admit it. Once I did, I wouldn't be able to go anywhere. So as far as I'm concerned, everything's completely changed."

"I think I understand," I said.

A brief pause hovered between us.

It was she who broke the silence. "When was the last time you saw him?" she asked.

"Spring, five years ago, right before he up and left."

"And did he tell you anything? I mean about why he was leaving town . . . ?"

"Nope."

"So he left you with no warning either?"

"That's right."

"And what did you think? At the time, I mean."

"About him up and leaving like that?"

"Yeah."

I got up from the bed and leaned against the wall. "Well, for sure I thought he'd give up and come back after six months. He never struck me as the stick-with-it type."

"But he didn't come back."

"No, he didn't."

There was a slight hesitation on her end of the line.

"Where is it you're staying now?" she asked.

I told her the name of the hotel.

"I'll meet you there tomorrow at five. The coffee lounge on the eighth floor all right?"

"Fine," I said. "I'll be wearing a white sports shirt and green cotton slacks. I've got short hair and . . ."

"I've got the picture," she said, cheerfully cutting me off. Then she hung up.

I replaced the receiver. What did she mean, she got the picture? *I* didn't get the picture, but then again, there are lots of things I don't know anything about. Age certainly hasn't conferred any smarts on me. Character maybe, but mediocrity is a constant, as one Russian writer put it. Russians have a way with aphorisms. They probably spend all winter thinking them up.

I took a shower, washed my rain-soaked hair, and with the towel wrapped around my waist, I watched an old American submarine movie on television. The creaking plot had the captain and first officer constantly at each other's throat. The submarine was a fossil, and one guy had claustrophobia. But all that didn't stop everything from working out well in the end. It was an everything-works-out-in-the-end-so-maybe-war's-not-so-bad-after-all sort of film. One of these days they'll be making a film where the whole human race gets wiped out in a nuclear war, but everything works out in the end.

I switched off the television, climbed into bed, and was asleep in ten seconds.

The drizzle still hadn't let up by five o'clock the next evening. The rain had been preceded by four or five days of crisp, clear early summer skies, fooling people into thinking the rainy season was over. From the eighth-floor window, every square inch of ground looked dark and damp, and a traffic jam stretched for several miles on the eastbound lanes of the elevated expressway.

As I stared out long and hard, things began to melt in the rain. In fact, everything in town was melting. The breakwater, the cranes, the rows of buildings, the figures beneath their black umbrellas, everything. Even the greenery was flowing down from the hills. Yet when I shut my eyes for a few seconds and opened them again, the town was back the way it had been. Six cranes loomed in the dark haze, trains headed east as if their engines had just restarted, flocks of umbrellas dodged back and forth across the streets of shops, the green hills soaked up their fill of June rain.

In a sunken area in the middle of the coffee lounge, a woman wearing a bright pink dress sat at a cerulean blue grand piano playing quintessential hotel-coffee-lounge numbers filled with arpeggios and syncopation. Not bad actually, though not an echo lingered in the air beyond the last note of each number.

It was past five o'clock and she hadn't arrived. Since I had nothing better to do, I had a second cup of coffee and watched the piano player. She was about twenty, her shoulder-length hair immaculately coiffed like whipped cream atop a cake. The coif swayed merrily, left and right, to the rhythm, bouncing back to center when the song ended. Then the next number would begin.

She reminded me of a girl I used to know in the third grade, when I was taking piano lessons. The same age, the same class. We sometimes had to play duets together. But her name and face, entirely forgotten. All I remember about her are her tiny pale hands and pretty hair and fluffy dress.

It's disturbing to realize this. Have I stripped her of her hands and hair and dress? Is the rest of her still living unattached somewhere else? Of course, this can't be. The world goes on without me. People cross streets through no intervention on my part, sharpen pencils, move fifty yards a minute west to east, fill coffee lounges with music that's refined into nothingness.

The "world"—the word always makes me think of a tortoise and elephants tirelessly supporting a gigantic disc. The elephants have no knowledge of the tortoise's role, the tortoise unable to see what the elephants are doing. And neither is the least aware of the world on their backs.

"Sorry to keep you waiting," a woman's voice from behind me said. "Work ran late, and I just couldn't get free."

"No problem. I didn't have anything to do today anyway."

She dropped her keys down on the table and ordered an orange juice without bothering to look at the menu. Her age was not easy to tell. If she hadn't mentioned it to me over the phone, I probably would not have known. If she had said she was thirty-three, she would have looked thirty-three to me. If she'd said twenty-seven, then she'd have looked twenty-seven. At face value.

Her taste in clothes was nicely succinct. Ample white cotton slacks, an orange-and-yellow checkered blouse, sleeves rolled up to the elbows, and a leather shoulder bag. None of them new, but all well cared for. She wore no rings or necklace or bracelet or earrings. Her bangs were short and brushed casually to the side.

The tiny wrinkles at the corners of her eyes might have been there from birth rather than acquired with age. Only her slender, fair neckline, visible from the button open at her collar, and the backs of her hands hinted at her age. People start aging from early, very early, on. Gradually it spreads over their entire body like a stain that cannot be wiped away.

"What sort of work?" I ventured to ask.

"Drafting work at an architectural office. I've been there for a long time now."

The conversation trailed off. I slowly took out a cigarette and lit up. The piano player stopped playing, brought the lid down, and retired somewhere for her break. I envied her.

"How long have you been friends with him?" she asked.

"Eleven years, I guess. And you?"

"Two months, ten days," she answered right off. "From the time I first met him to the time he disappeared. Two months and ten days. I remember because I keep a diary."

The orange juice came and my empty coffee cup was spirited away.

"I waited three months after he disappeared. December, January, February. The coldest time of the year. Maybe it was a cold winter that year?"

"I don't recall," I said, though the cold of winter five years ago now seemed like yesterday's weather.

"Have you ever waited for a woman like that?"

"No," I said.

"You concentrate on waiting for someone and after a certain

time it hardly matters what happens anymore. It could be five years or ten years or one month. It's all the same."

I nodded.

She drank half her orange juice.

"It was that way when I was first married," she said. "I was always the one who waited, until I got tired of waiting, and in the end I didn't care. Married at twenty-one, divorced at twenty-two. Then I came here."

"It was the same with my wife."

"What was?"

"Married at twenty-one, divorced at twenty-two."

She studied my face awhile. Then stirred her orange juice with her swizzle stick. I'd spoken unnecessarily, it seemed.

"When you're young, it's hard getting married then getting divorced right away," she said. "The thing is you're looking for something two-dimensional and not quite real. It never lasts. But you can't expect something unreal to last anyway, can you?"

"I suppose not."

"In the five years between my divorce and when I met him, I was all alone in this town. Living a life that was, well, rather unreal. I hardly knew anyone, rarely went out, had no romance. I'd get up in the morning, go to the office, draft plans, stop by the supermarket on the way home to shop, and eat dinner at home alone. I'd listen to FM radio, read, write in my diary, wash my stockings in the bath. My apartment's near the ocean, so there's always the sound of the surf. It was cold and lonely."

She finished the rest of her orange juice.

"It seems I'm boring you."

I shook my head.

Past six. The lights in the lounge dimmed for cocktail hour. The lights of town began to blink on. Red lights lit up on the cranes. Fine needles of rain became visible through the gathering dusk.

"Care for a drink?" I asked.

"What do you call vodka with grapefruit juice?"

"A salty dog."

I called the waiter and ordered a salty dog and a Cutty Sark on the rocks.

"Where were we?"

"Your cold and lonely life."

"Well, if you really want to know, it hasn't been all that cold and lonely," she said. "Just the sound of the waves is. That alone puts a chill on things. When I moved in, the superintendent said I'd get used to it soon enough, but I still haven't."

"The ocean's no longer there."

She smiled softly. A hint of movement came to the wrinkles at the corners of her eyes. "True. As you say, the ocean's no longer there. But even so, I swear I can sometimes still hear the waves. It's probably imprinted into my ears over the years."

"Then the Rat appeared."

"Yes. Although I never called him that."

"What did you call him?"

"By his name. Like everybody else."

Come to think it, "The Rat" did sound a bit childish, even for a nickname. "Hmm," I said.

They brought our drinks. She took a sip of her salty dog, then wiped the salt from her lips with the napkin. The napkin came away with the slightest trace of lipstick. Then she folded the lipstick-blushed napkin deftly and laid it down.

"He was, what can I say . . . unreal enough. Do you know what I mean?"

"I think so."

"I guess it took someone as unreal as him to break through my own unreality. It struck me the very first time I met him. That's why I liked him. Or maybe I only thought so after I got to like him. It amounts to the same thing either way."

The piano player returned from her break and began to play themes from old film scores. Perfect: the wrong background music for the wrong scene.

"I sometimes think maybe, in the end, I was only using him. And maybe he sensed it all along. What do you think?"

"I wouldn't know," I said. "That's between you and him."

She said nothing.

After a full twenty seconds of silence, I realized she'd run out of things to say. I downed the last of my whiskey and retrieved the Rat's letters from my pocket, placing them in the center of the table. Where they sat for a while.

"Do I have to read them here?"

"Please take them home and read them. If you don't want to read them, then do whatever you want with them."

She nodded. She put the letters in her bag, which she fastened with a snap of the clasp. I lit up a second cigarette and ordered another whiskey. The second whiskey is always my favorite. From the third on, it no longer has any taste. It's just something to pour into your stomach.

"You came all the way from Tokyo for this reason?" she asked.

"Pretty much so."

"You're very kind."

"I've never thought about it that way. A matter of habit. If the tables were turned, I'm sure he'd do the same for me."

"Have you ever asked something like this of him?"

I shook my head. "No, but we go back a long time imposing

our unrealities on each other. Whether we've managed to take care of things realistically or not is another question."

"Maybe nobody really can."

"Maybe not."

She smiled and got up, whisking away the bill. "Let me take care of this. I was forty minutes late, after all."

"If you're sure, then by all means," I said. "But one more thing, I was wondering if I could ask you a question."

"Certainly."

"Over the phone you said you could picture how I looked."

"I meant there was something I could sense about you."

"And that was enough for you to spot me right away?"

"I could tell in no time at all."

The rain kept falling at the same rate. From my hotel window, through the neon signs of the building next door, a hundred thousand strands of rain sped earthward through a green glow. If I looked down, the rain seemed to pour straight into one fixed point on the ground.

I plopped down on the bed and smoked a couple cigarettes, then called the front desk to make a reservation for a train the following morning. There was nothing left for me to do in town.

The rain kept falling until midnight.

Part Six

A Wild Sheep Chase, II

The Strange Man's Strange Tale

The black-suited secretary took his chair and looked at me without saying a word. He didn't seem to be sizing me up, nor did his eyes betray any disdain, nor was his a pointed stare to bore right through me. Neither cool nor hot, not even in the mid-range. That gaze held no hint of any emotion known to me. The man was simply looking at me. He might have been looking at the wall behind me, but as I was situated in front of it, the end result was that the man was looking at me.

The man picked up the cigarette case from the table, opened the lid and withdrew a plain-cut cigarette, flicked the tip a few times with his fingernail, lit up with the tabletop lighter, and blew out the smoke at an oblique angle. Then he returned the lighter to the table and crossed his legs. His gaze did not waver one blink the whole time.

This was the same man my partner had told me about. He was overdressed, his fingers overly graceful. If not for the sharp curve of his eyelids and the glass-bead chill of his pupils, I would surely have thought him homosexual. Not with those eyes, though. So what did he look like? He didn't resemble any sort, anything.

If you took a good look at his eyes, they were an arresting color. Dark brown with the faintest touch of blue, the hue of the left eye, moreover, different from the right. Each seemed to focus on a wholly different subject.

His fingers pursued scant movements on his lap. Hauntingly, as if separated from his hand, they moved toward me. Tense, compelling, nerve-racking, beautiful fingers. Slowly reaching across the table to crush out the cigarette not one-third smoked. I watched the ice melt in the glass, clear ice water mixing with the grape juice. An unequally variegated mix.

The room was utterly silent. Now there is the silence you encounter on entering a grand manor. And there is the silence that comes of too few people in too big a space. But this was a different quality of silence altogether. A ponderous, oppressive silence. A silence reminiscent, though it took me a while to put my finger on it, of the silence that hangs around a terminal patient. A silence pregnant with the presentiment of death. The air faintly musty and ominous.

"Everyone dies," said the man softly with downcast eyes. He seemed to have an uncanny purchase on the drift of my thoughts. "All of us, whosoever, must die sometime."

Having said that, the man fell again into a weighty silence. There was only the frantic buzzing of the cicadas outdoors. Bodies scraping out their last dying fury against the ending season.

"Let me be as frank as possible with you," the man spoke up. His speech had the ring of a direct translation from a formulaic text. His choice of phrase and grammar was correct enough, but there was no feeling in his words.

"Speaking frankly and speaking the truth are two different

things entirely. Honesty is to truth as prow is to stern. Honesty appears first and truth appears last. The interval between varies in direct proportion to the size of ship. With anything of size, truth takes a long time in coming. Sometimes it only manifests itself posthumously. Therefore, should I impart you with no truth at this juncture, that is through no fault of mine. Nor yours."

How was one to respond to this? He acknowledged my silence and continued to speak.

"You're probably wondering why I called you all this way here. It was to set the ship in forward motion. You and I shall move it forward. By discussing matters in all honesty, we shall proceed one step at a time closer to the truth." At that point, he coughed and glanced over at his hand resting on the arm of the sofa. "But enough of these abstractions, let us begin with real concerns. The issue here is the newsletter you produced. I believe you have been told this much."

"I have."

The man nodded. Then after a moment's pause, continued, "I'm sure all this came as quite a surprise to you. Anyone would be unhappy about having the product of his hard labors destroyed. All the more if it's a vital link in his livelihood. It may mean a very real loss of no mean size. Isn't that right?"

"That it is," I said.

"I would like to have you tell me about such real losses."

"In our line of work, real losses are part of business. It's not like clients never suddenly reject what's been produced. But for a small operation like ours, it can be a threat to our existence. So in order to prevent that, we honor the client's views one hundred percent. In extreme cases, this means checking through an entire bulletin line by line together with the client. That way we avoid all risks. It's not easy work, but that's the lot of the lone wolf."

"Everyone has to start somewhere," sympathized the man. "Be that as it may, am I to interpret from what you say that your company has incurred a severe financial setback as a result of the cessation of your bulletin?"

"Yes, I guess you could say that. It was already printed and bound, so we have to pay for the paper and printing within the month. There're also writers' fees for articles we farmed out. In monetary terms that comes to about five million yen, and we had planned to use it to pay off our debt. We borrowed money to invest in our facilities a year ago."

"I know," said the man.

"Then there is the question of our ongoing contract with the client. Our position is very weak, and once there's been trouble with an advertising agency, clients avoid you. We were under a one-year contract with the life insurance company, and if that's scrapped because of this, then effectively our company is sunk. We're small and without connections, but we've got a good reputation that's spread by word of mouth. If one bad word gets out, we're done for."

Even after I'd finished, the man stared at me without comment. Then he spoke up. "You speak most honestly. Moreover, what you tell me conforms to our investigations. I commend you on that. What if I had them offer you unconditional payment for those canceled insurance company bulletins and suggest to them that they continue your present contract?"

"There would be nothing more to tell. We'd go back to our boring everyday affairs, left wondering what this was all about."

"And with a premium on top of that? I have but to write one word on the back of a name card and you would have your work cut out for you for the next ten years. And none of those measly handbills either."

"A deal, in other words."

"A friendly transaction. I out of my own goodwill have done your partner the favor of informing him that the P.R. bulletin has ceased publication. And should you show me your goodwill, I would favor you with a further display of goodwill. Do you think you could do that? My favor could prove quite beneficial. Certainly you don't expect to go on working with a dull-witted alcoholic forever."

"We're friends," I said.

There ensued a brief silence, a pebble sent plunging down a fathomless well. It took thirty seconds for the pebble to hit bottom.

"As you wish," said the man. "That is your affair. I went over your vita in some detail. You have an interesting history. Now people can generally be classified into two groups: the mediocre realists and the mediocre dreamers. You clearly belong to the latter. Your fate is and will always be the fate of a dreamer."

"I'll remember that," I said.

The man nodded. I drank half the watered-down grape juice.

"Very well, then, let us proceed to particulars," said the man. "Particulars about sheep."

The man changed positions to pull a large black-and-white photograph out of an envelope, setting it on the table before me. The slightest breath of reality seemed to filter into the room.

"This is the photograph you used in your bulletin."

For a direct blowup of the photograph without using the negative, the image was surprisingly clear. Probably some special technology.

"As far as we know, the photo is one you personally came upon and then used in the bulletin. Is that not so?"

"That is correct."

"According to our investigations, the photograph was taken within the last six months by a total amateur. The camera, a cheap pocket-size model. It was not you who took the photograph. You have a Nikon SLR and take better pictures. And you haven't been to Hokkaido in the past five years. Correct?"

"You tell me," I said.

The man cleared his throat, then fell silent. This was a definitive silence, one you could judge the qualities of other silences by. "Anyway, what we want is a few pieces of information: namely, where and from whom did you receive that photograph, and what was your intention in using such a poor image in that bulletin?"

"I'm afraid I'm not at liberty to say," I tossed out the words with a cool that impressed even myself. "Journalists rightfully do not reveal their sources."

The man stared me in the eyes and stroked his lips with the middle finger of his right hand. Several passes, then he returned his hand to his lap. The silence continued for a while. I couldn't help thinking what perfect timing it would be if at that instant a cuckoo started to sing. But, of course, no cuckoo was to be heard. Cuckoos don't sing in the evenings.

"You are a fine one," said the man. "You know, if I felt like it, I could stop all work from coming your way. That would put an end to your claims of journalism. Supposing, of course, that your miserable pamphlets and handbills qualify as journalism."

I thought it over. Why is it that cuckoos don't sing at nightfall?

"What's more, there are ways to make people like you talk."

"I suppose there are," I said, "but they take time and I wouldn't talk until the last minute. Even if I did talk, I wouldn't spill everything. You'd have no way of knowing how much is everything. Or am I mistaken?"

Everything was a bluff, but it made sense the way things were going. The uncertainty of the silence that followed showed I had earned myself a few points.

"It is most amusing talking with you," said the man. "Your dreamer's scenario is delightfully pathetic. Ah well, let us talk about something else."

The man pulled a magnifying glass out of his pocket and set it on the table.

"Please examine the photograph as much as you care to."

I picked up the photo with my left hand and the magnifying glass with my right, and inspected the photo methodically. Some sheep were facing this way, some were facing in other directions, some were absorbed in eating grass. A scene that suggested a dull class reunion. I spot-checked each sheep one by one, looked at the lay of the grass, at the birch wood in the background, the mountains behind that, the wispy clouds in the sky. There was not one thing unusual. I looked up from the photo and magnifying glass.

"Did you notice anything out of the ordinary?"

"Not at all," I said.

The man showed no visible sign of disappointment.

"I seem to recall that you majored in biology at university," the man said. "How much do you know about sheep?"

"Practically nothing. I did mostly useless specialist stuff."

"Tell me what you know."

"A cloven-hoofed, herbivorous social animal. Introduced to Japan in the early Meiji era, I believe. Used as a source of wool and meat. That's about it."

"Very good," said the man. "Although I should like to make one small correction: sheep were not introduced to Japan in the early Meiji era, but during the Ansei reign. Prior to that, however, it is as you say: there were no sheep in Japan. True, there is some argument that they were brought over from China during the Heian period, but even if that were the case, they had long since died off in the interim. So up until Meiji, few Japanese had ever seen a sheep or understood what one was. In spite of its relatively popular standing as one of the twelve zodiacal animals of the ancient Chinese calendar, nobody knew with any accuracy what kind of animal it was. That is to say, it might as well have been an imaginary creature on the order of a dragon or phoenix. In fact, pictures of sheep drawn by pre-Meiji Japanese look like wholly fabricated monstrosities. One might say they had about as much knowledge of their subject as H. G. Wells had about Martians.

"Even today, Japanese know precious little about sheep. Which is to say that sheep as an animal have no historical connection with the daily life of the Japanese. Sheep were imported at the state level from America, raised briefly, then promptly ignored. That's your sheep. After the war, when importation of wool and mutton from Australia and New Zealand was liberalized, the merits of sheep raising in Japan plummeted to zero. A tragic animal, do you not think? Here, then, is the very image of modern Japan.

"But of course I do not mean to lecture you on the vainglory of modern Japan. The points I wish to impress upon you are two: one, that prior to the end of the late feudal period there probably was not one sheep in all of Japan; and two, that once imported, sheep were subjected to rigorous government checks. And what do these two things mean?"

The question wasn't rhetorical; it was addressed to me. "That every variety of sheep in Japan is fully accounted for," I stated.

"Precisely. To which I might add that breeding is as much a point with sheep as it is with racehorses, making it a simple matter to trace their genealogy several generations. In other words, here we have a thoroughly regulated animal. Crossbreeding with other strains can be easily checked. There is no smuggling. No one is curious enough to go to all the trouble to import sheep. By way of varieties, there are in Japan the Southdown, Spanish Merino, Cotswold, Chinese, Shropshire, Corriedale, Cheviot, Romanovsky, Ostofresian, Border Leicester, Romney Marsh, Lincoln, Dorset Horn, Suffolk, and that's about all. With this in mind," said the man, "I would like to have you take another look at the photograph."

Once again I took photo and magnifying glass in my hands.

"Be sure to look carefully at the third sheep from the right in the front row."

I brought the magnifying glass to bear upon the third sheep from the right in the front row. A quick look at the sheep next to it, then back to the third sheep from the right.

"And what can you tell now?" asked the man.

"It's a different breed, isn't it?" I said.

"That it is. Aside from that particular sheep, all the others are ordinary Suffolks. Only that one sheep differs. It is far more stocky than the Suffolk, and the fleece is of another color. Nor is the face black. Something about it strikes one as howsoever more powerful. I showed this photograph to a sheep specialist, and he concluded that this sheep did not exist in Japan. Nor probably anywhere else in the world. So what you are looking at now is a sheep that by all rights should not exist."

I grabbed the magnifying glass and looked once more at the third sheep from the right. On close examination, there, in the middle of its back, appeared to be a light coffee stain of a mark. Hazy and indistinct, it could have been a scratch on the film. Maybe my eyes were playing tricks again. Or maybe somebody actually did spill coffee on that sheep's back.

"There's this faint stain on its back."

"That is no stain," said the man. "That is a star-shaped birthmark. Compare it with this."

The man pulled a single-page photocopy out of the envelope and handed it over directly to me. It was a copy of a picture of a sheep. Drawn apparently in heavy pencil, with black finger smudges all over the rest of the page. Infantile, yet there was something about it that commanded your attention. The details were drawn with great care. Moreover, the sheep in the photograph and the sheep in the drawing were without a doubt the same sheep. The star-shaped birthmark *was* the stain.

"Now look at this," said the man, taking a lighter from his pocket and handing it to me. It was a specially made, heavy, solid silver Dupont, engraved with the same sheep emblem I'd seen in the limo. Sure enough, the star-shaped birthmark was there on the sheep's back, plain as day.

My head began to ache.

18

The Strange Man's Strange Tale Goes On

"Just a while ago, I made reference to mediocrity," said the man. "This was by no means a criticism of you. Or to put it more simply, it is because the world itself is so mediocre that you are mediocre as such. Do you not agree?"

"Excuse me?"

"The world is mediocre. About that there is no mistake. Well then, has the world been mediocre since time immemorial? No. In the beginning, the world was chaos, and chaos is not mediocre. The mediocratization began when people separated the means of production from daily life. For when Karl Marx posited the proletariat, he thereby cemented their mediocrity. And precisely because of this, Stalinism forms a direct link with Marxism. I affirm Marx. He was one of those rare geniuses whose memory extended back to primal chaos. And by the same token, I have high regard for Dostoyevsky. Nonetheless, I do not hold with Marxism. It is far too mediocre."

The man forced back a low sound in the back of his throat.

"I am, right now, speaking with extreme honesty. I mean this as a gesture of gratitude for your previous honesty. Furthermore, I will agree to clarify whatever so-called honest doubts you might have. But know that by the time I am through talking, the options left open to you will have become extremely limited. Please understand this in advance. Quite simply, you are raising the stakes. Are we agreed?"

"What choice have I?" I said.

"Right now, an old man lies dying within this estate," he began. "The cause is clear. It is a giant blood cyst in his brain. A cyst big enough to distort the very shape of his brain. How much do you know about neurology?"

"Next to nothing."

"To put it simply then, it is a blood bomb. A blockage of circulation causing an irregular swelling. Like a snake that has swallowed a golf ball. If it explodes, the brain will cease to function. Yet an operation is out of the question. The slightest stimulus might cause it to explode. Realistically speaking, we can only wait and watch him die. He might die in another week, or it might be another month. No one can say."

The man pursed his lips and let out a slow breath.

"There is nothing odd about him dying. He is an old man, his ailment pinpointed. What is odd is that he has lived this long."

I hadn't the foggiest notion what he was trying to say.

"The fact is, there would have been nothing amiss had he died thirty-two years ago," the man continued. "Or even forty-two years ago. That blood cyst was first discovered by U.S. Army doctors conducting health examinations on Class A war criminals. This was back in the autumn of 1946, before the Tokyo War Crimes Tribunal. The doctor who discovered it was rather alarmed when he saw the X rays. To have such an enormous cyst in one's brain and still be alive—and more active than the average person at that—challenged all medical common sense. He was transferred from Sugamo to the then-army hospital, St. Luke's, for special tests.

"The tests went on for a year, though ultimately they learned nothing. Only that his death would come as no surprise to anyone, since the fact that he was alive at all was a total mystery. Still he showed no signs of disability thereafter; he kept on living with singular vitality. All brain activities were, moreover, exceedingly normal. They were at a loss for explanations. A dead end. Here was a man who theoretically should have been dead, yet was alive and walking about.

"Certainly they shed light on a number of specific symptoms. He had three-day headaches that came and went on a forty-day cycle. By his own account, these headaches began in 1936, which they conjectured was around the time his blood cyst first appeared. His headaches were so intolerable that he required painkillers. In short, narcotics. The narcotics eased the pain all right, but they also resulted in hallucinations. Highly compressed hallucinations. Only he himself knows what exactly he experienced, but it seems they were far from pleasant. The U.S. Army still retains the detailed accounts of these hallucinatory experiences. The doctors apparently made meticulous observations. I obtained these by special means and have read them through several times, and in spite of their clinical language they describe a rather grueling series of events. I doubt there are many who could take such regular punishment as those hallucinatory experiences.

"No one has any idea why these hallucinations occurred. Perhaps the cyst gave off some periodic energy and the headaches were the body's reaction. So that when that reactive buffer was removed, the energy directly stimulated specific parts of the brain, resulting in hallucinations. Of course, this is only one hypothesis, but it is a hypothesis that interested the Americans. Enough that they initiated thorough tests. Top-secret tests by Intelligence. Even now it is not clear why American Intelligence should have jumped into investigations of one man's blood cyst; however, we can imagine several possibilities.

"As the first possibility, might they not have conducted certain more delicate interrogations under the cover of medical tests? To wit, the securing of spying routes and opium routes on the Chinese mainland. Remember, Chiang Kai-shek's eventual defeat meant the loss of the Chinese connection for the U.S. But needless to say, these inquiries could not be made public. In fact, after this series of tests, the Boss was released without having to stand trial. It is conceivable that an arrangement was made behind the scenes. An exchange of information for freedom, shall we say.

"The second possibility was to lay bare an interrelationship between his marked eccentricity as the leader of the right wing and the blood cyst. I will go more into this with you later, but it is a more bemusing turn of thought. Though I doubt they ever learned anything. Did they really imagine they could uncover something of that order when the more basic fact of his living remained a mystery? Short of an autopsy, there was no way they would find anything out. Here, then, another dead end.

"The third possibility concerns brainwashing. The idea being that, perhaps, by sending one predetermined set of stimulus waves into the brain they might elicit a particular reaction. They were doing that kind of experimentation in those days. It has come to light that there was, in fact, such a brainwashing research group at the time.

"It is not clear which of these three lines of thought represented the main Intelligence directive. Nor is it clear whether their efforts, shall we call them, bore any fruit. Everything is buried in history. The only ones who know the facts are a handful of the U.S. Army elite at the time and the Boss himself. So far, the Boss has never spoken a word about this to anyone, myself included, and it is doubtful he ever will."

When he finished talking, the man cleared his throat. I had lost all track of how much time had passed since entering the room.

"In the winter of 1932, the Boss was imprisoned on charges of complicity in a plot to assassinate a key figure. His imprisonment lasted until June 1936. The official prison records and medical register still exist, and he on occasion has touched upon the subject. These glimpses tell us this: that for virtually the entire length of his stay in prison, the Boss suffered from severe insomnia. Or perhaps it was more than simple insomnia. This was insomnia raised to an exceedingly dangerous level. For three days, four days at a time, sometimes close to a week, he would not close his eyes once. In those days, the police forced confessions out of political criminals by depriving them of sleep. So the Boss must have undergone especially punishing interrogations, implicated as he was with the resistance to the Imperial rule and the controlling faction. If the prisoner tried to sleep, they would throw water on him or beat him with bamboo sticks or shine strong lights on him, anything to dash the sleeping patterns to pieces. Most humans break down if such a regimen is kept up for several months. Their sleeping mind is effectively destroyed. They die or they go crazy or they become extreme insomniacs. The Boss went the last route. It was the spring of 1936 before he had completely recovered from his insomnia. That is, around the same time as the blood cyst appeared. What do you make of that?"

"Extreme lack of sleep for some reason disrupted the flow of blood in his brain, thereby creating the cyst, is that it?"

"That would seem the most plausible, commonsense hypothesis. And since a nonprofessional can think that far, you can be sure that it occurred to the U.S. Army doctors as well. Still, that explanation alone is not quite adequate. There is something missing here. I cannot help thinking that the phenomenon of the blood cyst was the secondary manifestation of a more significant factor. Consider, for example, that among the several other people known to have had such blood cysts, not one displayed the same symptoms. Nor, furthermore, does the explanation offer sufficient reason why the Boss went on living."

Undoubtedly, there was a logic to what the man was saying.

"One more curious fact about the blood cyst. Starting from the spring of 1936, the Boss was proverbially born again, a new man. Up to that point the Boss had been, in a word, a mediocre right-wing activist. Born the third son of a poor farming household in Hokkaido, he left home when he was twelve and went to Korea, but he found no place there either so he returned to his homeland and joined a right-wing group. An angry young man, it seems, who was forever brandishing his samurai sword. Very probably he could barely read. Yet by the summer of 1936, when he was released from prison, he had risen to the top, in every sense of the word, of the right wing. He had charisma, a solid ideology, powers of speech making to command a passionate response, political savvy, decisiveness, and above all the ability to steer society by using the weaknesses of the masses for leverage."

The man took a breath and cleared his throat again.

"Of course, as a right-wing thinker his theories and conception of the world were rather silly. Still, that scarcely mattered. The real question was how far he could organize his ranks behind them. Look at the way that Hitler took half-baked notions of *lebensraum* and racial superiority and organized them on the national level. The Boss, however, did not take that path. The path he chose was more covert—a shadow path. Never out in the open, his was to be a presence that manipulated society from behind the scenes. And for that reason, in 1937 he headed over to the Chinese mainland. But even so—well, let us leave it at that. To return to the cyst, what I mean to say is that the period in which the cyst appeared coincided precisely with the period in which he underwent a miraculous self-transformation."

"In your hypothesis," I said, "there was no causal relationship between the cyst and the self-transformation; instead the two were governed in parallel by some mysterious overriding factor."

"You catch on quickly," said the man. "Precise and to the point."

"So when does the sheep appear in your story?"

The man removed a second cigarette from the tabletop case and flicked it with his fingernail before putting it to his lips. He did not light it. "Let us take things in order," he said.

A weighty silence ensued.

"We built a kingdom," the man began again. "A powerful underground kingdom. We pulled everything into the picture. Politics, finance, mass communications, the bureaucracy, culture, all sorts of things you would never dream of. We even subsumed elements that were hostile to us. From the establishment to the anti-establishment, everything. Very few if any of them even noticed they had been co-opted. In other words, we had ourselves a tremendously sophisticated organization. All of which the Boss built single-handedly after the war. It is as if the Boss commandeered the hull of a giant ship of state. If he pulls out the plug, the ship goes down. Passengers and all, lost at sea, and surely before anyone becomes aware of that fact."

At that the man lit his cigarette.

"Nonetheless, this organization has its limits. Namely, the

king's death. When the king dies, the kingdom crumbles. The kingdom, you see, was built and maintained on this one man's genius. Which in my estimation is to say it was built and sustained by that mysterious factor. If the Boss dies, it means the end of everything, inasmuch as our organization was not a bureaucracy, but a perfectly tuned machine with one mind at its apex. Herein is the strength and weakness of our organization. Or rather, was. The death of the Boss will sooner or later bring a splintering of the organization, and like a Valhalla consumed by flames, it will plunge into a sea of mediocrity. There is no one to take over after the Boss. The organization will fall apart—a magnificent palace razed to make way for a public housing complex. A world of uniformity and certainty. Though perhaps you would think it fitting and proper. Fair allotment and all that. But think about it. The whole of Japan, leveled of mountains, coastlines or lakes, sprawling with uniform rows of public housing. Would that be the right thing?"

"I wouldn't know," I said. "I don't even know if the question itself makes sense."

"An intelligent answer," said the man, folding his fingers together on his lap. The tips of the fingers tapped out a slow rhythm. "All this talk of public housing is, as you know, merely for the sake of argument. More precisely, our organization can be divided into two elements. The part that moves ahead and the part that drives it ahead. Naturally, there are other parts managing other functions. Still, roughly divided, our organization is made up of these two parts. The other parts hardly amount to anything. The part at the forefront is the Will, and the part that backs up the forefront is the Gains. When people talk about the Boss, they make an issue only out of his Gains. And after the Boss dies, it will be only his Gains that people will clamor for a share of. Nobody wants the Will, because no one understands it. Herein we see the true meaning of what can and cannot be shared. The Will cannot be shared. It is either passed on in toto, or lost in toto."

The man's fingers kept drumming out that same slow rhythm on his lap. Other than that, everything about him had remained unchanged from the beginning. Same stare, same cold pupils, same smooth, expressionless face. That face had stayed turned toward me at the exact same angle the whole time.

"What is this Will?" I asked.

"A concept that governs time, governs space, and governs possibility."

"I don't follow."

"Of course. Few can. Only the Boss had a virtually instinctual understanding of it. One might even go so far as to say he negated self-cognition, thereupon realizing in its place something entirely revolutionary. To put it in simple terms for you, his was a revolution of labor incorporating capital and capital incorporating labor."

"A fantasy."

"Quite the contrary. It is cognition that is the fantasy." The man paused. "Granted, everything I tell you now is mere words. Arrange them and rearrange them as I might, I will never be able to explain to you the form of Will the Boss possesses. My explanation would only show the correlation between myself and that Will by means of a correlation on the verbal level. The negation of cognition thus correlates to the negation of language. For when those two pillars of Western humanism, individual cognition and evolutionary continuity, lose their meaning, language loses meaning. Existence ceases for the individuum as we know it, and all becomes chaos. You cease to be a unique entity unto yourself, but exist simply as chaos. And not just the chaos that is you; your chaos is also my chaos. To wit, existence is communication, and communication, existence."

All of a sudden the room grew cold, and I had the inexplicable feeling that a nice warm bed had been readied for me there off to one side. Someone was beckoning me under the covers.

An illusion, of course. It was still September. Outside, countless thousands of cicadas were screeching away.

"The expansion of consciousness your generation underwent or at least sought to undergo at the end of the sixties ended in complete and utter failure because it was still rooted in the individual. That is, the attempt to expand consciousness alone, without any quantitative or qualitative change in the individual, was ultimately doomed. This is what I mean by mediocrity. How can I make you understand this? Not that I particularly expect you to understand. I am merely endeavoring to speak honestly.

"About that picture I handed you earlier," said the man. "It is a copy of a picture from the U.S. Army hospital medical records. It is dated July 27, 1946. The picture was drawn by the Boss himself at the request of the doctors. As one link in the process of documenting his hallucinatory experiences. In fact, according to the medical records, this sheep appeared with remarkably high frequency in the Boss's hallucinations. To put it in numerical terms, sheep figured in approximately eighty percent of his hallucinations, or in four out of five hallucinations. And not just any sheep. It was this chestnut-colored sheep with the star on its back.

"So it was that the Boss came to use this sheep, that is engraved on the lighter, as his own personal crest from 1936 on. I believe you will have noticed that this sheep is one and the same as the sheep in the medical records. Which is again the same as the one in your photograph. Most curious, do you not think?"

"Mere coincidence," I tossed out. I had meant to sound cool, but it didn't quite come off.

"There is more," the man continued. "The Boss was an avid collector of all available reference materials on sheep, domestic and foreign. Once a week he reviewed at length clippings concerning sheep gleaned from every newspaper and magazine published that week in Japan. I always lent him a hand in this. The Boss was emphatic about his sheep clippings. It was as if he were looking for some one thing. And ever since the Boss took ill, I've continued this effort on a personal level. I have actually taken an interest in this pursuit. Who knows what might come to light? That is how you came into the picture. You and your sheep. Any way one looks at it, this is no coincidence."

I balanced the lighter in my hand. It had an excellent feel to it. Not too heavy, not too light. To think that there was such perfect heft in the world.

"And why do you suppose the Boss was so intent on finding that sheep? Any ideas?"

"None whatsoever," I said. "It would be quicker to ask the Boss."

"If I could ask him, I would. The Boss has been in a coma for two weeks now. Very probably he will never regain consciousness. And if the Boss dies, the mystery of the sheep with the star on its back will be buried with him forever. I, for one, am not about to stand by and let that happen. Not for reasons of my own personal loss, but for the greater good of all."

I cocked open the lid of the lighter, struck the flint to light the flame, then closed the lid.

"I am sure you think that all I am saying is a load of nonsense. And perhaps it is. It might well turn out to *be* total nonsense. But just consider, this may be the sum total of all that is left to us. The

Boss will die. That one Will shall die. Then everything around that Will shall perish. All that shall remain will be what can be counted in numbers. Nothing else will be left. That is why I want to find that sheep."

He closed his eyes a few seconds for the first time, saying nothing for a moment. Then: "If I might offer my hypothesis—a hypothesis and nothing more, forget I ever said a thing if it does nothing for you—I cannot help but feel that our sheep here formed the basic mold of the Boss's Will."

"Sounds like animal crackers," I said.

The man ignored my comment.

"Very probably the sheep found its way into the Boss. That would have been in 1936. And for the next forty years or so, the sheep remained lodged in the Boss. There inside, it must have found a pasture, a birch forest. Like the one in that photograph. What think you?"

"An extremely interesting hypothesis," I said.

"It is a special sheep. A v-e-r-y special sheep. I want to find it and for that I will need your help."

"And what do you plan to do with it once you find it?"

"Nothing at all. There is probably nothing I could do. The scale of things is far too vast for me to do much of anything. My only wish is to see it all out at last with my own eyes. And if that sheep should wish anything, I shall do all in my power to comply. Once the Boss dies, my life will have lost almost all meaning anyway."

At that he fell silent. I too was silent. Only the cicadas kept at it. They and the trees in the garden rustling their leaves in the near-dusk breeze. The house itself was agonizingly quiet. As if spores of death were drifting about in some unpreventable contagion. I tried to picture the pasture in the Boss's head. A pasture forlorn and forsaken, the grass withered, the sheep all gone.

"I will ask you one more time: tell me by what route you obtained the photograph," the man said.

"I cannot say," I said.

The man heaved a sigh. "I have attempted to talk to you honestly. Therefore I had hoped that you would talk to me honestly as well."

"I am not in a position to talk. If I were to talk, it might pose problems for the person who provided it."

"Which is to say," interposed the man, "that you have some reasonable grounds to believe that some problems might come to this person in connection with the sheep."

"No grounds whatsoever. I'm playing my hunches. There's got to be a catch. I've felt that the whole time I've been talking to you. Like there's a hook somewhere. Call it sixth sense."

"And therefore you cannot speak."

"Correct," I said. Giving the situation further thought, I went on: "I'm something of an authority on troublemaking. I can claim to be second to none in the ways and means of creating problems for others. I live my life trying my best to avoid things ever coming to that. Which ultimately only creates more problems. It's all the same. That's the way things go down. Yet, no matter that I know it's all the same, it doesn't change anything. Nothing gets that way from the start. It's only a pretext."

"I am not sure I follow you."

"What I am saying is, mediocrity takes many forms."

I put a cigarette to my lips, lit it with the lighter in my hand, and took a puff. I felt ever so slightly more at ease.

"You do not have to speak if you do not want to," said the man. "Instead, I will send you out in search of the sheep. These are our final terms. If within two months from now you succeed in finding the sheep, we are prepared to reward you however you would care to request. But if you should fail to find it, it will be the end of you and your company. Agreed?"

"Do I have any choice?" I asked. "And what if no such sheep with a star on its back ever existed in the first place?"

"It is still the same. For you and for me, there is only whether you find the sheep or not. There are no in-betweens. I am sorry to have to put it this way, but as I have already said, we are taking you up on your proposition. You hold the ball, you had better run for the goal. Even if there turns out not to have been any goal."

"So that's how it stands?"

The man took a fat envelope out of his pocket and placed it before me. "Use this for expenses. If you run out, give us a call. There is more where this came from. Any questions?"

"No questions, but one comment."

"Which is?"

"This all has got to be, patently, the most unbelievable, the most ridiculous story I have ever heard. Somehow coming from your mouth, it has the ring of truth, but I doubt anyone would believe me if I told them what happened today."

Almost imperceptibly, the man curled his lip. He conceivably could have been smiling. "From tomorrow, you're on the case. As I said, you have two months from today."

"It's a tough job. Two months might not be enough. I mean you're asking me to seek out one sheep from the entire countryside."

The man stared me straight in the face and said nothing. Making me feel like an empty pool. A filthy, cracked, empty pool that might never see another year's use. He looked at me a full thirty seconds without blinking. Then slowly he opened his mouth.

"It is time for you to be going," he said.

It sure seemed that way.

19

The Limo and Its Driver, Again

"Will you be returning to your office? Or to somewhere else?" the chauffeur asked. It was the same chauffeur from the trip out, but his manner seemed a bit more personable now. Guess he took to people easily.

I gave my arms and legs a full stretch on the roomy backseat and considered where I should go. I had no intention of returning to the office. Technically I was still on leave, and I wasn't about to try to explain all this to my partner. I wasn't about to go straight home either. Right now I needed a good dose of regular people walking on two legs in a regular way in a regular place.

"Shinjuku Station, west exit," I said.

Traffic was jammed solid in the direction of Shinjuku. Evening rush hour, among other things. Past a certain point the cars seemed practically glued in place, motionless. Every so often a wave would pass through the cars, budging them forward a few inches. I thought about the rotational speed of the earth. How many miles an hour was this road surface whirling through space? I did a quick calculation in my head but couldn't figure out if it was any faster than the Spinning Teacup at a carnival. There're many things we don't really know. It's an illusion that we know anything at all. If a group of aliens were to stop me and ask, "Say, bud, how many miles an hour does the earth spin at the equator?" I'd be in a fix. Hell, I don't even know why Wednesday follows Tuesday. I'd be an intergalactic joke.

I've read *And Quiet Flows the Don* and *The Brothers Karamazov* three times through. I've even read *Ideologie Germanica* once. I can even recite the value of *pi* to sixteen places. Would I still be a joke? Probably. They'd laugh their alien heads off.

"Would you care to listen to some music, sir?" asked the chauffeur.

"Good idea," I said.

And at that a Chopin ballade filled the car. I got the feeling I was in a dressing room at a wedding reception.

"Say," I asked the chauffeur, "you know the value of *pi*?"

"You mean that 3.14 whatzit?"

"That's the one. How many decimal places do you know?"

"I know it to thirty-two places," the driver tossed out. "Beyond that, well . . ."

"Thirty-two places?"

"There's a trick to it, but yes. Why do you ask?"

"Oh, nothing really," I said, crestfallen. "Never mind."

So we listened to Chopin as the limousine inched forward ten yards. People in cars and buses around us glared at our monster vehicle. None too comfortable, being the object of so much attention, even with the opaque windows.

"Awful traffic," I said.

"That it is, but sure as dawn follows night, it's got to let up sometime."

"Fair enough, but doesn't it get on your nerves?"

"Certainly. I get irritated, I get upset. Especially when I'm in a hurry. But I see it all as part of our training. To get irritated is to lose our way in life."

"That sounds like a religious interpretation of a traffic jam if there ever was one."

"I'm a Christian. I don't go to church, but I've always been a Christian."

"Is that so? Don't you see any contradiction between being a Christian and being the chauffeur for a major right-wing figure?"

"The Boss is an honorable man. After the Lord, the most godly person I've ever met."

"You've met God?"

"Certainly. I telephone Him every night."

"Excuse me?" I stammered. Things were starting to jumble up in my head again. "If everyone called God, wouldn't the lines be busy all the time? Like directory assistance right around noon."

"No problem there. God is your simultaneous presence. So even if a million people were to telephone Him at once, He'd be able to speak with everyone simultaneously."

"I'm no expert, but is that an orthodox interpretation? I mean, theologically speaking."

"I'm something of a radical. That's why I don't go to church."

"I see," I said.

The limousine advanced fifty yards. I put a cigarette to my lips and was about to light up when I saw I'd been holding the lighter in my hand the whole time. Without realizing it, I'd walked off with the sheep-engraved silver Dupont. It felt molded to my palm as naturally as if I'd been born with it. The balance and feel couldn't have been better. After a few seconds' thought, I decided it was mine. Who's going to miss a lighter or two? I opened and closed the lid a few times, lit up, and put the lighter in my pocket. By way of compensation, I slipped my Bic disposable into the pocket of the door.

"The Boss gave me it a few years ago," said the chauffeur out of nowhere.

"Gave you what?"

"God's telephone number."

I let out a groan so loud it drowned out everything else. Either I was going crazy or they were all Looney Tunes.

"He told just you, alone, in secret?"

"Yes. Just me, in secret. He's a fine gentleman. Would you care to get to know Him?"

"If possible," I said.

"Well, then, it's Tokyo 9-4-5- . . ."

"Just a second," I said, pulling out my notebook and pen. "But do you really think it's all right, telling me like this?"

"Sure, it's all right. I don't go telling just anyone. And you seem like a good person."

"Well, thank you," I said. "But what should I talk to God about? I'm not Christian or anything."

"No problem there. All you have to do is to speak honestly about whatever concerns you or troubles you. No matter how trivial you might think it is. God never gets bored and never laughs at you."

"Thanks. I'll give him a call."

"That's the spirit," said the chauffeur.

Traffic began to flow smoothly as the Shinjuku skyscrapers came into view. We didn't speak the rest of the way there.

20

Summer's End, Autumn's Beginning

By the time the limousine reached its destination, a pale indigo dusk had spread over the city. A brisk wind blew between the buildings bearing tidings of summer's end, rustling the skirts of women on their way home from work.

I went to the top of a high-rise hotel, entered the spacious bar, and ordered a Heineken. It took ten minutes for the beer to come. Meanwhile, I planted an elbow on the armrest of my chair, rested my head on my hand, and shut my eyes. Nothing came to mind. With my eyes closed, I could hear hundreds of elves sweeping out my head with their tiny brooms. They kept sweeping and sweeping. It never occurred to any of them to use a dustpan.

When the beer finally arrived, I downed it in two gulps. Then I ate the whole dish of peanuts that came with it. The sweeping had all but stopped.

I went over to the telephone booth by the register and tried calling my girlfriend, her with the gorgeous ears. But she wasn't at her place and she wasn't at mine. She'd probably stepped out to eat. She never ate at home.

Next I tried my ex-wife. I reconsidered and hung up after the second ring. I didn't have anything to say to her after all, and I didn't want to come off like a jerk.

After them, there was no one to call. Smack in the middle of a city with a million people out roaming the streets, and no one to talk to. I gave up, pocketed the ten-yen coin, and exited the booth. Then I put in an order with a passing waiter for two more Heinekens.

And so the day came to an end. I could hardly have spent a more pointless day. The last day of summer, and what good had it been? Outside, an early autumn darkness had come over everything. Strings of tiny yellow streetlamps threaded everywhere below. Seen from up here, they looked ready to be trampled on.

The beer came. I polished off the one, then dumped the dish of peanuts into the palm of my hand and proceeded to eat them, bit by bit. Four middle-aged women, finished with swimming lessons at the hotel pool, sat at the next table chatting over colorful tropical cocktails. A waiter stood by, rigidly upright, crooking his neck to yawn. Another waiter explained the menu to a middle-aged American couple. After the peanuts, I moved on to my third Heineken. After it was gone, I didn't know what to do with my hands.

I fished the envelope out of the hip pocket of my Levi's, tore open the seal, and started to count the stack of ten-thousand-yen notes. It looked more like a deck of cards than a bound packet of new bills. Halfway through, my fingers began to tire. At ninety-six, an elderly waiter came to clear away my empty bottles, asking whether to bring another. I nodded as I continued counting. He seemed totally uninterested in what I was doing.

There were one hundred and fifty bills. I stuck them back into the envelope and shoved it back into my hip pocket just as the new beer came. Again I ate the whole dish of peanuts, and only then did it occur to me that I was hungry. But why was I so hungry? I'd only eaten one slice of fruitcake since morning.

I called the waiter, ordered a cheese and cucumber sandwich. Hold the chips, double the pickles. Might they have nail clippers? Of course, they did. Hotel bars truly have everything you could ever want. One place even had a French-Japanese dictionary when I needed it.

I took my time with this beer, took a long took at the night scenery, took my time trimming my nails over the ashtray. I looked back at the scenery, then I filed my nails. And so on into the night. I'm well on the way to veteran class when it comes to killing time in the city.

A built-in ceiling speaker called my name. At first it didn't sound like my name. Only a few seconds after the announcement was over did it sink in that I'd heard the special characteristics of my name, and only gradually then did it come to me that my name was my name.

The waiter brought a cordless transceiver-phone over to the table.

"There has been a small change in plans," said the voice I knew from somewhere. "The Boss's condition has taken a sudden turn for the worse. There is not much time left, I fear. So we are curtailing your time limit."

"To how long?"

"One month. We cannot wait any longer. If after one month you have not found that sheep, you are finished. You will have nowhere to go back to."

One month. I thought it over. But my head was beyond dealing with concepts of time. One month, two months, was there any real difference? And who had any idea, any standard, of how much time it should take to find one sheep in the first place?

"How did you know to find me here?" I asked.

"We are on top of most things," said the man.

"Except the whereabouts of one sheep," I said.

"Exactly," said the man. "Anyway, get on it, you waste too much time. You should take good account of where you now stand. You have only yourself to blame for driving yourself into that corner."

He had a point. I used the first ten-thousand-yen note out of the envelope to pay the check. Down on the ground, people were still walking about on two legs, but the sight no longer gave me much relief.

21

One in Five Thousand

Returning to my apartment from the hotel bar, I found three pieces of mail together with the evening paper in my mailbox. A balance statement from my bank, an invitation to what promised to be a dud of a party, and a direct-mail flyer from a used-car dealership. The copy read: "BRIGHTEN UP YOUR LIFE—MOVE UP TO A CLASSY CAR." Thanks, but no thanks. I put all three envelopes together and tore them in half.

I took some juice out of the refrigerator and sat down at the kitchen table with it. On the table was a note from my girlfriend: "Gone out to eat. Back by 9:30." The digital clock on the table read 9:30. I watched it flip over to 9:31, then to 9:32.

When I got bored with watching the clock, I got out of my clothes, took a shower, and washed my hair. There were four types of shampoo and three types of hair rinse in the bathroom. Every time she went to the supermarket, she stocked up on something. Step into the bathroom and there was bound to be a new item. I counted four kinds of shaving cream and five tubes of toothpaste. Quite an inventory. Out of the shower, I changed into jogging shorts and a T-shirt. Gone was the grime of one bizarre day. At last I felt refreshed.

At 10:20 she returned with a shopping bag from the supermarket. In the bag were three scrub brushes, one box of paperclips, and a well-chilled six-pack of canned beer. So I had another beer.

"It was about sheep," I said.

"Didn't I tell you?" she said.

I took some sausages out of the refrigerator, browned them in a frying pan, and served them up for us to eat. I ate three and she ate two. A cool breeze blew in through the kitchen window.

I told her about what happened at the office, told her about the limo ride, the estate, the steely-eyed secretary, the blood cyst, and the heavyset sheep with the star on its back. I was talking forever. By the time I'd finished talking, it was eleven o'clock.

All that said and done, she didn't seem taken aback in the least. She'd cleaned her ears the whole time she listened, yawning occasionally.

"So when do you leave?"

"Leave?"

"You have to find the sheep, don't you?"

I looked up at her, the pull-ring of my second beer still on my finger. "I'm not going anywhere," I said.

"But you'll be in a lot of trouble if you don't."

"No special trouble. I was planning on quitting the company anyway. I'll always be able to find enough work to get by, no matter who interferes. They're not about to kill me. Really!"

She pulled a new cotton swab out of the box and fingered it awhile. "But it's actually quite simple. All you have to do is find one sheep, right? It'll be fun."

"Nobody's going to find anything. Hokkaido's a whole lot bigger than you think. And sheep—there've got to be hundreds of thousands of them. How are you going to search out one single sheep? It's impossible. Even if the sheep's got a star marked on its back."

"Make that five thousand sheep."

"Five thousand?"

"The number of sheep in Hokkaido. In 1947, there were two hundred seventy thousand sheep in Hokkaido, but now there are only five thousand."

"How is it you know something like that?"

"After you left, I went to the library and checked it out."

I heaved a sigh. "You know everything, don't you?"

"Not really. There's lot more that I don't know."

I snorted, then opened the second beer and split it between us.

"In any case, there are only five thousand sheep in Hokkaido. According to government surveys. How about it? Aren't you even a little relieved?"

"It's all the same," I said. "Five thousand sheep, two hundred seventy thousand sheep, it's not going to make much difference. The problem is still finding one lone sheep in that vast landscape. On top of which, we haven't a lead to go on."

"It's not true we don't have a lead. First, there's the photograph, then there's your friend up there, right? You're bound to find out something one way or another."

"Both are awfully vague as leads go. The landscape in the photograph is absolutely too ordinary, and you can't even read the postmark on the Rat's letter!"

She drank her beer. I drank my beer.

"Don't you like sheep?" she asked.

"I like sheep well enough."

I was starting to get confused again.

"Besides," I went on, "I've already made up my mind. Not to go, I mean." I meant to convince myself, but the words didn't come out right.

"How about some coffee?"

"Good idea," I said.

She cleared away the beer cans and glasses and put the kettle on. Then while waiting for the water to boil, she listened to a cassette in the other room. Johnny Rivers singing "Midnight Special" followed by "Roll Over Beethoven." Then "Secret Agent Man." When the kettle whistled, she made the coffee, singing along with "Johnny B. Goode." The whole while I read the evening paper. A charming domestic scene. If not for the matter of the sheep, I might have been very happy.

As the tape wound on, we drank our coffee and nibbled on a few crackers in silence. I went back to the evening paper. When I finished it, I began reading it again. Here a coup d'état, there a film actor dying, elsewhere a cat who does tricks—nothing much that related to me. It didn't matter to Johnny Rivers, who kept right on singing. When the tape ended, I folded up the paper and looked over at her.

"I can't figure it out. You're probably right that it's better to do something than nothing. Even if it's futile in the end, at least we looked for the sheep. On the other hand, I don't like being ordered and threatened and pushed around."

"To a greater or lesser extent, everybody's always being ordered and threatened and pushed around. There may not be anything better we could hope for."

"Maybe not," I said, after a moment's pause.

She said nothing and started to clean her ears again. From time to time, her fleshy earlobes showed through the long strands of hair.

"It's beautiful right now in Hokkaido. Not many tourists, nice weather. What's more, the sheep'll all be out and about. The ideal season."

"I guess."

"If," she began, crunching on the last cracker, "if you wanted to take me along, I'd surely be a help."

"Why are you so stuck on this sheep hunt?"

"Because I'd like to see that sheep myself."

"But why should I go breaking my back over this one lousy sheep? And then drag you into this mess on top of it?"

"I don't mind. Your mess is my mess," she said, with a cute little smile. "I've got this thing about you."

"Thanks."

"That's all you can say?"

I pushed the newspaper over to a corner of the table. The slight breeze coming in through the window wafted my cigarette smoke off somewhere.

"To be honest, there's something about this whole business that doesn't sit right with me. There's a hook somewhere."

"Like what?"

"Like everything but everything," I said. "The whole thing's so damn stupid, yet everything has a painful clarity to it, and the picture all fits together perfectly. Not a good feeling at all."

She paused a second, picked up a rubber band from the table, and started playing with it.

"But isn't that friend of yours already up to his neck in trouble? If not, why would he have gone out of his way to send you that photo?"

She had me there. I'd laid all my cards out on the table, and they'd all been trumped. She'd seen straight through me.

"I really think it has to be done. We'll find that sheep, you'll see," she said, grinning.

She finished her ear-cleaning ritual and wrapped up the cotton swabs in a tissue to throw away. Then she picked up a rubber band and tied her hair back behind her ears.

"Let's go to bed," she said.

22

Sunday Afternoon Picnic

I woke up at nine in an empty bed. No note. Only her handkerchief and underwear drying by the washbasin. Probably gone out to eat, I guessed, then to her place.

I got orange juice out of the refrigerator and popped three-day-old bread into the toaster. It tasted like wall plaster.

Through the kitchen window I could see the neighbor's oleander. Far off, someone was practicing piano. It sounded like tripping down an up escalator. On a telephone pole, three plump pigeons burbled mindlessly away. Something had to be on their mind to be going on like that, maybe the pain from corns on their feet, who knows? From the pigeons' point of view, probably it was I who looked mindless.

As I stuffed the second piece of toast down my gullet, the pigeons disappeared, leaving only the telephone pole and the oleander.

It was Sunday morning. The newspaper's weekend section included a color photo of a horse jumping a hedge. Astride the horse, an ill-complexioned rider in a black cap casting a baleful glare at the next page, which featured a lengthy description of what to do and what not to do in orchid cultivation. There were hundreds of varieties of orchids, each with a history of its own. Royalty had been known to die for the sake of orchids. Orchids had an ineffable aura of fatalism. And on the article went. To all things, philosophy and fate.

Now that I'd made up my mind to go off in search of the sheep, I was charged up and raring to go. It was the first time I'd felt like this since I'd crossed the great divide of my twentieth year. I piled the dishes into the sink, gave the cat his breakfast, then dialed the number of the man in the black suit. After six rings he answered.

"I hope I didn't wake you," I said.

"Hardly the question. I rise quite early," he said. "What is it?"

"Which newspaper do you read?"

"Eight papers, national and local. The locals do not arrive until evening, though."

"And you read them all?"

"It is part of my work," said the man patiently. "What of it?"

"Do you read the Sunday pages?"

"Of necessity, yes," he said.

"Did you see the photo of the horse in the weekend section?"

"Yes, I saw the horse photo," said the man.

"Don't the horse and rider seem to be thinking of two totally different things?"

Through the receiver, a silence stole into the room. There wasn't a breath to be heard. It was a silence strong enough to make your ears hurt.

"This is what you called me about?" asked the man.

"No, just small talk. Nothing wrong with a little topic of conversation, is there?"

"We have other topics of conversation. For instance, sheep."

He cleared his throat. "You will have to excuse me, but I am not as free with my time as you. Might you simply get on with your concern as quickly as possible?"

"That's the problem," I said. "Simply put, from tomorrow I'm thinking of going off in search of that sheep. I thought it over a lot, but in the end that's what I decided. Still, I can only see myself doing it at my own pace. When I talk, I will talk as I like. I mean I have the right to make small talk if I want. I don't like having my every move watched and I don't like being pushed around by nameless people. There, I've said my piece."

"You obviously do not know where you stand."

"Nor do you know where you stand. Now listen, I thought it over last night. And it struck me. What have I got to feel threatened about? Next to nothing. I broke up with my wife, I plan to quit my job today, my apartment is rented, and I have no furnishings worth worrying about. By way of holdings, I've got maybe two million yen in savings, a used car, and a cat who's getting on in years. My clothes are all out of fashion, and my records are ancient. I've made no name for myself, have no social credibility, no sex appeal, no talent. I'm not so young anymore, and I'm always saying dumb things that I later regret. In a word, to borrow your turn of phrase, I am an utterly mediocre person. What have I got to lose? If you can think of anything, clue me in, why don't you?"

A brief silence ensued. In that interval, I picked the lint from a shirt button and with a ballpoint pen drew thirteen stars on a memo pad.

"Everybody has some one thing they do not want to lose," began the man. "You included. And we are professionals at finding out that very thing. Humans by necessity must have a midway point between their desires and their pride. Just as all objects must have a center of gravity. This is something we can pinpoint. Only when it is gone do people realize it even existed." Pause. "But I am getting ahead of myself. All this comes later. For the present, let me say that I do not turn an uncomprehending ear toward your speech. I shall take your demands into account. You can do as you like. For one month, is that clear?"

"Clear enough," I said.

"Well then, cheers," said the man.

At that, the phone clicked off. It left a bad aftertaste, the click of the receiver. In order to kill that aftertaste, I did thirty push-ups and twenty sit-ups, washed the dishes, then did three days' worth of laundry. It almost had me feeling good again. A pleasant September Sunday after all. Summer had faded to a distant memory almost beyond recall.

I put on a clean shirt, a pair of Levi's without a ketchup stain, and a matching pair of socks. I brushed my hair. Even so, I couldn't bring back the Sunday-morning feeling I used to get when I was seventeen. So what else was new? Guess I've put on my share of years.

Next, I took my near-scrap Volkswagen out of the apartment-house parking lot, headed to the supermarket, and bought a dozen cans of cat food, a bag of kitty litter, a travel razor set, and underwear. At the doughnut shop, I sat at the counter and washed down a cinnamon doughnut with some tasteless coffee. The wall directly in front of the counter was mirrored, giving me an unobstructed view of myself. I sat there looking at my face, half-eaten doughnut still in hand. It made me wonder how other people saw me. Not that I had any way of knowing, of course. I finished off the doughnut and left.

There was a travel agency near the train station, where I booked two seats on a flight to Sapporo the following day. Then into the station arcade for a canvas shoulder bag and a rain hat. Each time I peeled another ten-thousand-yen note from the wad of bills in my pocket. The wad showed no sign of going down no matter how many bills I used. Only I showed signs of wear. There's that kind of money in the world. It aggravates you to have it, makes you miserable to spend it, and you hate yourself when it's gone. And when you hate yourself, you feel like spending money. Except there's no money left. And no hope.

I sat down on a bench in front of the station and smoked two cigarettes, deciding not to think about the money. The station plaza was filled with families and young couples out for a Sunday morning. Casually taking it all in, I thought of my ex-wife's parting remark that maybe we ought to have had children. To be sure, at my age it wouldn't have been unreasonable to have kids, but me a father? Good grief. What kid would want to have anyone like me for a father?

I smoked another cigarette before pushing through the crowd, each arm around a shopping bag, to the supermarket parking lot. While having the car serviced, I popped into a bookstore to buy three paperbacks. There went another two ten-thousand-yen notes. My pockets were stuffed with loose change.

When I got back to the apartment, I dumped all the change into a glass bowl and splashed cold water on my face. It had been forever since I'd gotten up, but when I looked at the clock, it was still before noon.

At three in the afternoon, my girlfriend returned. She was wearing a checkered shirt with mustard-colored slacks and intensely dark sunglasses. She had a large canvas bag like mine slung over her shoulder.

"I came packed and ready to go," she said, patting the bulging bag. "Will it be a long trip?"

"I wouldn't be surprised."

She stretched out on the sofa by the window, stared off at the ceiling with her sunglasses still on, and smoked a clove cigarette. I fetched an ashtray and went over to sit beside her. I stroked her hair. The cat appeared and jumped up on the sofa, putting his chin and forepaws over her ankles. When she'd had enough of her smoke, she transplanted what remained of the cigarette to my lips.

"Happy to be going on a trip?" I asked.

"Uh-huh, very happy. Especially because I'm going with you."

"You know, if we don't find that sheep, we won't have any place to come back to. We might end up traveling the rest of our lives."

"Like your friend?"

"I guess. In a way, we're all in the same boat. The only difference is that he's escaping out of his own choice and I'm being ricocheted about."

I ground out the cigarette in the ashtray. The cat raised his head and yawned, then resumed his position.

"Finished with your packing?" she asked.

"No, haven't begun. But I don't have too much to pack. A couple changes of clothes, soap, towel. You really don't need that whole bag yourself. If you need anything, you can buy it there. We've got more than enough money."

"I like it this way," she said, again with that cute little smile of hers. "I don't feel like I'm traveling unless I'm lugging a huge bag."

"You've got to be kidding. . . ."

A piercing bird call shot in through the open window, a call I'd never heard before. A new season's new bird.

A beam of afternoon sun landed on her cheek. I lazily watched a white cloud move from one edge of the window to the other. We stayed like that for the longest time.

"Is anything wrong?" she asked.

"I don't know how to put it, but I just can't get it through my head that here and now is really here and now. Or that I am really me. It doesn't quite hit home. It's always this way. Only much later on does it ever come together. For the last ten years, it's been like this."

"Ten years?"

"There's been no end to it. That's all."

She laughed as she picked up the cat and let it down onto the floor. "Shall we?"

We made love on the sofa. A period piece of a sofa I'd bought at a junk store. Put your face up against it and you get the scent of history. Her supple body blended in with that scent. Gentle and warm like a vague recollection. I brushed her hair aside with my fingers and kissed her ear. The earth trembled. From that point on, time began to flow like a tranquil breeze.

I undid all the buttons of her shirt and cupped her breasts while I appreciated her body.

"Feeling really alive now," she said.

"You?"

"Mmm, my body, my whole self."

"I'm right with you," I said. "Truly alive."

How amazingly quiet, I thought. Not a sound anywhere around. Everybody but the two of us probably gone off somewhere to celebrate the first Sunday of autumn.

"You know, I really love this," she whispered.

"Mmm."

"It seems like we're having a picnic, it's so lovely."

"A picnic?"

"Yeah."

I wrapped both hands around her back and held her tight. Then I nuzzled my way through her bangs to kiss her ear again.

"It's been a long ten years for you?" she asked, down low by my ear.

"Long enough," I said. "A long, long time. Practically endless, not that I've managed to get anything over and done with."

She raised her head a tiny bit from the sofa armrest and smiled. A smile I'd seen somewhere before, but for the life of me I couldn't place where or on whom. Women with their clothes off have a frightening similarity. Always throws me for a loop.

"Let's go look for the sheep," she said, eyes closed. "Once we get to looking for that sheep, things'll fall into place."

I looked into her face a while, then I gazed at both her ears. A soft afternoon glow enveloped her body as in an old still life.

23

Limited but Tenacious Thinking

At six o'clock, she got dressed, brushed her hair, brushed her teeth, and sprayed on her eau de cologne. I sat on the sofa reading *The Adventures of Sherlock Holmes*. The story began: "My colleague Watson is limited in his thinking to rather narrow confines, but possesses the utmost tenacity." Not a bad lead-in sentence.

"I'll be late tonight, so don't wait up for me," she said.

"Work?"

"Afraid so. I actually should have had today off, but those are the breaks. They pushed it on me because I'm taking off from tomorrow."

She went out, then after a moment or two the door opened.

"Say, what're you going to do about the cat while we're gone?" she asked.

"Oops, completely slipped my mind. But don't worry, I'll take care of it."

I brought out milk and cheese snacks for the cat. His teeth were so weak, he had a hard time with the cheese.

There wasn't a thing that looked particularly edible for me in the refrigerator, so I opened up a beer and watched television. Nothing newsworthy on the news either. On Sunday evenings like this, it's always some zoo scene. I watched the rundown of giraffes and elephants and pandas, then switched off the set and picked up the telephone.

"It's about my cat," I told the man.

"Your cat?"

"Yes, I have a cat."

"So?"

"So unless I can leave the cat with someone, I can't go anywhere."

"There are any number of kennels to be had thereabouts."

"He's old and frail. A month in a cage would do him in for sure."

I could hear fingernails drumming on a tabletop. "So?"

"I'd like you to take care of him. You've got a huge garden, surely you could take care of one cat."

"Out of the question. The Boss hates cats, and the garden is there to attract birds. One cat and there go all the birds."

"The Boss is unconscious, and the cat has no strength to chase down birds."

"Very well, then. I will send a driver for the cat tomorrow morning at ten o'clock."

"I'll provide the cat food and kitty litter. He only eats this one brand, so if you run out, please buy more of the same."

"Perhaps you would be so kind as to tell these details to the driver. As I believe I told you before, I am a busy man."

"I'd like to keep communications to one channel. It makes it clear where the responsibility lies."

"Responsibility?"

"In other words, say the cat dies while I'm gone, you'd get nothing out of me, even if I did find the sheep."

"Hmm," said the man. "Fair enough. You are somewhat off base, but you do quite well for an amateur. I shall write this down, so please speak slowly."

"Don't feed him fatty meat. He throws it all up. His teeth are bad, so no hard foods. In the morning, he gets milk and canned cat food, in the evening a handful of dried fish or meat or cheese snacks. Also please change his litter box daily. He doesn't like it dirty. He often gets diarrhea, but if it doesn't go away after two days the vet will have some medicine to give him."

Having gotten that far, I strained to hear the scrawl of a ballpoint pen on the other end of the line.

"He's starting to get lice in his ears," I continued, "so once a day you should give his ears a cleaning with a cotton swab and a little olive oil. He dislikes it and fights it, so be careful not to rupture the eardrum. Also, if you're worried he might claw the furniture, trim his claws once a week. Regular nail clippers are fine. I'm pretty sure he doesn't have fleas, but just in case it might be wise to give him a flea bath every so often. You can get flea shampoo at any pet shop. After his bath, you should dry him off with a towel and give him a good brushing, then last of all a once-over with a hair dryer. Otherwise he'll catch cold."

Scribble scribble scribble. "Anything else?"

"That's about it."

The man read back the items from his notepad. A memo well taken.

"Is that it?"

"Just fine."

"Well then," said the man. And the phone cut off.

It was already dark out. I slipped some change, my cigarettes, and a lighter into my pocket, put on my tennis shoes, and stepped outside. At my neighborhood dive, I drank a beer while listening to the latest Brothers Johnson record. I ate my chicken cutlet while listening to a Bill Withers record. I had some coffee while listening to Maynard Ferguson's "Star Wars." After all that, I felt as if I'd hardly eaten anything.

They cleared away my coffee cup and I put three ten-yen coins into the pink public phone and rang up my partner. His eldest son, who was still in grammar school, answered.

"Good day," I said.

"It's 'good evening,'" he corrected. I looked at my watch. Of course, he was right.

After a bit, my partner came to the phone.

"How'd it go?" he asked.

"Is it all right to talk now? I'm not catching you in the middle of eating?"

"We're in the middle of eating, but it's okay. Wasn't much of a meal, and anyway your story's got to be more interesting."

I related snatches of the conversation with the man in the black suit. Then I talked about the huge limo and the dying Boss. I didn't touch on the sheep. He wouldn't have believed it, and already this was too long and involved. Which naturally made everything more confusing than ever.

"I can't begin to follow you," said my partner.

"This is all confidential, you understand. If it gets out, it could mean a lot of trouble for you. I mean, with your family and all. . . ." I trailed off, picturing his high-class four-bedroom condominium, his wife with high blood pressure, his two cheeky sons. "I mean, that's how it is."

"I see."

"In any case, I have to be going on a trip from tomorrow. A long trip, I expect. One month, two months, three months, I really don't know. Maybe I'll never come back to Tokyo."

"Er . . . umm."

"So I want you to take over things at the company. I'm pulling out. I don't want to cause you any trouble. My work is pretty much done, and for all its being a co-venture, you hold down the important part. I'm only half playing there."

"But I need you there to take care of all the details."

"Consolidate your battle line, and go back to how it used to be. Cancel all advertising and editing work. Turn it back into a translation office. Like you were saying the other day yourself. Keep one secretary and get rid of the rest of the part-timers. You don't need them anymore. Nobody's going to complain if you give them two months' severance. As for the office, you can move to a smaller place. The income will go down, sure, but so will the outlay. And minus my take, yours'll increase, so in actual terms you won't be hurting. You won't have to worry about exploiting anyone so much, and taxes will be less of a problem. It'd be ideal for you."

"No go," he said, after some silence. "It won't work, I know it won't work."

"It'll be fine, I tell you. I've been through it all with you, so I know, no problem."

"It went well because we went into it together," he said. "Nothing I've tried to do by myself has ever come off."

"Now listen. I'm not talking about expanding business. I'm telling you to consolidate. The pre-industrial-revolution translation business we used to do. You and one secretary, plus five or six freelancers you can farm out work to. There's no reason why you can't do fine."

There was a click as the last ten-yen coin dropped into the machine. I fed the phone another three coins.

"I'm not you," he said. "You can make it on your own. Not

me. Things don't go anywhere unless I have someone to complain to or bounce ideas off of."

I put my hand over the receiver and sighed. The same old royal runaround. Black goat eats white goat's letter unread, white goat eats black goat's letter . . .

"Hello, hello?" said my partner.

"I'm listening," I said.

On the other end of the line, I could hear his two kids fighting over which television channel to watch. "Think of your kids," I said. Not exactly fair, but I didn't have another card to play. "You can't afford to be sniveling. If you call it quits, it's all over for everybody. If you wanted to strike out against the world, you don't go having children. Straighten up, square away the business, stop drinking."

He fell silent for a long time. The waitress brought me an ashtray. I gestured with my hand for another beer.

"You've got me pinned," he came back. "I'll do my best. I have no confidence it'll go, but . . ."

I filled my glass with beer and took a sip. "It'll go fine. Think of six years ago. No money or connections, but everything came through, didn't it?" I said.

"Like I said, you have no idea how secure I felt because we started the thing together," said my partner.

"I'll be calling in again."

"Umm."

"Thanks for everything. All this time, it's been great," I said.

"Once you're finished with what you've got to do and come back to Tokyo, let's do some business together again."

"Sure thing."

I hung up.

Both he and I knew the probability of my returning to the job. Work together six years and that much you understand.

I took my beer back to the table.

With the job out of the picture, I felt a surge of relief. Slowly but surely I was making things simpler. I'd lost my hometown, lost my teens, lost my wife, in another three months I'd lose my twenties. What'd be left of me when I got to be sixty, I couldn't imagine. There's no thinking about these things. There's no telling even what's going to happen a month from now.

I headed home and crawled into bed with my *Sherlock Holmes.* Lights out at eleven and I was fast asleep. I didn't wake once before morning.

24

One for the Kipper

At ten in the morning, that ridiculous submarine of an automobile was waiting outside my apartment building. From my third-story window, the limo looked more like an upside-down metal cookie cutter than a submarine. You could make a gigantic cookie that would take three hundred kids two weeks to eat. She and I sat on the windowsill looking down at the car.

The sky was appallingly clear. A sky from a prewar expressionist movie. Utterly cloudless, like a monumental eye with its eyelid cut off. A helicopter flying high off in the distance looked minuscule.

I locked all the windows, switched off the refrigerator, and checked the gas cock. The laundry brought in, bed covered with spread, ashtrays rinsed out, and an absurd number of medicinal items put in proper order by the washbasin. The rent paid two months in advance, the newspaper canceled. I looked back from the doorway into the lifeless apartment. For a moment, I thought about the four years of married life spent there, thought about the kids my wife and I never had.

The elevator door opened, and she called to me. I shut the steel door.

The chauffeur was intently polishing the windshield with a dry cloth as he waited for us. The car, not one single mark anywhere, gleamed in the sun to a burning, unearthly brilliance. The slightest touch of the hand and you'd get burned.

"Good morning," said the chauffeur. The very same religious chauffeur from two days ago.

"Good morning," said I.

"Good morning," said my girlfriend.

She held the cat. I carried the cat food and bag of kitty litter.

"Fabulous weather, isn't it?" said the chauffeur, looking up at the sky. "It's—how can I put it?—crystal clear."

I nodded.

"When it gets this clear, God's messages must have no trouble getting through at all," I offered.

"Nothing of the kind," said the chauffeur with a grin. "There are messages already in all things. In the flowers, in the rocks, in the clouds . . ."

"And cars?"

"In cars too."

"But cars are made by factories." Typical me.

"Whosoever makes it, God's will is worked into it."

"As in ear lice?" Her contribution.

"As in the very air," corrected the chauffeur.

"Well then, I suppose that cars made in Saudi Arabia have Allah in them."

"They don't produce cars in Saudi Arabia."

"Really?" Again me.

"Really."

"Then what about cars produced in America for export to Saudi Arabia? What god's in them?" queried my girlfriend.

A difficult question.

"Say now, we have to tell him about the cat," I launched a lifeboat.

"Cute cat, eh?" said the chauffeur, also relieved.

The cat was anything but cute. Rather, he weighed in at the opposite end of the scale, his fur was scruffy like an old, threadbare carpet, the tip of his tail was bent at a sixty-degree angle, his teeth were yellowed, his right eye oozed pus from a wound three years before so that by now he could hardly see. It was doubtful that he could distinguish between a tennis shoe and a potato. The pads of his feet were shriveled-up corns, his ears were infested with ear lice, and from sheer age he farted at least twenty times a day. He'd been a fine young tom the day my wife found him under a park bench and brought him home, but in the last few years he'd rapidly gone downhill. Like a bowling ball rolling toward the gutter. Also, he didn't have a name. I had no idea whether not having a name reduced or contributed to the cat's tragedy.

"Nice kitty-kitty," said the chauffeur, hand not outstretched. "What's his name?"

"He doesn't have a name."

"So what do you call the fella?"

"I don't call it," I said. "It's just there."

"But he's not a lump just sitting there. He moves about by his own will, no? Seems mighty strange that something that moves by its own will doesn't have a name."

"Herring swim around of their own will, but nobody gives them names."

"Well, first of all, there's no emotional bond between herring and people, and besides, they wouldn't know their name if they heard it."

"Which is to say that animals that not only move by their own will and share feelings with people but also possess sight and hearing qualify as deserving of names then?"

"There, you got it." The chauffeur nodded repeatedly, satisfied. "How about it? What say I go ahead and give the little guy a name?"

"Don't mind in the least. But what name?"

"How about 'Kipper'? I mean you were treating him like a herring after all."

"Not bad," I said.

"You see?" said the chauffeur.

"What do you think?" I asked my girlfriend.

"Not bad," she said. "It's like being witness to the creation of heaven and earth."

"Let there be Kipper," I said.

"C'mere, Kipper," said the chauffeur, picking up the cat. The cat got frightened, bit the chauffeur's thumb, then farted.

The chauffeur took us to the airport. The cat rode quietly up front next to the driver. Farting from to time to time. The driver kept opening the window, so we knew. Meanwhile, I cranked out instructions to the chauffeur about the cat. How to clean his ears, stores that sold litter-box deodorant, the amount of food to give him, things like that.

"Don't worry," said the chauffeur. "I'll take good care of him. I'm his godfather, you know."

The roads were surprisingly empty. The car raced to the airport like a salmon shooting upstream to spawn.

"Why do boats have names, but not airplanes?" I asked the chauffeur. "Why just Flight 971 or Flight 326, and not the *Bellflower* or the *Daisy*?"

"Probably because there're more planes than boats. Mass production."

"I wonder. Lots of boats are mass-produced, and they may outnumber planes."

"Still . . . ," said the chauffeur, then nothing for a few seconds. "Realistically speaking, nobody's going to put names on each and every city bus."

"I think it'd be wonderful if each city bus had a name," said my girlfriend.

"But wouldn't that lead to passengers choosing the buses they want to ride? To go from Shinjuku to Sendagaya, say, they'd ride the *Antelope* but not the *Mule*."

"How about it?" I asked my girlfriend.

"For sure, I'd think twice about riding the *Mule*," she said.

"But hey, think about the poor driver of the *Mule*," the chauffeur spoke up for drivers everywhere. "The *Mule*'s driver isn't to blame."

"Well put," said I.

"Maybe," said she, "but I'd still ride the *Antelope*."

"Well there you are," said the chauffeur. "That's just how it'd be. Names on ships are familiar from times before mass production. In principle, it amounts to the same thing as naming horses. So that airplanes treated like horses are actually given names too. There's the *Spirit of St. Louis* and the *Enola Gay*. We're looking at a full-fledged conscious identification."

"Which is to say that life is the basic concept here."

"Exactly."

"And that purpose, as such, is but a secondary element in naming."

"Exactly. For purpose alone, numbers are enough. Witness the treatment of the Jews at Auschwitz."

"Fine so far," I said. "So let's just say that the basis of naming is this act of conscious identification with living things. Why then do train stations and parks and baseball stadiums have names, if they're not living?"

"Why? Because it'd be chaos if stations didn't have names."

"No, we're not talking on the purposive level. I'd like you to explain it to me in principle."

The chauffeur gave this serious thought. He failed to notice that the traffic light had turned green. The camper van behind us honked its horn to the overture to the *The Magnificent Seven.*

"Because they're not interchangeable, I suppose. For instance, there's only one Shinjuku Station and you can't just replace it with Shibuya Station. This non-interchangeability is to say that they're not mass-produced. Are we clear on these two points?"

"Sure would be fun to have Shinjuku Station in Ekoda, though," said my girlfriend.

"If Shinjuku Station were in Ekoda, it would be Ekoda Station," countered the chauffeur.

"But it'd still have the Odakyu Line attached," she said.

"Back to the original line of discussion," I said. "If stations were interchangeable, what would that mean? If, for instance, all national railway stations were mass-produced fold-up type buildings and Shinjuku Station and Tokyo Station were absolutely interchangeable?"

"Simple enough. If it's in Shinjuku, it'd be Shinjuku Station; if it's in Tokyo, it'd be Tokyo Station."

"So what we're talking about here is not the name of a physical object, but the name of a function. A role. Isn't that purpose?"

The chauffeur fell silent. Only this time he didn't stay silent for very long.

"You know what I think?" said the chauffeur. "I think maybe we ought to cast a warmer eye on the subject."

"Meaning?"

"I mean towns and parks and streets and stations and ball fields and movie theaters all have names, right? They are all given names in compensation for their fixity on the earth."

A new theory.

"Well," said I, "suppose I utterly obliterated my consciousness and became totally fixed, would I merit a fancy name?"

The chauffeur glanced at my face in the rearview mirror. A suspicious look, as if I were laying some trap. "Fixed?"

"Say I froze in place, or something. Like Sleeping Beauty."

"But you already have a name."

"Right you are," I said. "I nearly forgot."

We received our boarding passes at the airport check-in counter and said goodbye to the chauffeur. He would have waited to see us off, but as there was an hour and a half before departure time, he capitulated and left.

"A real character, that one," she said.

"There's a place I know with no one but people like that," I said. "The cows there go around looking for pliers."

"Sounds like 'Home on the Pampas.'"

"Maybe so," I said.

We went into the airport restaurant and had an early lunch. Shrimp au gratin for me, spaghetti for her. I watched the 747s and Tristars take flight and swoop down to earth with a gravity that seemed fated. Meanwhile, she dubiously inspected each strand of spaghetti she ate.

"I thought that they always served meals on planes," she said, disgruntled.

"Nope," I said, waiting for the hot lump of gratin in my mouth to cool down, then gulping down some water. No taste but hot. "Meals only on international flights. They give you something to eat on longer domestic routes. Not exactly what you'd call a special treat, though."

"And movies?"

"No way. C'mon, it's only an hour to Sapporo."

"Then they give you nothing."

"Nothing at all. You sit in your seat, read your book, and arrive at your destination. Same as by bus."

"But no traffic lights."

"No traffic lights."

"Just great," she said with a sigh. She put down her fork, leaving half the spaghetti untouched.

"The thing is you get there faster. It takes twelve hours if you go by train."

"And where does the extra time go?"

I also gave up halfway through my meal and ordered two coffees. "Extra time?"

"You said planes save you over ten hours. So where does all that time go?"

"Time doesn't go anywhere. It only adds up. We can use those ten hours as we like, in Tokyo or in Sapporo. With ten hours we could see four movies, eat two meals, whatever. Right?"

"But what if I don't want to go to the movies or eat?"

"That's your problem. It's no fault of time."

She bit her lip as we looked out at the squat bodies of the 747s on the tarmac. 747s always remind me of a fat, ugly old lady in the neighborhood where I used to live. Huge sagging breasts, swollen legs, dried-up neckline. The airport, a likely gathering place for the old ladies. Dozens of them, coming and going, one after the other. The pilots and stewardesses, strutting back and forth in the lobby with heads held high, seemed quaintly planar. I couldn't help thinking how it wasn't like the DC-7 and Friendship-7 days, but maybe it was.

"Well," she went on, "does time expand?"

"No, time does not expand," I answered. I had spoken, but why didn't it sound like my voice? I coughed and drank my coffee. "Time does not expand."

"But time is actually increasing, isn't it? You yourself said that time adds up."

"That's only because the time needed for transit has decreased. The sum total of time doesn't change. It's only that you can see more movies."

"If you wanted to see movies," she added.

As soon as we arrived in Sapporo, we actually did see a double feature.

Part Seven

The Dolphin Hotel Affair

25

Transit Completed at Movie Theater; On to the Dolphin Hotel

The entire flight, she sat by the window and looked down at the scenery. I sat next to her reading my *Adventures of Sherlock Holmes*. Not a single cloud in the sky the whole time, the airplane riding on its shadow over the earth. Or more accurately, since we were in the plane, our shadows figured as well inside the shadow of the airplane skimming over mountain and field. Which would mean we too were imprinted into the earth.

"I really liked that guy," she said after drinking her orange juice.

"That guy who?"

"The chauffeur."

"Hmm," I said, "I liked him too."

"And what a great name, 'Kipper.' "

"For sure. A great name. The cat might be better off with him than he ever was with me."

"Not 'the cat,' 'Kipper.' "

"Right. 'Kipper.' "

"Why didn't you give the cat a name all this time?"

"Why indeed," I puzzled. Then I lit up a cigarette with the

sheep-engraved lighter. "I think I just don't like names. Basically, I can't see what's wrong with calling me 'me' or you 'you' or us 'us' or them 'them.' "

"Hmm," she said. "I do like the word 'we,' though. It has an Ice Age ring to it."

"Ice Age?"

"Like 'We go south' or 'We hunt mammoth' or . . ."

When we stepped outside at Chitose Airport, the air was chillier than we'd expected. I pulled a denim shirt over my T-shirt, she a knit vest over her shirt. Autumn had come over this land one whole month ahead of Tokyo.

"We weren't supposed to run into an Ice Age, were we?" she asked on the bus to Sapporo. "You hunting mammoths, me raising children."

"Sounds positively inviting," I said.

She soon fell asleep, leaving me gazing through the bus windows at the endless procession of deep forest on both sides of the road.

We hit a coffee shop first thing on arriving in the city.

"Right off, let's set our prime directives," I said. "We'll have to divide up. That is, I go after the scene in the photograph. You go after the sheep. That way we save time."

"Very pragmatic."

"If things go well," I amended. "In any case, you can cover the major former sheep ranches of Hokkaido and study up on sheep breeds. You can probably find what you need at a government office or the local library."

"I like libraries," she said.

"I'm glad."

"Do I start right away?"

I looked at my watch. Three-thirty. "Nah, it's already getting late. Let's start tomorrow. Today we'll take it easy, find a place to stay, have dinner, take a bath, and get some sleep."

"I wouldn't mind seeing a movie," she said.

"A movie?"

"What with all that time we saved by flying."

"Good point," I said. So we popped into the first movie theater that caught our eye.

What we ended up seeing was a crime-occult double feature. There was hardly a soul in the place. It'd been ages since I'd been in a theater that empty. I counted the people in the audience to pass the time. Eight, including ourselves. There were more characters in the films.

The films were exemplars of the dreadful. The sort of films where you feel like turning around and walking out the instant the title comes on after the roaring MGM lion. Amazing that films like that exist.

The first was the occult feature. The devil, who lives in the dripping, dank cellar of the town church and manipulates things through the weak preacher, takes over the town. The real question, though, was why the devil wanted to take over the town to begin with. All it was was a miserable nothing of a few blocks surrounded by cornfields.

Nonetheless, the devil had this terrible obsession with the town and grew furious that one last little girl refused to fall under his spell. When the devil got mad, his body shook like quivering green jelly. Admittedly, there was something endearing about that rage.

In front of us a middle-aged man was snoring away like a foghorn. To the extreme right there was some heavy petting in progress. Behind, someone let out a huge fart. Huge enough to stop the middle-aged man's snoring for a moment. A pair of high school girls giggled.

By reflex, I thought of Kipper. And it was only when I did that it came to me that we'd really left Tokyo and were now in Sapporo.

Funny about that.

Amid these thoughts I fell asleep. In my dreams, I encountered that green devil, but he wasn't endearing in the least. He remained silent and I just observed his machinations.

Meanwhile, the film ended, the lights came on, and I woke up. Each member of the audience yawned as if in predetermined order. I went to the snack bar and bought ice cream for us. It was hard as a rock, probably left over from last summer.

"You slept through the whole thing?"

"Uh-huh," I said. "How was it?"

"Pretty interesting. In the end, the whole town explodes."

"Wow."

The movie theater was deathly quiet. Or rather everything around us was deathly quiet. Not a common occurrence.

"Say," she said, "doesn't it seem like your body's in a state of transit or something?"

Now that she mentioned it, it actually did.

She held my hand. "Let's just stay like this. I'm worried."

"Okay."

"Unless we stay like this, we might get transported somewhere else. Someplace crazy."

As the theater interior grew dark again and the coming attractions began, I brushed her hair aside and kissed her ear. "It's all right. Don't worry."

"You're probably right," she said softly. "I guess we should have ridden in transportation with names after all."

For the next hour and a half, from the beginning to the end of the film, we stayed in a state of quiet transport in the darkness. Her head resting on my shoulder the whole time. My shoulder became warm and damp from her breath.

We came out of the movie theater and strolled the twilit streets, my arm around her shoulder. We felt closer than ever before. The commotion of passersby was comforting; faint stars were shining through in the sky.

"Are we really in the right city, the two of us?" she asked.

I looked up at the sky. The polestar was in the right position, but somehow it looked like a fake polestar. Too big, too bright.

"I wonder," I said.

"I feel like something's out of place," she said.

"That's what it's like, coming to a new city. Your body can't quite get used to it."

"But after a while you do get used to it, don't you?"

"After two or three days, you'll be fine," I said.

When we tired of walking, we went into the first restaurant we saw, drank draft beer, and ordered some salmon and potatoes. We'd walked in willy-nilly off the street and gotten lucky. The beer really hit the spot, and the food was actually good.

"Well then," I said after coffee, "what say we settle on a place to stay?"

"I've already got an image of a place," she said.

"Like what?"

"Never mind. Get a list of hotels and read off the names in order."

I asked a waiter to bring over the yellow pages and started reading the names listed in the "Hotels, Inns" section. After forty names, she stopped me.

"That's the one."

"Which one?"

"The last one you read."

"Dolphin Hotel," I said.

"That's where we're staying."

"Never heard of it."

"But I can't see us staying at any other hotel."

I returned the phone book, then called the Dolphin Hotel. A man with an indistinct voice answered, indicating they had double and single rooms available. And did they have other types of rooms besides doubles and singles? No. Doubles and singles were all. Confused, I reserved a double. The price: forty percent less than what I'd expected.

The Dolphin Hotel was located three blocks west and one block south of the movie theater we'd gone to. A small place, totally undistinguished. Its undistinguishedness was metaphysical. No neon sign, no large signboard, not even a real entryway. The glass front door, which resembled an employees' kitchen entrance, had next to it only a copper plate engraved with DOLPHIN HOTEL. Not even a picture of a dolphin.

The building was five stories tall, but it might as well have been a giant matchbox stood on end. It wasn't particularly old; still it was strikingly run-down. Most likely it was run-down when it was built.

This was our Dolphin Hotel.

Yet she apparently fell in love with the place the moment she set eyes on it.

"Not a bad hotel, eh?" she said.

"Not bad?" I tossed back her words.

"Cozy, no frills."

"No frills," I repeated. "By frills, I'm sure you mean clean sheets or a sink that doesn't leak or an air conditioner that works or reasonably soft toilet paper or fresh soap or curtains that prevent sunstroke."

"You always look at the dark side of things," she laughed. "Anyway, we didn't come here as tourists."

On opening the door, I found the lobby bigger than expected. In the middle of it was a set of parlor furniture and a large color TV; there was a quiz show on. Not a soul was in sight.

Large potted ornamentals sat on both sides of the front door, their leaves faded, nearly brown. I stood there taking everything in. The lobby was actually a lot less spacious than it had initially seemed. It appeared large because there were so few pieces of furniture. The parlor set, a grandfather clock, and a mirror. Nothing else.

I walked over and checked out the clock and mirror. Both were commemorative presents of some event or another. The clock was seven minutes off; the mirror made my head crooked on my body.

The parlor set was about as run-down as the hotel itself. The sofa was an unappealing orange, the sort of orange you'd get by leaving a choicely sunburnt weaving out in the rain for a week, then throwing it into the cellar until it mildewed. This was an orange from the early days of Technicolor.

On closer inspection, a balding middle-aged man lay, stretched out like a dried fish, asleep on the parlor set chaise longue. At first, I thought he was dead, but his nose twitched. There were the indentations of eyeglasses on the bridge of his nose, but no glasses anywhere. Which would mean that he hadn't fallen asleep while watching television. It didn't make sense.

I stood at the front desk and peeked over the counter. Nobody there. She rang the bell. It chimed across the expanse of lobby.

We waited thirty seconds and got no response. The man on the chaise longue didn't stir.

She rang the bell again.

Now the man on the chaise longue grunted. A self-accusing grunt. Then he opened his eyes and looked us over vacantly.

She gave the bell a third, serious ring.

The man sprang up and dashed across the lobby. He edged by me and went behind the counter. He was the desk clerk.

"Terrible of me," he said. "Really terrible of me. Fell asleep waiting for you."

"Sorry to wake you," I said.

"Not at all," said the desk clerk. He brought out a registration card and a ballpoint pen. He was missing the tips of the little and middle fingers on his left hand.

I wrote my name on the card but had second thoughts and crumpled it up and stuffed it in my pocket. I took another card and wrote a fake name and a fake address. An ordinary name and address, but not bad for a spur-of-the-moment name and address. I put down my occupation as real estate.

The desk clerk picked up his thick celluloid-rimmed glasses from beside the telephone and peered intently at the registration card.

"Suginami, Tokyo, . . . 29 years old, realtor."

I took a tissue from my pocket and wiped the ink from my fingers.

"Here on business?" asked the clerk.

"Uh, sort of," I said.

"How many nights?"

"One month," I said.

"One month?" He gave me a blank-white-sheet-of-drawing-paper look. "You'll be staying here one whole month?"

"Is there something wrong with that?"

"No, uh, nothing wrong, but well, we like to settle up payment three days at a time."

I set my satchel on the floor, counted out twenty ten-thousand-yen notes, and laid them on the counter.

"There's more if that runs out," I said.

The clerk scooped up the bills with the three fingers of his left hand and counted them with his right. Then he made out a receipt. "Would there be anything special you might care to see in the way of a room?"

"A corner room away from the elevator, if possible."

The clerk turned around and squinted at the keyboard. After much ado, he chose room 406. The keyboard was almost entirely full. A real success story, the Dolphin Hotel.

There was no such thing as a bellboy, so we carried our bags to the elevator. As she said, no frills. The elevator shook like a large dog with lung disease.

"For an extended stay, there's nothing like your small, basic hotel."

"Your small, basic hotel"—not a bad turn of phrase. Like something from the travel pages of a women's fashion magazine: "After a long trip, your small, basic hotel is just the thing."

Nonetheless, the first thing I did upon opening the door to our small, basic hotel room was to grab a slipper to smash a cockroach that was creeping along the window frame. Then I picked up two pubic hairs lying by the foot of the bed and disposed of them in the trash. A new experience for me, seeing a cockroach in Hokkaido. Meanwhile, she ran the bath to temperature. And believe me, it was one noisy faucet.

"I tell you, we should've stayed in a better hotel," I opened the bathroom door and yelled in her direction. "We've got more than enough money."

"It's not a question of money. Our sheep hunt begins here. No argument, it had to be here."

I stretched out on the bed and smoked a cigarette, switched on the television and ran through all the channels, then turned it off. The only thing decent was the reception. Presently, the bathwater stopped and her clothes came flying out, followed by the sound of the hand shower.

Parting the window curtains, I looked out across the way onto a sordid menagerie of buildings every bit as incomprehensible as our Dolphin Hotel. Each one a dingy ash gray and reeking of piss just by their looks. Although it was already nine o'clock, I could see people in the few lit windows, busily working away. I couldn't tell what line of work it was, but none of them looked terribly happy. Of course, to their eyes, I probably looked a bit forlorn too.

I drew the curtains shut and returned to the bed, rolled over on the hard-as-asphalt starched sheets, and thought about my ex-wife. I thought about the man she was living with now. I knew almost everything there was to know about him. He'd been my friend, after all, so why shouldn't I know? Twenty-seven years old. A not very well-known jazz guitarist, but regular enough as not very well-known jazz guitarists go. Not a bad guy. No style, though. One year he'd drift between Kenny Burrell and B.B. King, another year between Larry Coryell and Jim Hall.

Why she'd up and choose him after me, I couldn't figure. Granted, you can pick out certain characteristics among individuals. Yet the only thing he had over me was that he could play guitar, and the only thing I had over him was that I could wash dishes. Most guitarists can't wash dishes. Ruin their fingers and there goes everything.

Then I found myself thinking about sex with her. By default, I tried to calculate the number of times we'd had sex in our four years of married life. An approximate count at best, and admittedly, what would be the point of an approximate count? I should have kept a diary. Or at least made some mark in a notebook. That way I'd have an accurate figure. Accurate figures give things a sense of reality.

My ex-wife kept precise records about sex. Not that she kept a diary per se. She recorded in a notebook exact data about her periods from her first year on and included sex as a supplementary reference. Altogether there were eight of these notebooks, all kept in a locked drawer together with important papers and photographs. These she showed to no one. That she kept records about sex is the full extent of my knowledge. What and how much she wrote, I have no idea. And now that we're no longer together, I'll probably never know.

"If I die," she told me, "burn these notebooks. Douse them in kerosene and let them burn till ash, then bury them. I'd never forgive you if one word remained."

"But I'm the one who's been sleeping with you. I pretty much know every inch of your body. What's there to be ashamed of at this late date?"

"Body cells replace themselves every month. Even at this very moment," she said, thrusting a skinny back of her hand before my eyes. "Most everything you think you know about me is nothing more than memories."

The woman—save for the month or so prior to our divorce—

was singularly methodical in her thinking. She had an absolutely realistic grasp on her life. Which is to say that no door once closed ever opened again, nor as a rule was any door left wide open.

Now all I know about her is my memories of her. And these memories fade further and further into the distance like displaced cells. Now I have no way of knowing precisely how many times she and I had sex.

26

Enter the Sheep Professor

We woke the next morning at eight, donned our clothes, headed down in the elevator, and out to a nearby coffee shop for breakfast. No, the Dolphin Hotel had no coffee shop.

"Like I said yesterday, we'll split up," I said, passing her a copy of the sheep photo. "I'll use the mountains in the background as a handle toward searching out the place. You'll research places where they raise sheep. You know what to do. Any clue, anything, it doesn't matter how small, is fine. Anything is an improvement over scouring the entire island of Hokkaido totally blind."

"I'm fine. Leave it up to me."

"Okay, let's meet back at the hotel in the evening."

"Don't worry so much," she said, putting on sunglasses. "Finding it's going to be a piece of cake."

Of course, it was no piece of cake. Things never happen that way. I went to the Territorial Tourist Agency, did the rounds of various tourist information centers and travel agents, inquired at the Mountaineering Association. In general, I checked all the places that had anything to do with tourism and mountains. Nobody could recall ever having seen the mountains in the photograph.

"They're such ordinary-looking mountains too," they all said. "Besides, the photo shows only a small part of them."

One whole day on the pavement and that was about as close to progress as I got. That is, the realization that it'd be difficult to identify mountains with nothing to distinguish them and with only a partial view of them.

I stopped into a bookstore and bought *The Mountains of Hokkaido* and a Hokkaido atlas, then went into a café, had two ginger ales, and skimmed through my purchases. As far as mountains were concerned, there was an unbelievable number in Hokkaido, all of them about the same in color and in shape. I tried comparing the mountains in the Rat's photograph with every mountain in the book; after ten minutes, I was dizzy. It was no comfort to learn that the number of mountains in the book represented but a tiny fraction of all the mountains in Hokkaido. Complicated by the fact that a mountain viewed from one angle gave a wholly different impression than from another angle.

"Mountains are living things," wrote the author in his preface to the book. "Mountains, according to the angle of view, the season, the time of day, the beholder's frame of mind, or any one thing, can effectively change their appearance. Thus, it is essential to recognize that we can never know more than one side, one small aspect of a mountain."

"Just great," I said out loud. An impossible task. At the five o'clock bell, I went out to sit on a park bench and eat corn with the pigeons.

Her efforts at information gathering fared better than mine, but ultimately they were futile too. We compared notes of the day's trials and tribulations over a modest dinner at a restaurant behind the Dolphin Hotel.

"The Livestock Section of the Territorial Government knew next to nothing," she said. "They've stopped keeping track of sheep. It doesn't pay to raise sheep. At least not by large-scale ranching or free-range grazing."

"In a way that makes the search easier."

"Not really. Ranchers still raise sheep quite actively and even have their own union, which the authorities keep tabs on. With middle- and small-scale sheep raising, however, it's difficult to keep any accurate count going. Everyone keeps a few sheep pretty much like they do cats and dogs. For what it's worth, I took down the addresses of the thirty sheep raisers they had listings for, but the papers were four years old and people move around a lot in four years. Japan's agricultural policies change every three years just like that, you know."

"Just great," I sighed into my beer. "Seems like we've come to a dead end. There must be more than a hundred similar mountains in Hokkaido, and the state of sheep raising is a total blank."

"This is the first day. We've only just begun."

"Haven't those ears of yours gotten the message yet?"

"No message for the time being," she said, eating her simmered fish and miso soup. "That much I know. I only get despairing messages when I'm confused or feeling some mental pinch. But that's not the case now."

"The lifeline only comes when you're on the verge of drowning?"

"Right. For the moment, I'm satisfied to be going through all this with you, and as long as I'm satisfied, I get no such message. So it's up to us to find that sheep on our own."

"I don't know," I said. "In a sense, if we don't find that sheep we'll be up to our necks in it. In what, I can't say, but if those guys say they're going to get us, they're going to get us. They're pros. No matter if the Boss dies, the organization will remain and their network extends everywhere in Japan, like the sewers. They'll have our necks. Dumb as it sounds, that's the way it is."

"Sounds like *The Invaders.*"

"Ridiculous, I know. But the fact is we've gotten ourselves smack in the middle of it, and by 'ourselves' I mean you and me. At the start it was only me, but by now you're in the picture too. Still feel like you're not on the verge of drowning?"

"Hey, this is just the sort of thing I love. Let me tell you, it's more fun than sleeping with strangers or flashing my ears or proofreading biographical dictionaries. This is living."

"Which is to say," I interjected, "we're not drowning so we have no rope."

"Right. It's up to us to find that sheep. Neither you nor I have left so much behind, really."

Maybe not.

We returned to the hotel and had intercourse. I like that word *intercourse.* It poses only a limited range of possibilities.

Our third and fourth days in Sapporo came and went for naught. We'd get up at eight, have breakfast, split up for the day, and when evening came we'd exchange information over supper, return to the hotel, have intercourse, and sleep.

I threw away my old tennis shoes, bought new sneakers, and went around showing the photograph to hundreds of people. She made up a long list of sheep raisers based on sources from the government offices and the library, and started phoning every one of them. The results were nil. Nobody could place the mountain, and no sheep raiser had any recollection of a sheep with a star on its back. One old man said he remembered seeing that mountain in southern Sakhalin before the war. I wasn't about to believe that the Rat had gone to Sakhalin. No way can you send a letter special delivery from Sakhalin to Tokyo.

Gradually, I was getting worn down. My sense of direction had evaporated by our fourth day. When south became opposite east, I bought a compass, but going around with a compass only made the city seem less and less real. The buildings began to look like backdrops in a photography studio, the people walking the streets like cardboard cutouts. The sun rose from one side of a featureless land, shot up in a cannonball arc across the sky, then set on the other side.

The fifth, then the sixth day passed. October lay heavy on the town. The sun was warm enough but the wind grew brisk, and by late in the day I'd have to put on a thin cotton windbreaker. The streets of Sapporo were wide and depressingly straight. Up until then, I'd had no idea how much walking around in a city of nothing but straight lines can tire you out.

I drank seven cups of coffee a day, took a leak every hour. And slowly lost my appetite.

"Why don't you put an ad in the papers?" she proposed. "You know, 'Friends want to get in touch with you' or something."

"Not a bad idea," I said. It didn't matter if we came up empty-handed; it had to beat doing nothing.

So I placed a three-line notice in the morning editions of four newspapers for the following day.

> Attention: Rat
> Get in touch. Urgent!
> Dolphin Hotel, Room 406

For the next two days, I waited by the phone. The day of the ad there were three calls. One was a call from a local citizen.

"What's this 'Rat'?"

"The nickname of a friend," I answered.

He hung up, satisfied.

Another was a prank call.

"Squeak, squeak," came a voice from the other end of the line. "Squeak, squeak."

I hung up. Cities are damn strange places.

The third was from a woman with a reedy voice.

"Everybody always calls me Rat," she said. A voice in which you could almost hear the telephone lines swaying in the distant breeze.

"Thank you for taking the trouble to call. However, the Rat I'm looking for is a man," I explained.

"I kind of thought so," she said. "But in any case, since I'm a Rat too, I thought I might as well give you a call."

"Really, thank you very much."

"Not at all. Have you found your friend?"

"Not yet," I said, "unfortunately."

"If only it'd been me you were looking for . . . but no, it wasn't me.

"That's the way it goes. Sorry."

She fell silent. Meanwhile, I scratched my nose with my little finger.

"Really, I just wanted to talk to you," she came back.

"With me?"

"I don't quite know how to put it, but I fought the urge ever since I came across your ad in the morning paper. I didn't mean to bother you . . ."

"So all that about your being called Rat was a made-up story."

"That's right," she said. "Nobody ever calls me Rat. I don't even have any friends. That's why I wanted to call you so badly."

I heaved a sigh. "Well, uh, thanks anyway."

"Forgive me. Are you from Hokkaido?"

"I'm from Tokyo," I said.

"You came all the way from Tokyo to look for your friend?"

"That's correct."

"How old is this friend?"

"Just turned thirty."

"And you?"

"I'll be thirty in two months."

"Single?"

"Yes."

"I'm twenty-two. I suppose things get better as time goes on."

"Well," I said, "who knows? Some things get better, some don't."

"It'd be nice if we could get together and discuss things over dinner."

"You'll have to excuse me, but I've got to stay here and wait for a call."

"Oh, yes," she said. "Sorry about everything."

"Anyway, thanks for calling."

I hung up.

Clever, very clever. A call girl, maybe, looking for some business. True, she might really have been just a lonely girl. Either way it was the same. I still had zero leads.

The following day there was only one call, from a mentally disturbed man. "A rat you say? Leave it to me." He talked for fifteen minutes about fending off rats in a Siberian camp. An interesting tale, but no lead.

While waiting for the telephone to ring, I sat in the half-sprung chair by the window and spent the day watching the work conditions on the third floor office across the street. Stare as I might all day long, I couldn't figure out what the company did. The company had ten employees, and people were constantly running in and out like in a basketball game. Someone would hand someone papers, someone would stamp these, then another someone would stuff them into an envelope and rush out the door. During the lunch break, a big-breasted secretary poured tea for everyone. In the afternoon, several people had coffee delivered. Which made me want to drink some too, so I asked the desk clerk to take messages while I went out to a coffee shop. I bought two bottles of beer on the way back. When I resumed my seat at the window, there were only four people left in the office. The big-breasted secretary was joking with a junior employee. I drank a beer and watched the office activities, but mainly her.

The more I looked at her breasts, the more unusually large they seemed. She must have been strapped into a brassiere with cables from the Golden Gate Bridge. Several of the junior staff seemed to have designs on her. Their sex drive came across two panes of glass and the street in between. It's a funny thing sensing someone else's sex drive. After a while, you get to mistaking it for your own.

At five o'clock, she changed into a red dress and went home. I closed the curtain and watched a Bugs Bunny rerun on television. So went the eighth day at the Dolphin Hotel.

"Just great," said I. This "just great" business was becoming a habit. "One-third of the month gone and we still haven't gotten anywhere."

"So it would seem," said she. "I wonder how Kipper's getting on?"

After supper, we rested on the vile orange sofa in the Dolphin

Hotel lobby. No one else around except our three-fingered clerk. He was keeping busy, up on a ladder changing a light bulb, cleaning the windows, folding newspapers. There may have been other guests in the place; perhaps they were all in their rooms like mummies kept out of the light of day.

"How's business?" the desk clerk asked timidly as he watered the potted plants.

"Nothing much to speak of," I said.

"Seems you placed an ad in the papers."

"That I did," I said. "I'm trying to track down this one person on some land inheritance."

"Inheritance?"

"Yes. Trouble is the inheritor's disappeared, whereabouts unknown."

"Do tell. Sounds like interesting work."

"Not really."

"I don't know, there's something of *Moby Dick* about it."

"*Moby Dick*?"

"Sure. The thrill of hunting something down."

"A mammoth, for example?" said my girlfriend.

"Sure. It's all related," said the clerk. "Actually, I named this place the Dolphin Hotel because of a scene with dolphins in *Moby Dick*."

"Oh-ho," said I. "But if that's the case, wouldn't it have been better to name it the Whale Hotel?"

"Whales don't have quite the image," he admitted with some regret.

"The Dolphin Hotel's a lovely name," said my girlfriend.

"Thank you very much," smiled the clerk. "Incidentally, having you here for this extended stay strikes me as most auspicious, and I'd like to offer you some wine as a token of my thanks."

"Delighted," she said.

"Much obliged," I said.

He went into a back room and emerged after a moment with a chilled bottle of white wine and three glasses.

"A toast. I'm still on the job, so just a sip for me."

We drank our wine. Not a particularly fine wine, but a light, dry, pleasant sort of wine. Even the glasses were swell.

"You a *Moby Dick* fan?" I thought to ask.

"You could say that. I always wanted to go to sea ever since I was a child."

"And that's why you're in the hotel business today?" she asked.

"That's why I'm missing fingers," he said. "Actually, they got mangled in a winch unloading cargo from a freighter."

"How horrible!" she exclaimed.

"Everything went black at the time. But life's a fickle thing. Somehow or other, I ended up owning this hotel here. Not much of a hotel, but I've done all right by it. Ten years I've had it."

Which would mean he wasn't the desk clerk, but the owner.

"I couldn't imagine a finer hotel," she encouraged.

"Thank you very much," said the owner, refilling our wineglasses.

"For only ten years, the building has taken on quite a lot of, well, character," I ventured forth unabashedly.

"Yes, it was built right after the war. I count myself most fortunate that I could buy it so cheaply."

"What was it used for before it was a hotel?"

"It went by the name of the Hokkaido Ovine Hall. Housed all sorts of papers and resources concerning . . ."

"Ovine?" I said.

"Sheep," he said.

"The building was the property of the Hokkaido Ovine Association, that is, up until ten years ago. What with the decline in sheep raising in the territory, the Hall was closed," he said, sipping his wine. "Actually, the acting director at the time was my own father. He couldn't abide the thought of his beloved Ovine Hall shutting down, and so on the pretext of preserving the sheep resources he talked the Association into selling him the land and the building at a good price. Hence, to this day the whole second floor of the building is a sheep reference room. Of course, being resource materials, most of the stuff is old and useless. The dotings of an old man. The rest of the place is mine for the hotel business."

"Some coincidence," I said.

"Coincidence?"

"If the truth be known, the person we're looking for has something to do with sheep. And the only lead we've got is this one photograph of sheep that he sent."

"You don't say," he said. "I'd like to have a look at it if I might."

I pulled out the sheep photo that I'd sandwiched between the pages of my notebook and handed it to him. He picked up his glasses from the counter and studied the photo.

"I do seem to have some recollection of this," he said.

"A recollection?"

"For certain." So saying, he took the ladder from where he'd left it under the light and leaned it up against the opposite wall. He brought down a framed picture. Then he wiped off the dust and handed the picture to us.

"Is this not the same scenery?"

The frame itself was plenty old, but the photo in it was even older, discolored too. And yes, there were sheep in it. Altogether maybe sixty head. Fence, birch grove, mountains. The birch grove was different in shape from the one in the Rat's photograph, but the mountains in the background were the same mountains. Even the composition of the photograph was the same.

"Just great," I said to her. "All this time we've been passing right under this photograph."

"That's why I told you it had to be the Dolphin Hotel," she blurted out.

"Well then," I asked the man, "exactly where is this place?"

"Don't rightly know," he said. "The photograph's been hanging in that spot since Ovine Hall days."

"Hmph," I grunted.

"But there's a way to find out."

"Like what?"

"Ask my father. He's got a room upstairs where he spends his days. He hardly ever comes out, he's so wrapped up in his sheep materials. I haven't set eyes on him for half a month now. I just leave his meals in front of his door, and the tray's empty thirty minutes later, so I know he's alive."

"Would your father be able to tell us where the place in the photograph is?"

"Probably. As I said before, he was the former director of Ovine Hall, and anyway he knows all there is to know about sheep. Everyone calls him the Sheep Professor."

"The Sheep Professor," I said.

27

The Sheep Professor Eats All, Tells All

According to his Dolphin Hotel–owner son, the Sheep Professor had by no means had a happy life.

"Father was born in Sendai in 1905, the eldest son of a land-holding family," the son explained. "I'll go by the Western calendar, if that's all right with you."

"As you please."

"They weren't independently wealthy, but they lived on their own land. An old family previously vested with a fief from the local castle lord. Even yielded a respected agriculturist toward the end of the Edo period.

"The Sheep Professor excelled in scholastics from early on, a child wonder known to everyone in Sendai. And not just schooling. He surpassed everyone at the violin and in middle school even performed a Beethoven sonata for the royal family when they came to the area, for which he was given a gold watch.

"The family tried to push him in the direction of law, but, the Sheep Professor flatly refused. 'I have no interest in law,' said the young Sheep Professor.

" 'Then go ahead with your music,' said his father. 'There ought to be at least one musician in the family.'

" 'I have no interest in music either,' replied the Sheep Professor.

"There was a brief pause.

" 'Well then,' his father spoke up, 'what path is it you want to take?'

" 'I am interested in agriculture. I want to learn agricultural administration.'

" 'Very well,' said his father a second later. What else could he say? The Sheep Professor was considerate and earnest, the sort of youth who once he said something would stick by his word. His own father couldn't get a word in edgewise.

"The following year, as per his wishes, the Sheep Professor matriculated at the Agriculture Faculty of Tokyo Imperial University. His child-wonder love of studies showed no sign of abating even there. Everyone, including his professors, was watching him. Scholastically he excelled as always, and he enjoyed tremendous popularity. He was, in a nutshell, one of your chosen few. Untainted by dissipation, reading every spare moment. If he tired of reading, he'd play his violin in the university courtyard, his gold watch ever in the pocket of his school uniform.

"He graduated at the top of his class and entered the Ministry of Agriculture and Forestry as one of the elite. His senior thesis was, simply stated, a unified scheme of large-scale agriculturalization for Japan, Korea, and Taiwan, which some decried as slightly too idealistic. It was, nonetheless, the talk of the time.

"After two years in the Ministry, the Sheep Professor went to the Korean peninsula to conduct research in rice cultivation. His report, published as *A Study on Rice Cropping on the Korean Peninsula*, was adopted by the government.

"In 1934, the Sheep Professor was called back to Tokyo and was introduced to a young army officer. For the big, imminent North China campaign, the Sheep Professor was asked to establish a self-sufficiency program based on sheep. This was to be the Sheep Professor's first encounter with sheep. The Sheep Professor concentrated on developing a general framework for ovine productivity in Japan, Manchuria, and Mongolia. The following spring, he embarked on a site-observation tour.

"The spring of 1935 passed uneventfully. The events happened in July. Setting out on horseback, unaccompanied, on his observation tour, the Sheep Professor disappeared. Whereabouts unknown.

"Three days, four days passed. Still no Professor. The army search team combed the terrain desperately, but he was nowhere to be found. Perhaps he had been attacked by wolves or abducted by tribesmen. Then at dusk a week later, just as everyone had given up hope, one utterly disheveled Sheep Professor wandered back into camp. His face was haggard, with cuts in several places, but his eyes retained their gleam. His horse was gone, his watch was gone. His explanation, which everyone seemed willing to accept, was that he'd lost his way and his horse fell injured.

"Not one month later, a bizarre rumor began to spread through the government offices. Word had gotten out that he enjoyed a 'special relationship' with sheep. What this 'special relationship' meant, no one knew. Whereupon his superior summoned him to his office and conducted an interrogation to set the record straight. Rumors are not to be tolerated in colonial societies.

" 'Did you in truth experience a special relationship with sheep?' queried his superior.

" 'I did,' answered the Sheep Professor.

"The interrogation went something like this:

Q: By this special relationship, do you mean you engaged in sexual relations with sheep?
A: No, that is not the case.
Q: Please explain.
A: It was a mental relationship.
Q: That is not an explanation.
A: It is difficult to find the right words, sir, but perhaps spiritual communion comes close.
Q: You would tell me you had spiritual communion with sheep?
A: That is correct.
Q: Are you telling me that during the week of your disappearance you had spiritual communion with sheep?
A: That is correct.
Q: Do you not think that is sufficient reason for dismissal from your offices?
A: It is my office to study sheep, sir.
Q: Spiritual communion is not a recognized course of study. Henceforth, I would ask that you amend your ways. Consider your graduation with honors from the Agriculture Faculty of Tokyo Imperial University, your brilliant work record upon entering the Ministry. There are great expectations of you as the standard-bearer of agricultural administration for tomorrow's East Asia.
A: I understand.
Q: Then forget about this spiritual communion nonsense. Sheep are livestock. Simply livestock.
A: It is impossible for me to forget.
Q: You will have to explain the circumstances.
A: The reason, sir, is that there is a sheep inside me.

Q: That is not an explanation.

A: Further explanation is impossible.

"February 1936. The Sheep Professor is ordered home to Japan. After undergoing numerous similar interrogations, he is transferred in the spring to the Ministry Reference Collection. There he catalogues reference materials and organizes bookshelves. In other words, he has been purged from the core elite of the East Asian agricultural administration.

" 'The sheep has now gone from inside me,' the Sheep Professor told a close friend at the time. 'But it used to be there inside.'

"1937. Sheep Professor retires from the Ministry of Agriculture and Forestry and, availing himself of a Ministry loan under the Japan-Manchuria Sheep Scheme, which used to be in his charge, moves to Hokkaido and becomes a shepherd. 56 head of sheep.

"1939. Sheep Professor marries. 128 head of sheep.

"1942. Eldest son born (present owner-operator of the Dolphin Hotel). 181 head of sheep.

"1946. American Occupation Forces appropriate Sheep Professor's sheep ranch as a training camp. 62 head of sheep.

"1947. Sheep Professor enters employ of Hokkaido Ovine Association.

"1949. Wife dies of bronchitis.

"1950. Sheep Professor assumes directorship of Hokkaido Ovine Association.

"1960. Eldest son loses fingers at Port of Otaru.

"1967. Hokkaido Ovine Hall closes.

"1968. Dolphin Hotel opens.

"1978. Young real estate agent inquires about sheep photograph."

Me, in other words.

"Just great," I said.

"By all means, I would like to meet your father," I said.

"I have no objection to your meeting him, but since my father dislikes me, you'll have to excuse me if I ask you to go alone," said the son of the Sheep Professor.

"Dislikes you?"

"Because I lost two fingers and am balding."

"I see," I said. "An eccentric man, your father."

"As his son, it's not for me to say, but yes, an eccentric man indeed. A completely changed man since he encountered sheep. Extremely difficult, sometimes even cruel. Deep down in his heart he's kind. If you heard him play his violin, you'd know that. Sheep hurt my father, and through my father, sheep have also hurt me."

"You love your father, don't you?" said my girlfriend.

"Yes, that I do. I love him very much," said the Dolphin Hotel owner, "but he dislikes me. He never once held me since the day I was born. Never once had a kind word for me. And since I lost my fingers and started going bald, he's done nothing but ridicule me."

"I'm sure he doesn't mean to ridicule you," she said.

"I can't believe that he would either," I said.

"You're too kind," said the hotel man.

"Shall we go and try to see him directly, then?" I asked.

"I don't know," said the hotel man. "Though I'm sure he'll see you if you're careful about two things. One is to state clearly that you wish to inquire about sheep."

"And the other?"

"Don't say that I told you about him."

"Fair enough," I said.

We thanked the Sheep Professor's son and headed up the stairs. The air at the top of the stairs was chilly and damp. The lights were dim, scarcely revealing the dust drifts in the corners of the hallway. The whole place smelled indistinctly of old papers and old body odors. We walked down the long hallway, as per the son's instructions, and knocked on the ancient door at the end. An old plastic plaque affixed to the door read DIRECTOR'S OFFICE. No answer. I knocked again. Again, no answer. At the third knock, there was a groan, and then the response—"Don't bother me. Go away."

"We've come to ask a few things about sheep, if we might."

"Eat shit!" yelled the Sheep Professor from inside. A mighty healthy voice for seventy-three.

"We really have to talk with you," I shouted through the door.

"Don't give me this you-want-to-talk-about-sheep crap," said the Sheep Professor.

"But it's something that probably ought to be discussed," I coaxed. "It's about a sheep that disappeared in 1936."

There was a brief silence, then the door flew open. Before us stood the Sheep Professor.

The Sheep Professor had long hair, white as snow. His eyebrows were also white, hanging down over his eyes like icicles. He stood five foot ten. A self-possessed figure. Sturdy-boned. His nose thrust out from his face at a challenging angle, like a ski jump.

His body odor permeated the entire room. No, I would hesitate to call it body odor. Beyond a certain point, it ceased to be body odor and blended into time, merged with the light. What had probably once been a large space was so packed with old books and papers you could hardly see the floor. Almost all the publications were scholarly tomes written in foreign languages. Without exception, all were covered with stains. On the right, against the wall, was a filthy bed, and before the window a huge mahogany desk and revolving chair. The desktop was in relative order, papers neatly stacked and surmounted by a paperweight in the shape of a sheep. The room was dark, the only illumination coming from a dust-covered lamp's sixty-watt bulb.

The Sheep Professor was wearing a gray shirt, black cardigan, and herringbone trousers that had all but lost their shape. In the light of the room, his gray shirt and black cardigan could have passed for a white shirt and gray cardigan. Maybe those had been the original colors, hard to say.

The Sheep Professor sat behind his desk, motioning with his finger for us to sit down on the bed. We made our way over, straddling books as if crossing a minefield, and sat down. The bed was so palpably grimy I was afraid my Levi's would stick to the sheets. The Sheep Professor folded his fingers on top of his desk and stared at us intently. His fingers were thick with black hair right up to his knuckles. The blackness in stark contrast to the brilliant white of his head.

Suddenly, the Sheep Professor picked up the telephone and shouted into the receiver: "Bring me my supper, quick!"

"Well now," said the Professor. "You say you have come to discuss a sheep that disappeared in 1936?"

"That's right," I said.

"Hmm," he said. Then abruptly, with great volume, he blew his nose into a wad of paper. "Is there something you wish to tell? Or something you wish to ask?"

"Both."

"First, let me hear what you have to tell."

"We know what became of the sheep that escaped you in the spring of 1936."

The Sheep Professor snorted. "Are you telling me that you know I threw away everything I had for a sheep I have been trying to track down for forty-two years?"

"We are aware of that," I said.

"You could be making this up."

I pulled out the silver lighter from my pocket and placed it on his desk together with the Rat's sheep photograph. He reached out a hairy hand, picked up the lighter and photograph, and examined them at length under the lamp. Particles of silence floated about the room for the longest time. The solid double-hung window shut out the city noise; only the sputter of the old lamp punctuated the silence.

The old man, having finished his examination of the lighter and photograph, turned off the lamp with a click and rubbed his eyes with stubby fingers. As if he were trying to press his eyeballs into his skull. When he removed his fingers, his eyes were murky red, like a rabbit's.

"Forgive me," said the Sheep Professor. "I've been surrounded by idiots for so long, I've grown distrustful of people."

"That's okay," I said.

My girlfriend smiled politely.

"Can you imagine what it's like to be left with a solitary thought when its embodiment has been pulled out from underneath you, roots and all?" asked the Professor.

"No, I can't."

"It's hell. A maze of a subterranean hell. Unmitigated by even one shaft of light or a single draft of water. That's been my life for forty-two years."

"Because of this sheep?"

"Yes, yes, yes. All because of that sheep. That sheep left me stranded in the thick of everything. In the spring of 1936."

"And it was to search for this sheep that you left the Ministry of Agriculture, am I correct?"

"Those paper pushers were all morons. They hadn't the slightest idea of the true value of things. Probably'll never catch on to the monumental significance of that sheep."

There came a knock on the door, followed by a woman's voice. "I've brought you your meal."

"Leave it," said the Sheep Professor.

The sound of the tray being set on the floor was followed by the echo of receding footsteps.

My girlfriend opened the door and brought the meal tray over to the Sheep Professor's desk. On the tray were soup, salad, a roll, and meatballs for the Professor, plus two coffees for us.

"You've eaten already?" asked the Sheep Professor.

"Yes, thank you," I said.

"What did you have?"

"Veal in wine sauce," I said.

"Shrimp, grilled," she said.

The Sheep Professor grunted. Then he ate his soup and crunched the croutons. "Excuse me if I eat while you talk. I'm hungry."

"By all means," we said.

The Sheep Professor ate his soup and we sipped our coffee. As he ate, the Professor stared headlong into his bowl.

"Would you know where the place in this photograph is?" I asked.

"I would indeed. I know it very well."

"Would you tell us?"

"Just hold on," said the Sheep Professor, setting aside his now-empty bowl. "One thing at a time. Let's start with the events of 1936. First I'll talk, then you talk."

I nodded.

The Sheep Professor began. "It was the summer of 1935 when the sheep entered me. I had lost my way during a survey of open-pasture grazing near the Manchuria-Mongolia border, when I happened across a cave. I decided to spend the night there. That night I dreamed about a sheep that asked, could it go inside me? Why not? I said. At the time, I didn't think much of it. It was a dream, after all." The old man chortled as he moved on to his salad.

"It was a breed of sheep I'd never set eyes on before. Because of my work I was acquainted with every breed of sheep in the world, but this one was unique. The horns were bent at a strange angle, the legs squat and stocky, eyes clear as spring water. The fleece was pure white, except for a brownish star on its back. There is no such sheep anywhere in the world. That's why I told the sheep it was all right to enter my body. As a sheep specialist, I was not about to let go of such a find."

"And what did it feel like to have this sheep inside your body?"

"Nothing special, really. It just felt like there was this sheep inside me. I felt it in the morning. I woke up and there was this sheep inside. A perfectly natural feeling."

"Do you experience headaches?"

"Never once since the day I was born."

The Sheep Professor went at his meatballs, glazing them in sauce before shoveling them into his mouth with gusto. "In parts of Northern China and Mongol territory, it's not uncommon to hear of sheep entering people's bodies. Among the locals, it's believed that a sheep entering the body is a blessing from the gods.

For instance, in one book published in the Yuan dynasty it's written that a 'star-bearing white sheep' entered the body of Genghis Khan. Interesting, don't you think?"

"Quite."

"The sheep that enters a body is thought to be immortal. And so too the person who hosts the sheep is thought to become immortal. However, should the sheep escape, the immortality goes. It's all up to the sheep. If the sheep likes its host, it'll stay for decades. If not—zip!—it's gone. People abandoned by sheep are called the 'sheepless.' In other words, people like me."

Chomp, chomp.

"Ever since that sheep entered my body, I began reading on ethnological studies and folklore related to sheep. I went around interviewing locals and checking old writings. Pretty soon talk went around that I'd been entered by a sheep, and word got back to my commanding officer. My commanding officer didn't take kindly to it. I was labeled 'mentally unfit' and promptly shipped home to Japan. Your typical 'colony case.'"

Having polished off three meatballs, the Sheep Professor moved on to the roll.

"The basic stupidity of modern Japan is that we've learned absolutely nothing from our contact with other Asian peoples. The same goes for our dealings with sheep. Sheep raising in Japan has failed precisely because we've viewed sheep merely as a source of wool and meat. The daily-life level is missing from our thinking. We minimize the time factor to maximize the results. It's like that with everything. In other words, we don't have our feet on solid ground. It's not without reason that we lost the war."

"That sheep came with you to Japan, I take it," I said, returning to the subject.

"Yes," said the Sheep Professor. "I returned by ship from Pusan. The sheep came with me."

"And what on earth do you suppose the sheep's purpose was?"

"I don't know," the Sheep Professor spat out. "The sheep didn't tell me anything. But the beast did have one major purpose. That much I do know. A monumental plan to transform humanity and the human world."

"One sheep planned to do all that?"

The Sheep Professor nodded as he popped the last morsel of his roll into his mouth and brushed the crumbs from his hands. "Nothing so alarming. Consider Genghis Khan."

"You have a point," I said. "But why now? Why Japan?"

"My guess is that I woke the sheep up. It probably would've gone on sleeping in that cave for hundreds of years. And stupid me, I had to go and wake it up."

"It's not your fault," I said.

"No," said the Professor, "it is my fault. I should have caught on a long time ago. I would have had a hand to play. But it took me a long time to catch on. And by the time I did, the sheep had already run off."

The Sheep Professor grew silent. He rubbed his icicled white brow with his fingers. It was as if the weight of forty-two years had infiltrated the furthest reaches of his body.

"One morning I awoke and the sheep was gone. It was then that I understood what it meant to be 'sheepless.' Sheer hell. The sheep goes away leaving only an idea. But without the sheep there is no expelling that idea. That is what it is to be 'sheepless.'"

Again the Sheep Professor blew his nose on a wad of paper. "Now it's your turn to talk."

I began with the route the sheep took after it left the Sheep Professor. How the sheep had entered the body of a rightist youth in prison. How as soon as this youth got out of prison he became a major right-wing figure. How he then crossed over to the Chinese continent and built up an intelligence network and a fortune in the process. How he'd been marked a Class A war criminal, but how he was released in exchange for his intelligence network on the continent. And how, utilizing the fortune he brought back from China, he'd laid claim to the whole underside of postwar politics, economics, information, etc., etc.

"I've heard of this man," the Sheep Professor said bitterly. "Somehow the sheep has an uncanny sense of the most competent targets."

"Only this spring, the sheep left his body. The man himself is in a coma, on the verge of death. Up until now, it seems that a brain dysfunction covered for the sheep."

"Such bliss. Better that the 'sheepless' be without this shell of half-consciousness."

"Why do you suppose the sheep left his body—after all this time building up a huge organization?"

The Sheep Professor let out a deep sigh. "You still don't understand? It's the same with that man as it was with me. He outlived his usefulness. People have their limits, and the sheep has no use for people who've reached their limit. My guess is that he did not fully comprehend all that the sheep had cut out for him. His role was to build a huge organization, and once that was complete, he was tossed. Just as the sheep used me as a means of transport."

"So what has the sheep been up to since?"

The Sheep Professor picked up the photograph from the desk and gave it a flick of his fingers. "It has roamed all over Japan to search out a new host. To the sheep, that would probably mean a new person to put on top of the organization by one scheme or another."

"And what is the sheep seeking?"

"As I said before, I can't express that in words with any precision. What the sheep seeks is the embodiment of sheep thought."

"Is that good?"

"To the sheep's thinking, of course it's good."

"And to yours?"

"I don't know," said the old man. "I really don't know. Ever since the sheep departed, I can't tell how much is really me and how much the shadow of the sheep."

"A while ago, you said something about having a hand to play. What would that be?"

"I have no intention of telling you that." The Sheep Professor shook his head.

Once again, silence shrouded the room. Outside, a hard rain began to fall. The first rain since we'd arrived in Sapporo.

"One last thing: could you tell us where the place in the photograph is?" I asked.

"The homestead where I lived for nine years. I raised sheep there. Appropriated right after the war by the American Forces, and when they repatriated the place to me I sold it to some rich man as a vacation home with pasture. Ought to still be the same owner."

"And would he still be raising sheep?"

"I don't know. But from the photograph it sure looks as if he's raising sheep. Whatever, it's a good remove from any settlements. Not another house in sight. The roads are blocked in the winter. I'm sure the owner uses the place only two, maybe three months a year. It's nice and quiet there."

"Does anyone look after the place when the owner's not there?"

"I doubt if anyone stays there over the winter. Other than myself, I can't imagine any other human staying there the winter through. You can pay the municipal shepherds in the town at the foot of the hills to look after the sheep. The roof of the house is sloped so that the snow naturally slides off onto the ground, and no worry about burglars. Even if somebody did steal something up there, it'd be a pain to get it to town. It's staggering, the amount of snow that falls there."

"So is anyone there now?"

"Hmm. Maybe not now. The snow's going to start soon and bears'll be roaming around for food before they go into hibernation. You're not planning to head up there?"

"Probably will have to. We have no other real lead."

The Sheep Professor sat for a while with his mouth shut. Tomato sauce from the meatballs at the corner of his mouth.

"You should probably know that prior to you one other person came here asking about the homestead. Around February it was. Age and appearance, well, kind of like you. He said he was interested in the photograph in the hotel lobby. I was pretty bored at the time, so I told him this and that. He said he was looking for material for a novel he was writing."

Out of my pocket I pulled a snapshot of the Rat and me together. It was taken in the summer eight years before, in J's Bar. I was in profile, smoking a cigarette, the Rat was looking at the camera, signaling thumbs up. Both of us were young and tan.

"This one's you, eh?" said the Sheep Professor, holding the snapshot under the lamp. "Younger than now."

"You're right—taken eight years ago."

"The other one's that man. He looked older than in this photo and had a moustache, but it was him."

"A moustache?"

"A neat little moustache and the rest stubble."

I tried to picture the Rat with a moustache, but couldn't quite see it.

The Sheep Professor drew us a detailed map to the homestead. You had to change trains near Asahikawa to a branch line and travel three hours to get to the town at the foot of the hills. From there it was three hours by car to the homestead.

"Thank you kindly for everything," I said.

"If you really want to know the truth, I think the fewer people that get involved with that sheep the better. I'm a prime example. There's not a soul the happier for having tangled with it. The values of one lone individual cannot bear up before the presence of that sheep. But well, I guess you've got your reasons."

"That I do."

"Be careful now," said the Sheep Professor. "And place the dishes by the door if you would."

28

Farewell to the Dolphin Hotel

We took one day to ready for our departure.

We got mountaineering supplies and portable rations at a sporting-goods store, and bought heavy fishermen's knit sweaters and woolen socks at a department store. At a bookstore, we bought a 1:50,000-scale map of the area we were headed for and a tome on the local history. We also settled on some rugged spiked boots and padded thermal underwear.

"All these layers do absolutely nothing for my line of work," she said.

"When you're out in the snow, you won't have time to think about that," I said.

"You planning to stay until the heavy snows?"

"Can't tell. But I do know it'll already be starting by the end of October. Better to be prepared. No telling what to expect."

We hauled our purchases back to the hotel and stuffed them into a large backpack, then we gathered together all the extra items we'd brought from Tokyo and left them with the Dolphin Hotel man. As a matter of fact, almost everything she'd brought in her bag was extra. A cosmetics set, five books and six cassettes, one paper bag full of stockings and underwear, T-shirts and shorts, a travel alarm clock, a sketchbook and set of twenty-four colored pencils, stationery and envelopes, bath towel, mini first-aid kit, hair dryer, cotton swabs.

"But why are you bringing your dress and high-heels with us?"

"What am I supposed to do if we go to a party?" she pleaded.

"What makes you think there's going to be a party?"

There was no reasoning with her. She managed to fit her dress, neatly folded, and high heels into our backpack along with our pared-down effects. For cosmetics, she switched to a travel compact she picked up at a nearby shop.

The hotel owner accepted the luggage graciously. I settled the bill up through the following day and told him we'd be back in a week or two.

"Was my father of any help?" he asked worriedly.

I said that he'd helped enormously.

"I sometimes wish I could go off in search of something," he declared, "but before getting even that far, I myself wouldn't have the slightest idea what to search for. Now my father, he's someone who's been searching for something all his life. He's still searching today. Ever since I was a little boy, my father's told me about the white sheep that came to him in his dreams. So I always thought that's what life is like. An ongoing search."

The lobby of the Dolphin Hotel was hushed as ever. An elderly maid was going up and down the stairs with a mop.

"My father's seventy-three now and still no sheep. I don't know if the thing even exists. I can't help thinking that it hasn't been such a good life for him. I want to see my father happy now more than ever, but he just belittles me and won't listen to a word I say. That's because I have no purpose in life."

"But you have the Dolphin Hotel," my girlfriend said sweetly.

"Besides, your father's stepped down from his sheep searching," I added. "We've taken up the rest."

The hotel owner smiled.

"If that's so, there's nothing more for me to say. We two ought to get on very happily."

"I sure hope so," I said.

Later, when we were alone, she asked me, "Do you really think those two deserve each other?"

"They've been together this long . . . They'll be all right. At least, after a forty-two-year gap, the Sheep Professor's role is finished. Now we have to track down the sheep."

"I like those two."

"I like them too."

We finished our packing and had intercourse, then went out and saw a movie. In the movie there were a lot of men and women having intercourse too. Nothing wrong with watching others having intercourse, after all.

Part Eight

A Wild Sheep Chase, III

29

The Birth, Rise, and Fall of Junitaki Township

It was an early morning train we took from Sapporo to Asahikawa. I opened a beer as I settled down to the voluminous, slip-cased *Authoritative History of Junitaki Township*. Junitaki was the township in which the Sheep Professor's homestead was located. Reading up on its history probably had no practical value, but it couldn't hurt.

The author was born in 1940 in Junitaki and, after graduating from the literature department of Hokkaido University, was active as a local historian, or so the cover copy said. For being so active, he had only one book to his name. Published in May 1970. First edition, probably the only edition.

According to the author, the first settlers arrived in what today is Junitaki early in the summer of 1881. Eighteen persons total, all poor dirt farmers from Tsugaru, meager farm tools, clothes, bedding, cook pots, and knives being the sum of their possessions.

They passed through an Ainu village near Sapporo, and with the little money they had, they engaged a lean, dark-eyed Ainu youth as a guide. The youth's name in Ainu translated into "Full Moon on the Wane" (suggesting a tendency toward manic depression, the author hypothesized).

Perhaps the youth was not cut out to be a guide; still, he proved far better than he might have at first appeared. Hardly understanding any Japanese, he led these eighteen grim, suspicious farmers north, up along the Ishikari River. He had a clean picture in mind where to go to find fertile land.

On the fourth day, the entourage arrived at this destination. Endowed with vast waters, the whole landscape was alive with beautiful flowers.

"Here is good," said the youth. "Few wild animals, fertile soil, plenty of salmon."

"Nothing doing," said the leader of the farmers. "We want farther in."

The youth understood the farmers to believe they'd find better land the farther in they went. Fine. If that's what they want, off into the interior.

So the entourage continued their march north for another two days. There the youth found a rise where, if the soil was not exactly as rich as the earlier spot, at least there was no fear of flooding.

"How about it?" asked the youth. "Here is also good."

The farmers shook their heads.

This scene repeated itself any number of times until finally they arrived at the site of present-day Asahikawa. Seven days and one hundred miles from Sapporo.

"What about here?" asked the youth, more uncertain than ever.

"No go," answered the farmers.

"But from here, we climb mountains," said the youth.

"We don't mind," said the farmers gleefully.

And so they crossed the Shiokari Pass.

Needless to say, there was a reason why the farmers had passed up the rich bottomland and insisted on going deep into the wilderness. The fact was, they were on the lam. They had skipped town, walking out on sizable debts, and wanted to get as far away from civilization as possible.

Of course, the Ainu youth had no way of knowing this. And so naturally his initial surprise at the farmers' rejection of fertile farmland soon turned to bewilderment, distress, and loss of self-confidence.

Nevertheless, the youth's character was sufficiently complex that by the time the entourage crossed the Shiokari Pass, he had given himself over to his incomprehensible fate, leading them northward, ever northward. He took pains to choose the most rough trails, the most perilous bogs, to please his patrons.

Four days north of the Shiokari Pass, the entourage came on to a west-flowing river. By consensus, it was decided they should head east.

This tack sent them up horrible trails through horrible terrain. They fought through seas of brush bamboo, hacked their way across fields of shoulder-high grass a half-day at a time, waded through mud up to their chests, squirmed up crags, anything to get farther east. At night, they spread their tarps over the river-bank and kept an ear out for the howling of wolves while they slept. Their arms, scraped raw from the bush bamboo, were beset at every turn by gnats and mosquitoes that would burrow into their ears to suck blood.

Five days east, they found their way blocked by mountains and could go no further. What lay beyond was not fit for human settlement, the youth declared. Upon hearing this, the farmers halted in their tracks. This was July 8, 1881, 150 miles overland from Sapporo.

First thing, they surveyed the lay of the land, tested the water, checked the soil. It was reasonably good farmland. Then they divided the land among the group and erected a communal log cabin in the center.

The Ainu youth came upon a band of Ainu hunters passing through the area. "What is this area called?" he asked them.

"Do you really think this asshole of a terrain even deserves a name?" they replied.

So for the time being, this frontier was without a name. As another dwelling (or at least another dwelling that desired human contact) did not exist for forty miles, the settlement had no need for a name. In fact, when in 1889 an official census taker from the Territorial Government pressed the group for a name, the settlers remained steadfastly indifferent. Sickle and hoe in hand, they met in the communal hut and decided against naming the settlement. The official was literally up a creek. All he could do was to count the falls in the nearby river, twelve, and report the name of Junitaki-buraku, or Twelve Falls Settlement, to the Territorial Government. From then on, the settlement bore the formal appellation Junitaki-buraku (and later, Junitaki-mura, Twelve Falls Village).

The area fanned a sixty-degree arc between two mountains and was cut down the middle by a deep river gorge. An asshole of a terrain for sure. The ground was covered with brush bamboo while huge evergreens spread their roots far and wide. Wolves and elk and bears and muskrats and birds competed in the wilderness for the meager food available. Everywhere flies and mosquitoes swarmed.

"You all really want to live here?" asked the Ainu youth.

"You bet," replied the farmers.

It is not obvious why the Ainu youth, instead of returning to his own home, chose to stay on with the settlers. Perhaps he was curious, hypothesized the author (who loved to hypothesize). Whatever the case, if he had not remained, it's doubtful the settlers could have made it through the winter. The youth taught the settlers how to root for winter vegetables, how to survive the snow, how to fish in the frozen river, how to lay traps for the wolves, how to escape the attention of bears before hibernation, how to determine the weather from the direction of the wind, how to prevent chilblains, how to roast bush bamboo roots for food, how to fell evergreen trees in a set direction. Soon, everyone came to recognize the youth's value, and the youth himself regained his confidence. He eventually took a Japanese name and married the daughter of one of the settlers, with whom he had three children. No more "Full Moon on the Wane."

Yet, even with the practical knowledge of the Ainu youth, the settlers' lot was miserable. By August, each family had built its own hut, which being a hurriedly thrown together affair of split logs did next to nothing to keep out the winter wind. It was not uncommon to awaken and find a foot of snow by one's pillow. Most families had but one set of bedding besides, so the menfolk typically had to sleep curled up by the fire. When their store of food was used up, the settlers went out in search of fish and whatever shriveled-up wild plants they could find deep beneath the snow. It was an especially cold winter. No one died, however.

There was no fighting, no tears. Their strength was their inbred poverty.

Spring came. Two children were born and the settlers' number rose to twenty-one. Two hours before giving birth the mothers were working in the fields, and the morning after giving birth they were working in the fields.

The group planted corn and potatoes. The men felled trees and burned the roots to clear more land. New life came over the face of the earth, young plants bore fruit, but just when the settlers were sighing with relief, they were beset by swarm after swarm of locusts.

The locusts swept in over the mountains. At first, they looked like a giant black cloud. Then there came a rumbling. No one had any idea what was about to overtake them. Only the Ainu youth knew. He ordered the men to build fires in their fields. Dousing their last piece of furniture in their last drop of oil, the men burned everything they could lay their hands on. The womenfolk banged pots with pestles. They did everything in their power, but everything was not enough. Hundreds of thousands of locusts swooped down on their crops and laid them to waste. Nothing was left in their wake.

When the locusts departed, the youth went out into the fields and wept. Not one of the settlers shed a tear. They gathered up the dead locusts and burned them, and as soon as they were in ashes, the settlers continued to clear land.

They went back to eating fish and wild vegetables all through the next winter. In spring, another three children were born. People planted the fields. In summer, they were visited by locusts again. And again all the crops were chewed down to the roots. This time, however, the Ainu youth did not weep.

The onslaught of the locusts finally stopped the third year. A long spell of rain had gotten to the locust eggs. But the excessive rain damaged the crops. The following year saw an unusual infestation of beetles, and the summer after that was unusually cold.

Having read that far, I shut the book, opened another beer, and pulled a box lunch of salmon roe out of my pack.

She sat across from me with folded arms, fast asleep. The autumn morning sun, slanting in through the train window, spread a thin blanket of light over her lap. A tiny moth blew in from somewhere and fluttered about like a scrap of paper. The moth ended up on her breast and stayed there before flying off again. Once the moth had flown off, she looked the slightest bit older.

I smoked a cigarette, then resumed reading the *Authoritative History of Junitaki Township*.

By the sixth year, the settlement was at last holding its own. The crops were bearing, the cabins refurbished, and everyone had adjusted to life in a cold climate. Sawed-board houses took their place among the log cabins, hearths were built, lamps hung. People loaded up a boat with what little they had in the way of extra produce and dried fish and elk antlers, traveled two days to market in the nearest town, and bought salt and clothing and oil in exchange. Some learned how to make charcoal from the timber felled in clearing fields. A number of similar settlements sprang up downstream and trade was established.

As groundbreaking continued, it became apparent that the settlement was sorely short of hands, so the group convened the village council, and after two days decided to call in reinforcements from the old hometown. The question of the reneged loans arose, but from replies to inquiries carefully couched in their letters home, they learned that their creditors had long since given up on trying to collect. The eldest of the settlers then sent off notes to their old buddies, asking that they join the settlers in working the new land. In 1889, the census was conducted, the same year the settlement was officially named.

The following year, six new families, comprising nineteen new settlers, came to the settlement. They were greeted with upgraded log cabins. A tearful reunion was had by all. The new residents were given land, and with the help of the first settlers they planted crops and built their own houses.

By 1893, four more new families had arrived with sixteen people. By 1897, seven more new families had arrived with twenty-four people.

The number of settlers rose steadily. The communal hut was expanded into a more formal meeting hall, and next to it they built a small shrine. The settlement officially became a village. From Junitaki-buraku to Junitaki-mura. The postman began to make appearances, however infrequently. And while millet was the main diet of the villagers, they now occasionally mixed in real white rice.

Of course, they were not without their share of misfortune. Officials came through to levy taxes and enforce military service. The Ainu youth, by now in his mid-thirties, was particularly upset by these developments. He could not understand why such things as taxes and military service were at all necessary.

"It seems to me things were better off like they used to be," he said.

Even so, the village kept on developing.

In 1903, they discovered higher ground near the village suitable for grazing, and the village set up a communal sheep pasture. An official from the Territorial Government instructed them in building fences, supplying irrigation, and constructing livestock shelter.

Next, prison labor was called in to lay a road along the river, and as time went on, flocks of sheep, bought cheap from the government, were being herded up the road. The farmers had not the slightest idea why the government was being so generous. Well, why not? they thought. After so hard a struggle, this was welcome relief.

Of course, the government was not being generous for nothing, giving them these sheep. Prodded by the military's goal of self-sufficiency in thermal wool for the upcoming campaign on the continent, the government had ordered the Ministry of Agriculture and Business to increase efforts in sheep raising, and the Ministry had forced these plans on the Territorial Government. The Russo-Japanese War was drawing near.

In all the village, it was again the Ainu man, no longer a youth, who showed the greatest interest in sheep. He learned methods of sheep raising from the territorial official and took on the responsibility of the village pasture. There is no knowing exactly why he became so devoted to the sheep. It may have been the complexities of life brought on by a village population suddenly growing by leaps and bounds.

The pasture became home to thirty-six head of Southdowns and twenty-one head of Shropshires in addition to two Border collies. The Ainu man became an able shepherd, and with each passing year the number of sheep and dogs increased. He came to love his sheep and his dogs with all his heart. The officials were most satisfied. Puppies were farmed out as top sheepdogs to similar sheep farms established nearby.

When the Russo-Japanese War broke out, five village youths were conscripted and sent to the front line in China. Two were killed and one lost his left arm when an enemy grenade exploded in a skirmish over a small hill. When the fighting ended three days later, the other two gathered up the scattered bones of their fellow village youths. All had been sons of first- and second-wave settlers. One of the dead was the eldest son of the Ainu youth-turned-shepherd. He died wearing an army-issue wool overcoat.

"Why send boys off to war in a foreign land?" the Ainu shepherd went around asking people. By then he was forty-five.

Nobody would answer him. The Ainu shepherd broke off from the village and stayed out at the pasture, spending his waking and sleeping hours with the sheep. His wife had died from bronchitis five years earlier, and his two remaining daughters had both married. For his services in minding the sheep, the village provided him with scant wages and food.

After losing his son, the Ainu shepherd grew embittered. He died at age sixty-two. One winter morning, the boy who was his helper found him sprawled out dead on the floor of the sheephouse. Frozen. Two sorry-eyed grandpuppies of the original two Border collies whined at his side. The sheep, oblivious, were grazing away at the hay in their enclosure. The low grinding rhythm of sheep teeth sounded like a chorus of castanets.

The history of Junitaki went on, but history for the Ainu youth ended there. I got up to go to the john and piss two beers' worth. When I returned to my seat, she was awake and gazing distractedly out the window. Rice fields stretched far and wide. Occasionally there'd be a silo. Rivers drew near, then retreated. I smoked a cigarette, taking in the scenery together with her profile taking in the scenery. She spoke not a word. Once I finished my cigarette, I went back to the book. The shadow of a steel bridge flashed across the page.

After the unhappy tale of the Ainu youth who became a shepherd, got old, and died, the remaining history was rather boring fare.

An outbreak of sheep bloat claimed ten head, severe cold dealt a temporary blow to crops, but other than that everything went smoothly with the village. In the Taisho era it was incorporated as a township and newly renamed Junitaki-cho. Junitaki-cho did well, building more facilities, a primary school, a town hall, a postal service outpost. By this time, the settling of Hokkaido was nearly complete.

With arable land reaching its limit, several young men left Junitaki-cho to seek their fortune in the new worlds of Manchuria and Sakhalin. In 1937, the Sheep Professor made his appearance in town.

Read the history: "Ministry of Agriculture and Forestry technical administrator much recognized for his studies in Korea and Manchuria, Dr. _____ (aged 32) took leave of his post due to special circumstances and established his own sheep ranch in a mountain valley north of Junitaki-cho."

Nothing else about him was written.

The author himself seemed to have gotten bored by the events of the thirties on, his reportage becoming spotty and fragmentary. Even the writing style faltered, losing the clarity of his discussion of the Ainu youth.

I skipped the thirty-one years between 1938 and 1969 and jumped to the section entitled "Junitaki Today." Of course, the book's "today" being 1970, it was hardly today's "today." Still, writing the history of one town obviously imposed the necessity of bringing it up to a "today." And even if such a today soon ceases to be today, no one can deny that it is in fact a today. For if a today ceased to be today, history could not exist as history.

According to my *Authoritative History of Junitaki Township*, in 1969 the population had dropped to 15,000, a decrease of 6,000 from ten years prior, due almost entirely to a decline in farming. The unusually high rate of agrarian disenfranchisement came about in reaction, it stated, to changes within the national infrastructure in a period of rapid industrial growth, as well as to the peculiar nature of cold-climate farming in Hokkaido.

What became of their abandoned farmlands? They were reforested. The land that their forefathers had sweated blood clearing, the descendants now planted with trees. Strange how that worked.

Which was to say that the primary industry in Junitaki today was forestry and lumber milling. The town now boasted several small mills where they made television cabinets, vanities, and tourist-trade figurines of bears and Ainus. The former communal hut was converted into the Pioneer Museum, where the farming tools and eating utensils from early settlement days were kept on display. There were also keepsakes of the village youths who had died in the Russo-Japanese War. Also a lunch box bearing the teeth marks of a brown bear. And even the letter to the old hometown inquiring about the debt collectors.

But if the truth be known, Junitaki today was a dreadfully dull town. The townsfolk, when they came home from work, watched an average of four hours of television before going to bed each night. Balloting ran high, but it was never any surprise who won the election. The town slogan was "Bountiful Humanity in Bountiful Nature." Or so the sign in front of the station read.

I closed the book, yawned, and fell asleep.

30

The Further Decline of Junitaki and Its Sheep

We caught the connecting train in Asahikawa and headed north over the Shiogari Pass, traveling by largely the same route the Ainu youth and the eighteen dirt farmers had taken a century before.

The autumn sun shone brilliantly though the last vestiges of virgin forest and the blazing red leaves of the rowan ash. The air was still and clear. So much so just looking at the scenery made your eyes hurt.

The train was empty at first, but midway a whole carload of commuting high school students piled in and we were plunged into their commotion, their shouting and dandruff and body odors and incomprehensible conversations and sexual urges with no outlet. This went on for thirty minutes until they disappeared all at the same station. Once again, the train was empty, with not a voice to be heard.

We split a chocolate bar between us and munched on it as the scenery paraded before our eyes. A tranquil light spilled over the ground. Everything seemed so far away, as if we were looking through the wrong end of a telescope. She whistled snatches of "Johnny B. Goode." This may have been the longest we two had ever not spoken.

It was afternoon when we got off the train. Standing on the platform, I took a deep breath and gave myself a good stretch. The air was so fresh I felt as if my lungs were going to collapse. The sun on my arms was warm and sensuous, even as the air was three or four degrees cooler than in Sapporo.

A row of old brick warehouses lined the tracks, and alongside these was a pyramid stack of logs three yards long, soaked and dark from the rain of the previous night. After the train we'd come on pulled out of the station, there was no one in sight, only a flowerbed of marigolds that were swaying in the cool breeze.

From the platform, we could see a typical small-scale regional city. Complete with main street, modest department store, bus terminal, tourist information center. A singularly dull town, if first impressions were any indication.

"This is our destination?" she asked.

"No, not here. We've got another train ride from here. Our destination is a much, much smaller town than this."

I yawned and took another deep breath.

"This is our transit point. Here's where the first settlers turned eastward."

"First settlers?"

In the time before our connecting train arrived, we sat down in front of the heater in the waiting room, and I related snippets of the history of Junitaki-cho. The chronology got a bit confused, so I used a page from my notebook to make a simplified timeline based on the summary at the back of the *Authoritative History.* On the left side of the page, I listed dates and developments in the history of Junitaki-cho and on the right the major events in the history of Japan in the same period. A fairly respectable chronological table.

For example, in 1905 Port Arthur fell and the Ainu youth's son was killed in the war. And if my memory served me correctly, that was also the year the Sheep Professor was born. Incrementally, history linked up.

"Looking at things this way," she said, comparing the left and right sides of the chronology, "we Japanese seem to live from war to war."

"Sure seems that way," I said.

"How did things ever get like this?"

"It's complicated. I can't really say. Not just like that."

"Humph."

The waiting room, like most waiting rooms, was deserted and unremarkable. The benches were miserably uncomfortable, the ashtrays swollen with waterlogged cigarette butts, the air stale. On the walls were travel posters and most-wanted lists. The only other people there were an old man wearing a camel-color sweater and a mother with her four-year-old son. The old man sat glued in position, poring through a literary magazine. He turned the pages as slowly as if he were peeling away adhesive tape. Fifteen minutes from one page to the next. The mother and child looked like a couple whose marriage was on the rocks.

"What it comes down to is that everyone's poor, but we want to believe that if things work out, we'll be through with poverty."

"Like the people in Junitaki-cho."

"Exactly. That's why they worked themselves to death to break new ground. Even so, most of the settlers died poor."

"How come?"

"It's the territory. Hokkaido's cold country, every few years there's a killer frost. If their crops die, there's no food to eat, no income to buy oil. They can't even buy next year's seeds. So they put their land in hock and borrow money at high interest. But no agriculture in any region is productive enough to pay off that interest, and in the end the land is taken away from them. That's what reduces many farmers to tenant farming."

I flipped through the pages of my *Authoritative History* and read to her: "By 1930, the number of self-employed farmers had fallen to 46 percent of the population of Junitaki-cho. They had been dealt a double blow, a depressed market compounded by a killer frost."

"So after all their struggles to clear a new land for themselves to farm, they only got deeper in debt," she concluded.

As there were still forty minutes before our train, she decided to take a walk around town by herself. I stayed behind in the waiting room, had a Coke, and took up where I'd left off in another book I'd been reading. I was soon bored with it and put it away. I could not concentrate. My head was full of Junitaki-cho sheep chomping up all the print I could feed them. I closed my eyes and sighed. A passing freight train sounded its whistle.

A few minutes before departure time, she returned with a bag of apples. We ate them for lunch, then boarded the train.

The train had surely seen better days. Weak portions of the floorboards were buckled and worn. Walking the aisle was enough to make you sway from side to side. The seat coverings had lost their pile and the cushions were like month-old bread. An air of doom, mixed with toilet and kerosene smells, filled the car. I spent ten minutes trying to raise a window to let in some fresh air, but no sooner did I get it open than some fine sand blew in and I had to spend an equal amount of time closing the window.

The train had two cars. There was a total of fifteen passengers, lumped together by the common bonds of disinterest and ennui. The old man in the camel-color sweater was still reading his magazine. At his reading speed, the issue may have gotten to be three months old. One heavy middle-aged lady was training her gaze at a distant point in space outside, as if a critic listening to a Scriabin sonata.

The children were quiet too. They sat still and stared out the window. Occasionally, someone coughed with a dry rasp that sounded like a mummy tapped on the head with a pair of tongs.

Each time the train pulled into a station, someone got off. Whenever someone got off, the conductor also got off to collect the ticket, then the conductor would get back on. The conductor was so totally without expression he could have pulled off a bank robbery without covering his face. No new passengers ever got on.

Outside, the river stretched forever, muddy brown from the rains. Glinting in the autumn sun, it looked like a spillway of café au lait. An improved road along the river popped in and out of view, and infrequently there'd be a huge truck hurtling westward with a load of lumber. On the whole, though, the road seemed practically unused. Roadside billboards relayed their sponsors' messages to no one, nowhere. I warded off boredom by looking at each new billboard, noting the sharp, urban appeal. A terrifically tanned girl in a bikini pursed her lips over a Coke, a middle-aged character actor wrinkled his brow at a tilted glass of Scotch, a diver's watch lavishly splashed with water, a model in the midst of a slick, sophisticated interior, doing her nails. The new pioneers of advertising were carving a mean streak deep into the country.

It was 2:40 when the train reached its destination, Junitaki-cho. Somewhere along the line we had dozed off, apparently missing the station announcement. The diesel engine had squeezed out its last breath, and everything went silent. I woke with a start, the silence tingling on my skin. When I looked around, no other passengers were on board.

I brought our bags down from the rack, roused her with a couple of taps on the shoulder, and we got off. The wind that whisked the length of the platform was already tinged with a late-autumn chill. The dark shadows of the hills crept across the ground like fatal stains. Directly beyond the streets the two ranges of hills on either side of the town seemed to meet, neatly enfolding the town like two cupped hands protecting a match flame from the wind. The hills towered above the narrow station platform.

We stood there, rather at a loss, gazing at the scene for a few minutes.

"Where's the Sheep Professor's old homestead?" she asked.

"Up in the mountains. Three hours from here by car."

"Do we head straight out?"

"No," I said. "If we set out right now, it'll be the middle of the night before we get there. Let's stay here overnight and get a fresh start in the morning."

In front of the station was a small rotary, which was empty. No one milling about. No taxis picking up or letting off customers. Just, in the middle, a bird-shaped fountain with no water in it. The bird looked vacantly up at the sky with an open mouth and nothing to say. Around the fountain was planted a circular bank of marigolds. One glance told you the town was far more run-down than it had been a decade ago. Almost no one was out on the streets, and the few that were seemed to share the distracted run-down expression of a town on the wane.

To the left of the rotary were a half dozen old warehouses, from the days of shipping by rail. Of old-fashioned brick construction, they had high-pitched roofs and steel doors that had been painted countless times, only to have been abandoned in the end. Huge crows perched in rows along the roof ridges, silently surveying the town. Next came an empty lot under a thicket of weeds that could make you break out in hives up to your shoulder, in the center of which were the remains of two old cars left out to the elements. Both cars were missing tires, their guts ripped out from beneath pried hoods.

The GUIDE TO THE TOWN, posted next to the deserted rotary, was so weathered you could barely make it out. The only discernible words were JUNITAKI-CHO and NORTHERN LIMIT OF LARGE-SCALE RICE FARMING.

Directly in front of the rotary was a small street lined with shops. A street not unlike such streets anywhere in Japan except that the road was absurdly wide, giving the town an impression of even greater sparseness, and chill. On either side of the road was a line of rowan ashes, in brilliant foliage but somehow no less chill. It was a chill that infused every living thing, without regard for human fortune. The listless day-to-day goings-on of the town residents—everything—were engulfed in that chill.

I hiked my backpack up onto my shoulders and walked to the end of the five-hundred-yard-long commercial district, looking for a place to stay. There was no inn of any kind. A third of the shops had their shutters pulled down. A half-torn sign in front of a watch shop banged about in the wind.

Where the street of shops cut off abruptly, there was a large parking lot, again overgrown with weeds. In it were a cream-colored Honda Fairlady and a sports car, a red Toyota Celica. Both brand new. What a picture they made, their mint condition smack in the middle of a deadbeat town.

Beyond the shops, the road ambled down a slope to the river, where it split left and right at a T. Along this road were small one-story wood-frame houses, with dust-gray trees that thrust brambled limbs up into the sky. I don't know what it was, but every tree had the most eccentric array of branches. Each house had, at its front door, identical large fuel tanks with matching milk-delivery boxes. And on every rooftop stood unimaginably tall television antennas. These silver feelers groped about in the air, in defiance of the mountains that formed a backdrop to the town.

"But there's no inn," she said worriedly.

"Not to worry. Every town has got to have an inn."

We retraced our steps back to the station and asked the two attendants there where we could find one. Aged far enough apart to have been parent and child, they were obviously bored silly and explained the whereabouts of the lodgings in distressingly thorough detail.

"There are two inns," said the elder attendant. "One is on the expensive side, the other is fairly cheap. The expensive one is where we put up important officials from the Territorial Government and hold special banquets."

"The food is not bad at all there," said the younger attendant.

"The other is where traveling businessmen or young folk or, well, where regular people stay. The looks of it might put you off, but it's not unsanitary or anything. The bath is something else."

"Though the walls are thin," said the younger.

Whereupon the two them launched into debate over the thinness of the walls.

"We'll go for the expensive one," I said. No reason to economize. There was the envelope, still stuffed with money.

The younger attendant tore a sheet off a memo pad and drew a precise map of the way to the inn.

"Thank you," I said. "I guess you don't get as many people coming through here as you did ten years ago."

"No, that's for sure," said the elder. "Now there's only one lumber mill and no other industry to speak of. The bottom's fallen out of agriculture. The population's gone way down too."

"Hell, there aren't enough students to form proper classes at the school anymore," added the younger.

"What's the population?"

"They say it's around seven thousand, but really it's got to be less than that. More like five thousand, I'd guess," the younger said.

"Take this spur line, boy, before they shut us down, which may be any day. Come what may, we're the third deepest in the red of any line in the country," the elder said with finality.

I was surprised to hear that there were train lines more run-down than this one. We thanked them and left.

The inn was down the slope and to the right of the street of shops, three hundred yards along the river. An old inn, nice enough, with a glimmer of the charm it must have had in the heyday of the town. Facing the river, it had a well-cared-for garden. In one corner of the garden, a shepherd puppy buried its nose in a food dish, eating an early evening meal.

"Mountaineering is it?" asked the maid who showed us to our room.

"Mountaineering it is," I answered simply.

There were only two rooms upstairs. Each a spacious layout,

and if you stepped out into the corridor, you had a view of the same café-au-lait river we'd seen from the train.

My girlfriend wanted to take a bath, so I went to check out the Town Hall. Town Hall was located on a desolate street two blocks west of the street of shops, yet the building was far newer and in much better shape than I'd expected.

I walked up to the Livestock Section in Town Hall, introduced myself with a magazine namecard from two years before when I'd posed as a freelance writer, and broke into a spiel about needing to ask a few questions about sheep raising, if they didn't mind. It was pretty farfetched that a women's weekly magazine would have need for a piece on sheep, but the livestock officer bought the line immediately and conducted me into his office.

"At present, we have two-hundred-some sheep in the township, all Suffolks. That is to say, meat sheep. The meat is parceled out to nearby inns and restaurants, and enjoys considerable favor."

I pulled out my notebook and jotted down appropriate notes. No doubt this poor man would be buying the women's magazine for the next several issues. Which, admittedly, made me feel embarrassed.

"A cooking article, I assume?" he stopped to ask once he'd detailed the current state of sheep raising.

"Well, of course that's part of it," I said. "But more than that, we're looking to paint a total picture of sheep."

"A total picture?"

"You know, their character, habits, that sort of thing."

"Oh," said my informant.

I closed my notebook and drank the tea that had been served. "We'd heard there was an old sheep ranch up in the hills somewhere."

"Yes, there is. It was appropriated by the U.S. Army after the war and is no longer in use. For about ten years after the Americans returned it, a rich man from somewhere used the place for a villa, but it's so far out of the way that he finally stopped going up there. The house is as good as abandoned now. Which is why the ranch is on loan to the town. We ought to buy it and turn the place into a tourist ranch, but I'm afraid the finances of this township aren't up to it. First, we'd have to improve the road . . ."

"On loan?"

"In the summer, our municipal sheep farm takes about fifty head up into the mountains. There isn't enough grass in the municipal pasture and it's quite fine pastureland up there, as pastures go. When the weather starts turning bad around the latter half of September, the sheep are brought back down."

"Would you happen to know when it is that the sheep are up there?"

"It varies from year to year, but generally speaking it's from the beginning of May to the latter half of September."

"And how many men take the sheep up there?"

"One man. The same man's been doing it these ten years."

"Would it be possible to meet this man?"

The official placed a call to the municipal sheep farm.

"If you go there now, you can meet him," he said. "Shall we drive there?"

I declined politely at first, but I soon learned that I couldn't otherwise get to the sheep farm. There were no taxis or car rentals in town, and on foot it would have taken an hour and a half.

The livestock officer drove a small sedan. He passed our inn and headed west, taking a long concrete bridge to cross over a cold marshy area, then climbing up a mountain slope. Tires spun over the gravel.

"Coming from Tokyo, you probably think this is a ghost town."

I said something noncommittal.

"The truth is we are dying. We'll hold on as long as we have the railway, but if that goes we'll be dead for sure. It's a curious thing, a town dying. A person dying I can understand. But a whole town dying . . ."

"What will happen if the town dies?"

"What *will* happen? Nobody knows. They'll all just run away before that, not wanting to know. If the population falls below one thousand—which is well within the realm of possibility—we'll pretty much be out of a job, and we might be the ones who have to run out on everything."

I offered him a cigarette and gave him a light with the sheep-engraved Dupont lighter.

"There's plenty of good jobs in Sapporo. I've got an uncle who runs a printing company there, and he needs more hands. Work comes from the school system, so business is steady. Really, moving there would be the best thing. At least it'd beat monitoring shipments of sheep and cattle way out here."

"Probably," I said.

"But when it comes to actually packing up and leaving, I can't bring myself to do it. Can you see what I mean? If the town's really going to die, then the urge to stay on and see the town to its end wins out."

"Were you born here in this town?" I asked.

"Yes," he said, but did not go on. A melancholy-hued sun had already sunk a third of the way behind the hills.

Two poles stood at the entrance to the sheep farm and between them hung a sign: JUNITAKI-CHO MUNICIPAL SHEEP FARM. The road passed under the sign and led up a slope, disappearing into the dense autumn foliage.

"Beyond the woods there's the sheep house and behind that the caretaker's quarters. What shall we do about you getting back to town?"

"It's downhill. I can manage on foot. Thanks for everything."

The car pulled out of view, and I walked between the poles and up the slope. The last rays of the sun added an orange tinge to the already golden maple leaves. The trees were tall, patches of sunlight filtering down through the boughs and shimmering on the gravel road.

Emerging from the woods, I came upon a narrow building on the face of the hill, and with it the smell of livestock. The sheep house was roofed in red corrugated iron, pierced in three places by ventilation stacks.

There was a doghouse at the entrance to the house. No sooner had I seen it than a small Border collie came out on a tether and barked two or three times. It was a sleepy-eyed old dog with no threat in its bark. When I rubbed its neck, it calmed right down. Yellow plastic bowls of food and water were placed in front of the doghouse. As soon as I released my hand, the dog went back in the doghouse, satisfied, aligned its paws with the portal, and lay down on the floor.

The interior of the sheep house was dim. No one was around. A wide concrete walkway led down the middle, and to either side were the sheep pens. Along the walkway were gutters for draining off the sheep piss and wash water. Here and there windows cut through the wood-paneled walls, revealing the jaggedness of the hills. The evening sun cast red over the sheep on the right side, plunging the sheep on the left side into a murky blue shadow.

The instant I entered the sheep house, all two hundred sheep turned in my direction. Half the sheep stood, the other half lay on the hay spread over their pen floors. Their eyes were an unnatural blue, looking like tiny wellsprings flowing from the sides of their faces. They shone like glass eyes which reflected light from straight on. They all stared at me. Not one budged. A few continued munching away on the grass in their mouths, but there was no other sound. A few, their heads protruding from their pens, had stopped drinking water and had frozen in place, fixing their eyes on me. They seemed to think as a group. Had my standing in the entrance momentarily interrupted their unified thinking? Everything stopped, all judgment on hold. It took a move by me to restart their mental processes. In their eight separate pens, they began to move. The ewes gathered around the seed ram in the female pen; in the males-only pens, the rams vied for dominant position. Only a few curious ones stayed at the fence staring at me.

Attached to the long, level black ears that stuck out from the sides of the face were plastic chips. Some sheep had blue chips, some yellow chips, some red chips. They also had colored markings on their backs.

I walked on tiptoe so as not to alarm them. Feigning disinterest, I approached one pen and extended my hand to touch the head of a young ram. It flinched but did not move away. Tense, wide-eyed, rigid. Perhaps he would be the gauge of my intrusion. The other sheep glared at us.

Suffolk sheep are peculiar to begin with. They're completely black, yet their fleece is white. Their ears are large and stick flat out like moth wings, and their luminous blue eyes and long bony noses make them seem foreign. These Suffolks neither rejected nor accepted my presence, regarding me more as a temporary manifestation. Several pissed with a tinkling flourish. The piss flowed across the floor, under my feet, into the gutter.

I exited the sheep house, petting the Border collie again and taking a deep breath.

The sun had set behind the mountains. A pale violet gloom

spread over the slant of the hills like ink dispersing in water. I circled around the back of the sheep house, crossed a wooden bridge over a stream, and headed toward the caretaker's quarters. A cozy little one-story affair, dwarfed by a huge attached barn that stored hay and farm tools.

The caretaker was next to the barn, stacking plastic bags of disinfectant beside a yard-wide by yard-deep concrete trough. As I approached, he glanced up once, then returned to the task at hand, unaffected by my presence. Not until I was in front of him did he stop and wipe his face with the towel around his neck.

"Tomorrow's the day for disinfecting the sheep," he said, pulling out a crushed pack of cigarettes and lighting up. "This here's where we pour the liquid disinfectant and make the sheep swim from end to end. Otherwise, being indoors, they get all kinds of bugs over the winter."

"You do all this by yourself?"

"You kidding? I got two helpers. Them and me and the dog. The dog does most of the work, though. The sheep trust the dog. He ain't no sheepdog if the sheep don't trust him."

The man was a couple inches shorter than me, solidly built. He was in his late forties, with close-cropped hair, stiff and straight as a hairbrush. He pulled his rubber gloves off as if he were peeling off a layer of skin. Whacking himself on his pants, he stood with his hands in his patch pockets. He was more than a caretaker of sheep; he was rather like a drill sergeant at a military school.

"So you've come to ask something, eh?"

"Yes, I have."

"Well, do your askin'."

"You've been in this line of work a long time?"

"Ten years," he said. "If that's a long time, I don't know, but I do know my sheep. Before that I was in the Self-Defense Forces."

He threw his hand towel around his neck and looked up at the sky.

"You stay here through the winter?"

"Well, uh," he coughed, "I guess so. No other place for me to go. Besides, there's a lot of busywork to take care of over the winter. We get near to six feet of snow in these parts. It piles up and if the roof caves in, you got yourself some flat sheep. Plus I feed them, clean out the sheep house, and this and that."

"When summer comes around, you take half of them up into the mountains?"

"That's right."

"How difficult is it walking so many sheep?"

"Easy. That's what people used to do all the time. It's only in recent years you got sheep keepers, not sheep herders. Used to be they'd keep them on the move the whole year 'round. In Spain in the fifteen hundreds, they had roads all over the country no one but shepherds could use, not even the King."

The man spat phlegm onto the ground, rubbing it into the dirt with his shoe.

"Anyway, as long as they're not frightened, sheep are very cooperative creatures. They'll just follow the dog without asking any questions."

I took out the Rat's sheep photograph and handed it to the caretaker. "This is the place in the photo, right?"

"Sure is," said the man. "No doubt about it: they're our sheep too."

"What about this one?" I pointed with my ballpoint pen to the stocky sheep with the star on its back.

The man squinted at the photograph a second. "No, that's not one of ours. Sure is strange, though. There's no way it could've gotten in there. The whole place is fenced in with wire, and I check each animal morning and night. The dog would notice if a strange one got in. The sheep would raise a fuss too. But you know, never in my life have I ever seen this breed of sheep."

"Did anything strange happen this year when you were up in the mountains with the sheep?"

"Nothing at all," he said. "It was peaceful as could be."

"And you were up there alone all summer?"

"No, I wasn't alone. Every other day staffers came up from town, and then there'd be some official observers too. Once a week I went down to town, and a replacement looked after the sheep. Need to stock up on provisions and things."

"Then you weren't holed up there alone the whole time?"

"No. Summer lasts as long as the snow doesn't get too deep, and it's only an hour and a half to the ranch by jeep. Hardly more than a little stroll. Of course, once it snows and cars can't get through, you're stuck up there the whole winter."

"So nobody's up on the mountain now?"

"Nobody but the owner of the villa."

"The owner of the villa? But I heard that the place hasn't been used in ages."

The caretaker flicked his cigarette to the ground and stepped on it. "It *hasn't* been used in ages. But it is now. If you had half a mind to, no reason why you couldn't live there. I put in a little upkeep on the house myself. The electricity and gas and phone are all working. Not one pane of glass is broken."

"The man from Town Hall said nobody was up there."

"There's lots of stuff those guys don't know. I've gotten work on the side from the owner all along, never spilled a word to anyone. He told me to keep it quiet."

The man wanted another cigarette, but his pack was empty. I offered him my half-smoked pack of Larks, folding against it a ten-thousand-yen note. The man considered the gratuity for a second, then put one cigarette to his lips and pocketed everything else. "Much obliged," he said.

"So when did the owner show up?"

"Spring. Wasn't yet spring thaw, so it must've been March. It was maybe five years since he'd been up here. Don't rightly know why he came after all this time, but well, that's the owner's business and none of mine. He told me not to tell a soul. He must have had his reasons. In any case, he's been up there ever since. I buy him his food and fuel in secret and deliver it by jeep a little at a time. With all he's got, he could hold out for a year, easy."

"He wouldn't happen to be about my age, with a moustache, would he?"

"Uh-huh," said the caretaker. "That's the guy."

"Just great," I said. There was no need to show him the photograph.

31

Night in Junitaki

Negotiations with the caretaker went smoothly with supplementary monetary lubrication. The caretaker was to pick us up at the inn at eight in the morning, then drive us up to the sheep farm on the mountain.

"Disinfecting sheep can wait until afternoon, I figure," said the caretaker. A hard-line realist.

"There's one other thing that bothers me," he said. "The ground's going to be soft from yesterday's rain, and there's one place the car might not be able to get through. So I might have to ask you to walk from that point. Not through any fault of mine."

"That's okay," I said.

Walking back down the hill, I suddenly recalled that the Rat's father had a vacation villa in Hokkaido. Come to think of it, the Rat had said so a number of times years back. Up in the mountains, big pasture, old two-story house. I always remember important details long afterward. It should have struck me the moment I got the Rat's letter. If I'd thought of it first, there'd have been any number of ways to follow up on it.

Annoyed with myself, I trudged back to town down a mountain road that was growing darker and darker. In the hour and a half I walked, I encountered only three vehicles. Two were large diesel trucks loaded down with lumber, one a small tractor. All three were heading downhill, but no one called out to offer me a ride. So much the better as far as I was concerned.

It was past seven by the time I reached the inn, and the night was already pitch black. My body was chilled to the core. The shepherd puppy stuck its nose out of the doghouse and whined in my direction.

She was wearing jeans and my crew-neck sweater, totally absorbed in a computer game in the recreation room near the entrance of the inn. Apparently a remodeled old parlor, the room still boasted a magnificent fireplace. A real wood-burning fireplace. In addition, there were four computer games and two pinball tables; the pinball tables were old Spanish cheapies, models you'd never be able to find anywhere.

"I'm starved," she said.

I placed our order for dinner and took a quick bath. Drying off, I weighed myself, the first time in a long while. One hundred thirty-two pounds, same as ten years ago. The extra inch I put on around the middle had been neatly trimmed away over the last week.

When I got back to the room, dinner was laid out. Scooping morsels out of the steaming hot pot and washing them down with beer, I told her about the municipal sheep farm and the caretaker with the Self-Defense Forces background. She kicked herself for missing the sheep.

"Still," she said, "I think we're like one step away from our goal."

"I hope you're right," I said.

We watched a Hitchcock movie on TV, crawled into bed and turned out the light. The clock downstairs struck eleven o'clock.

"Maybe not tonight," I said. "We've gotta get up early."

She didn't say a thing. She was already asleep, breathing steadily. I set my travel alarm and had a smoke in the moonlight. The only sound was the rush of the river. The whole town seemed to be fast asleep.

After a day of running around, I felt physically drained, but my mind was going a mile a minute. There was no way I could get to sleep. The sound of the river was just another noise to me, and it fastened itself on my brain.

Holding my breath in the darkness, I let images of the town melt and ooze all around me. The houses rotted away, the rails rusted and were gone, weeds overwhelmed the farmland. The town came to the end of its short hundred-year history and sank into the earth. Time regressed like a film running backward. Once again Ainu deer, black bears, and wolves came to live on the plain, thick swarms of locusts filled the sky, an ocean of bamboo grass swayed in the autumn wind, and the luxurious evergreen forests hid the sun.

All the works of man faded into nothingness, yet still the sheep remained. They stood there, staring at me, eyes flashing in the darkness. Saying nothing, thinking nothing, they only stared and stared—directly at me. Tens of thousands of sheep. The monotonous clacking of their teeth covered the earth.

The clock struck two and they were gone.

And then I fell asleep.

32

An Unlucky Bend in the Road

The morning was hazy and cool. I sympathized with those sheep. Swimming though the cold disinfectant on a day like this could be brutal. Maybe sheep don't feel cold? Maybe they don't feel anything.

Hokkaido's short autumn season was drawing to a close. The thick gray clouds in the north were intimations of the snows to come. Flying from September Tokyo to October Hokkaido, I'd lost my autumn. There'd been the beginning and the end, but none of the heart of autumn.

I woke at six and washed my face. I sat alone in the corridor, looking out the window until breakfast was ready. The waters of the river had subsided somewhat since the day before and were now running clear. Rice fields spread out on the opposite bank, where irregular morning breezes traced random waves through the ripened, tall grassiness, as far as the eye could see. A tractor crossed the concrete bridge, heading toward the hills, its puttering engine faintly audible in the wind. Three crows flew out of the now-golden birch woods. Making a full circle above the river and landing on a railing of the building. Perched there, the crows acted the perfect bystanders from an avant-garde drama. Soon tiring of even that role, however, the crows flew off one by one and disappeared upstream.

The sheep caretaker's old jeep was parked outside the inn at eight o'clock sharp. The jeep had a box-shaped roof, apparently a surplus job if the Self-Defense Forces issue number legible on the front fender was any indication.

"You know, there's something funny going on," the caretaker said as soon as he saw me. "I tried to telephone ahead up on the mountain, but I couldn't get through."

She and I climbed into the backseat. It smelled of gasoline. "When was the last time you tried calling?" I asked.

"Well, around the twentieth of last month, I guess. I haven't gotten in touch once since then. A call generally comes in from him whenever there's something he needs. A shopping list or something."

"Did you get the phone to ring?"

"Not even a busy signal. Must be a line down somewhere. Not unlikely if there's been a big snow."

"But there hasn't been any snow."

The caretaker looked up at the roof of the jeep and rolled his head around to crack his neck. "Then we'll just have to go take a look, won't we?"

I nodded. The gasoline fumes were starting to get to me.

We crossed the concrete bridge and started up the hill by the same road I'd taken yesterday. Passing the Municipal Sheep Farm, all three of us turned to look at the two poles with the sign over the entrance. The farm was stillness itself. I could picture the sheep: each staring off into its own silent space with limpid blue eyes.

"You leave the disinfecting to the afternoon?"

"Yeah, well, no real hurry or nothin'. So long's it gets done before it snows."

"When does it start to snow?"

"Wouldn't be surprised if it snowed next week," said the caretaker. With one hand on the steering wheel, he looked down and coughed. "It'll be into November before it gets to piling up, though. Ever know a winter in these parts?"

"No," I said.

"Well, once it starts to collect, it piles up nonstop as if a dam's burst through. By then, there's nothin' you can do but crawl indoors and hang your head. People were never meant to live in these parts in the first place."

"But you've been living here all this time."

"That's because I like sheep. Sheep are good-natured creatures. They even remember people by their face. A year looking after sheep is over before you know it, and then it starts to add up. In the autumn they mate, spring they lamb, summer they graze. When the lambs get big, in the autumn they're mating. 'Round and 'round. It all repeats itself. The sheep change every year, it's only me getting older. And the older I get, the less I want to live in town again."

"What do sheep do over the winter?" asked my girlfriend.

His hands still on the steering wheel, the caretaker turned around and gazed at her, practically drinking in her face, as if he hadn't noticed her before. The road was paved and straight and there wasn't another car in sight; even so, I broke into a nervous sweat.

"They stay put indoors all winter long," said the caretaker, at last turning his eyes back to the road.

"Don't they get bored?"

"Do you get so bored with your own life?"

"I can't really say."

"Well, the same with sheep," said the caretaker. "They don't think about stuff like that, and it wouldn't do 'em any good if they did. They just pass the winter eating hay, pissing, getting into spats, thinking about the babies in their bellies."

The hills grew steeper and steeper, and the road started to curve into switchbacks. Pastoral scenery gradually gave way to sheer walls of dark primal forest on both sides of the road. Occasionally, there'd be an opening to a glimpse of the flatlands below.

"Under snow, we wouldn't be getting through here," said the caretaker. "Not that there's any need to."

"Aren't there any ski areas or mountaineering courses?" I asked.

"Not here, nothing. And that's why there's no tourists. Which is why the town's going nowhere fast. Up until the early sixties, the town was fairly active as a model for cold-zone agriculture. But ever since the rice surplus, everybody's lost interest in farming in an icebox. Stands to reason."

"What happened to the lumber mills?"

"Weren't enough hands to go around, so they moved to more convenient places. You can still find small mills in a few towns today, but not many. Now, trees cut here in the mountains pass right through town and are taken to Nayoro and Asahikawa. That's why the roads are in top shape while the town's going to pieces. A large truck with snow tires'll get through most any snowblock."

Unconsciously, I brought a cigarette to my lips, but before

lighting up I remembered the gasoline fumes and returned it to the pack. So I sucked on a lemon drop instead. The result: the uncommon taste of lemon gasoline.

"Do sheep quarrel?" asked my girlfriend.

"You bet they quarrel," said the caretaker. "It's the same with any animal that goes around in groups. Each and every sheep has a pecking order in the sheep society. If there's fifty sheep in a pen, then there's number one sheep right down to number fifty sheep. And each one knows exactly where it belongs."

"Amazing," she said.

"It makes managing 'em that much easier for me too. You pull on number one sheep, and the rest just follow along, no questions asked."

"But if they all know their place, why should they fight?"

"Say one sheep gets hurt and loses its strength, its position becomes unstable. So the sheep under it get feisty and try for better position. When that happens, they're at it for three days."

"Poor things."

"Well, it all evens out. The sheep that gets the boot, when it was young, gave some other sheep the boot, after all. And when it all comes down to the butcher block, there's no number one or number fifty. Just one happy barbecue."

"Humph," she said.

"But the real pitiful one is the stud ram. You know all about sheep harems, don't you?"

"No, I don't," I said.

"When you're raising sheep, the most important thing you got to keep an eye on is mating. So you keep 'em separate, the males with the males, the females with the females. Then you throw one male into the pen with the females. Generally, it's the strongest number one male. In other words, you're serving up the best seed.

After a month, when all the business is done, this stud ram gets returned to the males-only pen. But during the time the stud's been busy, the other males have worked out a new pecking order. And thanks to all that servicing, the stud is down to half his weight and there's no way he can win a fight. So all the other males gang up on him. Now there's a sad story."

"How do sheep fight?"

"They bump heads. Sheep foreheads are hard as steel and all hollow inside."

She said nothing, but seemed to be deep in thought. Probably trying to picture angry sheep beating their heads together.

After thirty minutes' drive, the paved surface suddenly disappeared, and the road narrowed to half its width. From both sides, dark primal forests rushed in like giant waves at our jeep. The temperature dropped.

The road was terrible. It bounced the jeep around like a seismographic needle, agitating the gasoline in the plastic tank at our feet. The gas made ominous sounds, as if someone's brains were sloshing about, ready to come flying out of their skull. Was I nervous about it? You bet.

The road went on like this for twenty or thirty minutes. I couldn't steady myself even to read my watch. The whole while nobody said a word. I held tight to the belt attached to the seat, as she clung to my right arm. The caretaker concentrated on holding on to the steering wheel.

"Left," the caretaker suddenly spoke up. Not knowing what to expect, I turned to see a wall in the dark forest torn wide open, the ground falling away. The valley was vast, and the view was spectacular. But without a hint of warmth. The rock face was sheer, stripped of every bit of life. You could smell its menacing breath.

Back straight ahead on the road a slick, conical mountain now appeared. At the tip, a tremendous force had twisted the cone out of shape.

Hands tight on the steering wheel, the caretaker jutted his chin forward in the direction of the cove.

"We're headed 'round the other side of that."

The strong wind that climbed the right slope from the valley sent the thick foliage sweeping upward, lightly spraying sand against the windows.

At some point near the top of the cone, the switchbacks came to an end, the slope on the right changing into volcanic crags, then eventually into a steep stone face. Squeezed on a narrow ledge chiseled into a featureless expanse of rock, the jeep crept along.

Suddenly, the weather took a turn for the worse. The blue-tinged patches of light-gray sky wearied of their fickle subtleties and turned dark, mixing in an uneven sooty black. Imparting a grim cast to the mountains.

In this caldron of a mountain, the winds whirled around, wheezing and moaning awfully. I wiped the sweat from my brow. Under my sweater, I was all cold sweat too.

The caretaker pursed his lips with each cut of the wheel, pulling right, right again. Then he leaned forward as if straining to hear something, slowing the jeep gradually until, where the road widened slightly, he stepped on the brake. He turned off the engine, and we sat, delivered into the midst of a frozen silence. There was only the wind taking its survey of the land.

The caretaker rested both hands on the wheel. A half hour seemed to pass before he got out of the jeep and tapped the ground with the sole of his work shoe. I climbed out of the jeep after him and stood beside him, looking down at the road surface.

"No good," said the caretaker. "It rained a lot harder than I thought."

The road did not seem all that damp to me. On the contrary, it looked hard-packed and dry.

"The core is damp," he explained. "It fools everyone. Things are different in these parts."

"Different?"

Instead of answering, he took a cigarette out of his pocket and lit up. "How about taking a short walk with me?"

We walked two hundred yards to the next bend. I could feel the nasty chill. I zipped my windbreaker all the way up and turned my collar, but the cold insisted.

Right where the road began to curve, the caretaker stopped. Facing the cliff on the right, cigarette still at his lips, he grimaced. Water, a light clayey brown, was trickling out of the middle of the cliff, flowing down the rock, and slowly crossing the road. I swiped my finger across the rock face. It was more porous than it seemed, the surface crumbling at the slightest touch.

"This here's one hell of a curve," said the caretaker. "The surface is loose, but that's not all. It's, well, bad luck. Even the sheep are afraid of it."

The caretaker coughed and tossed his cigarette to the ground. "I hate to do this to you, but I don't want to chance it."

I nodded.

"Think you can walk it the rest of the way?"

"Walking isn't the question. The point is the vibration."

The caretaker gave one more good hard stamp of his shoe. A split second later came a dull, depressing retort. "It's okay for walking."

We returned to the jeep.

"It's about another three miles from here," said the caretaker. "Even with the woman, you'll get there in an hour and a half. One straight road, not much of a rise. Sorry I can't take you the whole way."

"That's all right. Thanks for everything."

"You thinking to stay up there?"

"I don't know. I might be back down tomorrow. It might take a week. Depends on how things go."

He put another cigarette to his lips, but this time before he could even light up he started coughing. "You better watch out, though. The way things look, it'll probably be an early snow. And once the snow sets in, you're not gettin' out."

"I'll keep an eye out," I said.

"There's a mailbox by the front door. The key's wedged in the bottom. If nobody's there, use that."

We unloaded the jeep under the lead-gray skies. I took my windbreaker off and slipped on a heavy mountaineering parka. I was still cold.

With great difficulty, the caretaker managed to turn the jeep around, bumping into the cliff repeatedly. Each time he hit the cliff, it would crumble. Finally, he succeeded in turning completely around, honked his horn, and waved. I waved back. The jeep swung around the bend and was gone.

We were totally alone. As if we'd been dropped off at the edge of the world.

We set our backpacks on the ground and stood there saying nothing, trying to get our bearings. Below us a slender ribbon of silver river wound its way through the valley, both banks covered in dense green forest. Across the valley broke waves of low, autumn-tinged hills and beyond that a hazy view of the flatlands. Thin columns of smoke rose from the fields where rice straw was being burned after the harvest. A breathtaking panorama, but it made me feel no better. Everything seemed so remote, so . . . alien.

The sky was weighed down with a moist, uniform gray—clouds that seemed, as one, to blanket all light. Below, lumps of dense black cloud matter blew by, almost within touching distance. The clouds raced eastward from the direction of the Asian continent, cutting across the Japan Sea to Hokkaido on their way to the Sea of Okhotsk with remarkable speed. It all contributed to making us aware of the utter precariousness of where we stood. One passing gust and this whole crumbling curve plastered against the cliff could easily drag us to the bottom of the abyss.

"Let's get moving," I said, shouldering my monster backpack. Something awful, whether rain or sleet, was in the air, and I wanted to be near someplace with a roof. I sure didn't want to get drenched out here in the cold.

We hoofed it away from that "dead man's curve" on the double. The caretaker was right: the place was bad luck. There was a feeling of doom that first came over my body, then went on to strike a warning signal in my head. The sort of feeling you get when you're crossing a river and all of a sudden you sink your feet into mud of a different temperature.

In just the three hundred yards we walked, the sound of our footsteps on the road surface went through any number of changes. Time and again, spring-fed rivulets snaked across our path.

Even after we cleared the curve, we did not slow down, trying to create as much distance from the spot as we could. Only after thirty minutes did we relax as the cliff eased back into a less precipitous slope and trees came into view.

Having made it this far, we had no problem with the rest of the way. The road flattened out, and the mountains lost their sharp ridges. Gradually, we were in the midst of a peaceful highland scene.

In another thirty minutes, the cone was completely behind us, and we came onto a plateau surrounded by mountains that looked like cutouts. It was as if the top half of a gigantic volcano had collapsed. A sea of birch trees in their autumn foliage stretched forever. Among the birches were brilliantly hued shrubs and undergrowth, here and there a toppled birch, brown and rotting.

"Seems like a nice enough place," said my girlfriend.

After that curve, it looked like a nice place indeed.

The road led us straight up through this sea of birches. It was barely wide enough for a jeep and absolutely straight. Not one bend, no steep slopes. If you looked ahead, everything was sucked into one point. Even the black clouds passed directly over that point.

And it was quiet. The sound of the wind itself was swallowed by the grand expanse of forest. The air was split by the cry of a fat blackbird. Once the bird was out of sight, the silence flowed back in, a viscous fluid filling every opening. The leaves that had fallen on the road were saturated from the rain of two days before. The road seemed endless, like the birch forest around it. The low clouds, which had been terrifying only a short while before, now seemed surreal through the woods.

After another fifteen minutes, we came to a clear stream. There was a sturdy birch-trunk bridge with handrails, and nearby, a small clearing. We set down our packs, went down to the stream, and helped ourselves to a drink. It was the best-tasting water I'd ever had. Cold enough to redden my hands, and sweet, with a scant trace of earth.

The clouds kept on their appointed course, but unaccountably the weather was bearing up. She adjusted the laces of her mountain shoes, I sat back on the handrail and smoked a cigarette.

Downstream, I could hear a waterfall. Not a very big waterfall from the sound of it. A playful breeze blew in from the left, sending a ripple through the piles of leaves and scattering them.

I finished my cigarette and ground it out with my shoe, only to find another butt right next to my foot. I picked it up. A flattened Seven Stars. Not wet, so it had been from after the rains. Which meant either yesterday or today.

I tried to recall what brand of cigarette the Rat smoked. But I couldn't remember if he even smoked. I gave up and tossed the cigarette butt into the stream. The current whisked it off downstream in an instant.

"What is it?" she asked.

"I found a fresh cigarette butt, so somebody must have been sitting here having a smoke like me not too long ago."

"Your friend?"

"I wish I could say."

She sat herself down next to me and pulled back her hair, giving me the first view of her ears in a long time. The sound of the waterfall grew faint, then came back.

"You still like my ears?" she asked.

I smiled and quickly reached out my hand to touch them.

"You know I do," I said.

After yet another fifteen minutes, the road suddenly came abruptly to an end, just as the sea of birches suddenly stopped. Before us was a vast lake of a pasture.

Posts set at five-yard intervals surrounded the pasture. Wire connecting them, old, rusty wire. We had, it seemed, found our way to the sheep pasture. I pushed open the well-worn double gate and entered. The grass was soft, the soil dark and moist.

Black clouds were passing over the pasture. In the direction of their flight, a tall, jagged line of mountains. The angle was different, to be sure, but there was no mistaking: these were the same mountains in the Rat's photograph. I didn't need to pull out the photograph to check.

Still, it was unsettling seeing with my very own eyes a scene I had by now seen hundreds of times in a photograph. The depth of the actual place seemed artificial. Less my being there than the sense that the scene had been temporarily thrown together in order to match the photograph.

I leaned on the gate and heaved a sigh. This was it, what we'd been searching for. And whatever meaning that search might have had, we'd found it.

"We made it, eh?" she said, touching my arm.

"We made it," I said. Nothing more to say.

Straight on across the pasture stood an old American-style two-story wood-frame house. The house that the Sheep Professor had built forty years before and the Rat's father had then bought. Nothing was nearby to compare it to, so from a distance it was difficult to tell how big it was. It was, in any case, squat and expressionless. Painted white, beneath the overcast skies it looked a foreboding gray. From the middle of the mustard, almost rust-colored gabled roof a rectangular brick chimney protruded. Instead of a fence around the house, there was a stand of evergreens which protected it from the elements. The place seemed curiously uninhabited. An odd house the more I looked at it. It wasn't particularly inhospitable or cold, nor built in any unusual way, nor even much in disrepair. It was just . . . odd. As if a great creature had grown old without being able to express its feelings. Not that it didn't know how to express them, but rather that it didn't know what to express.

The smell of rain was suddenly everywhere. Time to get moving. We made a beeline across the pasture for the house. The clouds blowing in from the west were no longer gentle passing puffs; big threatening rain clouds were on the approach.

The pasture was huge. No matter how fast we walked, we seemed to make no progress. I couldn't get any feeling for the distance. Come to think of it, this was the first level ground we'd walked on, so even things far off seemed within reach.

A flock of birds crossed the course of the clouds on their way north.

When, after hours it seemed, we finally made it to the house, the patter of rain had already started. Up close, the house was bigger and older than it had appeared from a distance. The white paint was blistered and peeling, the flakes on the ground long since brown from the rain. At this point, you'd have to strip off all the dead layers of paint before you could think about putting on a new coat. The prospect of painting such a house—why was I even thinking of this?—made me wince. A house where no one lives goes to pieces, and this house, without a doubt, was on its way there.

The trees, in contrast to the ailing house, were thriving, enveloping it like the treehouse in *The Swiss Family Robinson.* Long untrimmed, their branches spread wildly.

With the road up the mountain so tortuous, what a feat it must have been for the Sheep Professor to build this house. Hauling the lumber, doing all the work, sinking his entire savings into it, no doubt. To think that this same Sheep Professor was now holed up in a dark room at the Dolphin Hotel! You couldn't ask for a better (or worse) personification of an unrewarded life.

I stood in the cold rain staring up at the house. Even up close, it showed no signs of habitation. Layers of fine sand had accumulated on the wooden shutters of the high, narrow double-hung windows. Rain had fixed the sand into configurations onto which another layer of sand had been blown, to be fixed in place by yet new rain.

In the middle of the front door at eye level was a four-inch-square windowpane covered on the inside with a cloth. The brass doorknob had been blasted with sand too, and grit crumbled off to the touch. The knob was as loose as an old molar, yet the door wouldn't open. Made of three planks of oak, it was sturdier than it looked. I knocked loudly on it a couple of times for the hell of it. As expected, no answer. All I did was hurt my hand. The boughs of the huge pin oak swayed in a gust of wind, producing a virtual sandslide.

As the caretaker had said, the key was in the bottom of the mailbox. An old-fashioned brass key, tarnished white where hands had touched it.

"Don't you think they're a little careless leaving the key like that?" asked my girlfriend.

"Know any burglars who'd come all this way, steal something, and haul it back down?"

The key fit the keyhole remarkably well. I turned it, there was a loud click, and the bolt unlocked.

It was dim, unnaturally dim. The shutters had been drawn for a long time, and it took a while for my eyes to adjust. There was gloom everywhere.

The room was large. Large, quiet, and smelling like an old barn. A smell I remembered from childhood. Old furniture and cast-off carpets. We closed the door behind us, shutting the sound of the wind out entirely.

"Hello?" I shouted. "Anybody home?"

Of course not. It was clear no one was there. Only the presence of a grandfather clock ticking away beside the fireplace.

For a brief instant, I felt a sense of vertigo. There in the darkness, time turned on its head. Moments overlapped. Memories crumbled. Then it was over. I opened my eyes and everything fell back into place. Before my eyes was a plain gray space, nothing more.

"Are you all right?" she asked worriedly.

"I'm all right," I said. "Let's check upstairs."

While she searched for a light switch, I checked the grandfather clock. It was the kind that had three weights you wound up on chains. Although all three had hit bottom, the clock was eking out its last increments of motion. Given the length of the chains, it would have taken about a week for the weights to hit bottom. Which meant that sometime during the week someone had been here to wind the clock.

I wound the three weights up to the top, then sat down on the sofa and stretched out my legs. An old prewar sofa, but quite comfortable. Not too soft, not too hard, and smelling like the palm of your hand.

A click, and the lights came on. She emerged from the kitchen, sat on the chaise, and lit up a clove cigarette. I lit up one myself. I'd learned to like them from her.

"Seems your friend was planning to spend the winter here," she said. "There's a whole winter's worth of fuel and food in the kitchen. A regular supermarket."

"But no sign of him."

"What about upstairs?"

We climbed the stairs next to the kitchen. They careened off at an angle halfway up. Emerging onto the second floor, we seemed to have entered a different atmospheric layer.

"My head aches," she said.

"Is it bad?"

"Oh, I'm all right. Don't worry about it. I'm used to this."

There were three bedrooms on the second floor. One big room to the left of a hallway and two smaller rooms to the right. Each room had a bare minimum of furniture, each room on the gloomy side. The big room had twin beds and a dresser. The beds were stripped down to their frames. Time was dead in the air.

Only in the farther small bedroom was there any lingering scent of human occupation. The bed was neatly made, the pillow with a slight indentation, and a pair of blue pajamas was folded at the head of the bed. An old-model lamp sat on the side table next to an overturned book. A Conrad novel.

Beside the bed was a heavy oak chest of drawers. In it an inventory of men's sweaters, shirts, slacks, socks, and underwear. The sweaters and slacks were well worn, invariably frayed somewhere, but good clothes. I could swear I'd seen some of them before. They were the Rat's, all right. Shirts with a fifteen-inch neck, slacks with a twenty-nine-inch waist.

Next to the window were an old table and chair of a singularly simple design you don't see often anymore. In the desk drawer, a cheap fountain pen, three boxes of ink cartridges, and a letter set, the stationery unused. In the second drawer, a half-used supply of cough drops and various and sundry small items. The third drawer, empty. No diary, no notebook, nothing. He'd done away with all extras. Everything was squared away. Too much. I ran my finger over the desktop, and it came up white with dust. Not a whole lot of dust. Maybe a week's worth.

I lifted up the double-hung window and pushed open the shutters. Low black clouds were swooping in. The wind had gathered strength, and you could almost see it cavorting through the pasture like a wild animal. Beyond that were the birches and beyond them the mountains. It was the exact same vista as in the photograph. Except there were no sheep.

We went back downstairs and sat on the sofa. The grandfather clock gave a command chime performance, then struck twelve times. We were silent until the last note was swallowed into the air.

"What do we do now?" she asked.

"We wait. What else?" I said. "The Rat was here a week ago. His things are still here. He's got to come back."

"But if the snow sets in before that, we'll be here all winter and our time will run out."

True enough.

"Don't your ears tell you anything?"

"They're out of commission. If I open my ears, I get a headache."

"Well, then, I guess we stretch out and wait for the Rat," I said.

Which was to say we'd run out of options.

While she went into the kitchen and made coffee, I took a quick once-around the big living room, inspecting it corner to corner. The fireplace, a real working fireplace set in the middle of the main wall, was clean and ready for use. But it had not been used recently. A few oak leaves, having gotten in through the chimney, sat in the hearth. A large kerosene heater stood nearby. The fuel gauge read full.

Next to the fireplace was a built-in glass-paneled bookcase completely filled with old books. I pulled out a few volumes and leafed through them. All were prewar editions, almost none of any value. Geography and science and history and philosophy and politics. Utterly useless, the lot of them, except maybe as documents of an intellectual's required reading forty years ago. There were postwar editions too, of similar worth. Only *Plutarch's Lives* and *Selected Greek Tragedies* and a handful of novels had managed to survive the erosion of years. This was a first for me: never before had I set eyes on so grand a collection of useless tomes.

To the side of the bookcase was a display shelf, likewise built-in, and on it a stereo hi-fi—bookshelf speakers, amplifier, turntable—the kind popular in the mid-sixties. Some two hundred old records, every one scratched beyond reckoning, but at least not worthless. The musical taste was not as eroded as the ideology. I switched on the vacuum-tube amplifier, picked a record at random, and lowered the needle. Nat King Cole's *South of the Border.* All at once the room felt transported back to the 1950s.

The wall opposite had four six-foot double-hung windows, equidistantly spaced. You could see the rain coming down in torrents now. A gray rain, which obscured the line of mountains in the distance.

The room was wood-floored, with an eight-by-twelve-foot carpet in the middle, on which were arranged a set of drawing-room furniture and a floor lamp. A dining table stood in one corner of the room, covered with dust.

The vacant aftermath of a room.

A door, set inconspicuously into the wall, opened into a fair-sized trunk room. It was stacked high and tight with surplus furniture, carpets, dishes, a set of golf clubs, a guitar, a mattress, overcoats, mountaineering boots, old magazines. Even junior high school exam reference books and a radio-controlled airplane. Mostly products of the fifties and sixties.

The house kept its own time, like the old-fashioned grandfather clock in the living room. People who happened by raised the weights, and as long as the weights were wound, the clock continued ticking away. But with people gone and the weights unattended, whole chunks of time were left to collect in deposits of faded life on the floor.

I took a few old screen magazines back to the living room. The photo feature of one was *The Alamo*. John Wayne's directorial debut with the all-out support of John Ford. I want to make a grand epic that lingers in the hearts of all Americans, John Wayne said. He looked corny as hell in a beaver cap.

My girlfriend appeared with coffee, and we faced each other as we drank. Drops of rain tapped intermittently on the windows. The time passed slowly as chill infiltrated the room. The yellow glow of the light bulbs drifted about the room like pollen.

"Tired?" she asked.

"I guess," I said, gazing absently out the window. "We've been running around searching like crazy all this time, and now we've ground to a halt. Can't quite get used to it. After all we did to find the scene in the photograph, there's no Rat and no sheep."

"Get some sleep. I'll make dinner."

She brought a blanket down from upstairs and covered me. Then she readied the kerosene heater, placed a cigarette between my lips, and lit it for me.

"Show a little spirit. Everything's going to be fine."

"Thanks," I said.

At that, she disappeared into the kitchen.

All alone, my body felt heavy. I took two puffs of the cigarette, put it out, pulled the blanket up to my neck, and shut my eyes. It only took a few seconds before I fell asleep.

33

She Leaves the Mountain; Hunger Strikes

The clock struck six and I woke up on the sofa. The lights were out, the room enveloped in dense evening gloom. Everything from the core of my being to the tips of my fingers was numb. Darkness had spread over my skin like ink.

The rain had let up, the nightbirds sang through the window glass. The flames of the heater cast faint, undulating, elongated shadows on the white walls of the room. I got up and switched on the floor lamp, walked into the kitchen, and drank two glasses of cold water. A pot of stew, still warm, was on the stove. An ashtray held two clove cigarettes, crushed out.

Immediately, instinctively, I knew she was gone.

I stood there, hands on the cooktop, and tried to sort out my thoughts.

She was no longer here, that much was certain. No argument or guesswork about it. She was, in fact, not here. The vacated atmosphere of the house was final, undeniable. It was a feeling I had known well in the couple of months between the time my wife left me and the time I met my girlfriend.

I went upstairs to check. I opened the closet doors. No sign of her. Her shoulder bag and down jacket had vanished. So had her boots in the vestibule. Without a doubt, she was gone. I looked in all the places where she might have left a note, but there was nothing. She was probably already down the mountain.

I could not accept the fact of her disappearance. I was barely awake, but even if I were totally lucid, this—and everything that was happening to me—was far beyond my realm of comprehension. There was almost nothing one could do except let things take their course.

Sitting on the sofa, I felt a sudden hunger. And not an ordinary hunger either.

I went from the kitchen into the provisions cellar and uncorked a bottle of red wine. Overchilled but drinkable. Returning to the kitchen, I cut a few slices of bread, then peeled an apple. As I waited for the stew to heat, I had three glasses of wine.

When the stew was ready, I moved to the living-room table and ate dinner listening to the Percy Faith Orchestra playing "Perfidia." After dinner, I drank the coffee left in the pot, and with a deck of cards that was sitting on the mantel I dealt myself a hand of solitaire. A game invented and fashionable in nineteenth-century England, it later became less popular and then forgotten due to its complicated rules. A mathematician once calculated the success rate as one in 250,000. I gave it three tries—without success, of course. I cleared away the cards and dishes. Then I finished off the rest of the wine.

Night had come. I closed the shutters and lay down on the sofa to listen to scratchy old records.

Would the Rat ever come back?

I had to assume he'd be back. After all, he'd stocked up on a winter's supply of fuel and provisions.

But that was assuming. The Rat might have given up on the place and returned to town. Or maybe he'd taken up with some woman. Practically anything was possible.

Which could mean that I was in a fine mess. My one-month time limit, now exactly half over, would soon be past. No Rat, no sheep, just the man in the black suit dragging me into his Götterdämmerung. Even though I was nobody, he'd do it. I had no doubt about it.

In the city, the second week of October is a most urbane time of year. If all this hadn't happened, I'd be eating omelettes and drinking whiskey now. A beautiful time in a beautiful season, in the evening as the rains lifted, chunks of ice and a solid-wood bar top, time flowing slowly, easily, like a gentle stream.

Turning all this over in my mind, I started to imagine another me somewhere, sitting in a bar, nursing a whiskey, without a care in the world. The more I thought about it, the more that other me became the real me, making this me here not real at all.

I shook my head clear.

Outside, night birds kept up a low cooing.

I went upstairs and made the bed in the small room that the Rat hadn't been using. Mattress and sheets and blankets were all neatly stacked in the closet by the stairs.

The furniture was exactly the same as in the Rat's room. Bedside table and desk and chair and lamp. Old-fashioned, but products of an age when things were made to be strong and functional. Without frills.

Predictably, the view from the window at the head of the bed looked out over the pasture. The rain had stopped, and the thick cloud cover was beginning to break. There was a lovely half-moon that illuminated the pasture now and again. A searchlight sweeping over what might as well have been the ocean floor.

Crawling under the covers, still in my clothes, I gazed at the scene that soon dissolved, soon reappeared. A faded image of my girlfriend rounding the unlucky bend in the road, heading alone down the mountain, came to mind. Then that disappeared, to be replaced by the flock of sheep and the Rat taking their photograph. Again the moon hid behind a cloud, and when it reemerged, even they had gone.

I read my *Sherlock Holmes* by lamplight.

34

A Find in the Garage; Thoughts in the Middle of the Pasture

Birds of a kind I'd never seen before clung like Christmas ornaments to the pin oaks by the front door, chirping away. The world shone moistly in the morning light.

I made toast in a primitive toaster, the type where you turn the slices of bread by hand. I coated a frying pan with butter, fried a couple eggs sunnyside-up, drank two glasses of grape juice. I was feeling lonely without her, but the fact that I could feel lonely at all was consolation. Loneliness wasn't such a bad feeling. It was like the stillness of the pin oak after the little birds had flown off.

I washed the dishes, then rinsed the egg yolk from my mouth and brushed my teeth for a full five minutes. After lengthy deliberations, I decided to shave. There was an almost new can of shaving cream and a Gillette razor at the washbasin. Toothbrush and toothpaste, soap, lotion, even cologne. Ten hand towels, each a different color, lay neatly folded on the shelf. Not a spot on mirror or washbasin. True to methodical Rat-form.

The same was pretty much true of the lavatory and the bathroom. The grouting between the tiles had been scrubbed with brush and cleanser. It was gleaming white, a work of art. The box sachet in the lavatory gave off the fragrance of a gin-with-lime you'd get at a fancy bar.

I went into the living room to smoke my morning cigarette. I had three packs of Larks left in my backpack. When those were gone, it'd be no smoking for me. I lit up a second cigarette and thought about what it'd be like without smokes. The morning sun felt wonderful, and sitting on the sofa, which molded itself to my body, was pure luxury. Before I knew it, a whole hour had passed. The clock struck a lazy nine o'clock.

I began to understand why the Rat had put the house in such order, scrubbed between the tiles, ironed his shirts, and shaved, though surely he had no one to meet. Unless you kept moving up here, you'd lose all sense of time.

I got up from the sofa, folded my arms, and walked once around the room, but I couldn't see anything that needed doing. The Rat had cleaned anything that was cleanable. He'd even brushed the soot from the ceiling.

I decided instead to go for a walk. It was spectacular weather. The sky was feathered with a few white brushstroke clouds, the air filled with the songs of birds.

In back of the house was a large garage. A cigarette butt lay on the ground in front of the old double doors. Seven Stars. This time, the cigarette butt turned out to be rather old. The paper had come apart, exposing the filter.

Ashtrays. I had seen only one in the house, and it had shown no trace of use. The Rat didn't smoke! I rolled the filter around in the palm of my hand, then threw it back onto the ground.

I undid the heavy bolt and opened the garage doors to find a huge interior. The sunlight slanted in through the cracks in the siding, creating a series of parallel lines on the dark soil. There was the smell of dirt and gasoline.

An old Toyota Land Cruiser sat there. Not a speck of mud on the body or tires. The gas tank was almost full. I felt under the dash where the Rat always hid his keys. As expected, the key was there. I inserted it in the ignition and gave it a turn. Right away the engine was purring. It was the same Rat, always good at tuning his automobiles. I cut the engine, put the key back, then looked around the driver's seat. There was nothing noteworthy—road maps, a towel, half a bar of chocolate. In the backseat, unusually dirty for the Rat, was a roll of wire and a large pair of pliers. I opened the rear door and swept the debris into my hand, holding it up to the sunlight leaking in through a knothole in the siding. Cushion stuffing. Or sheep wool. I pulled a tissue out of my pocket, wrapped up the debris, and put it in my breast pocket.

I couldn't understand why the Rat hadn't taken the car. The fact that the car was in the garage meant that he had walked down the mountain or that he hadn't gone down at all. Neither made sense. Up to three days ago the cliff road would have been easy to drive. Would he abandon the house to camp out up here?

Puzzled, I shut the garage doors and walked out into the pasture. There was no reasonable explanation possible from such unreasonable circumstances.

As the sun rose higher in the sky, steam rose from the pasture. The mountains seemed to mist over, and the smell of grass was overwhelming.

I walked through the damp grass to the middle of the pasture. There lay a discarded old tire, the rubber white and cracked. I sat down on it and surveyed my surroundings. From here the house looked like a white rock jutting out from the shoreline.

In this solitary state, the memory of the ocean swim meets I used to participate in when I was a kid came to me. On distance swims between two islands, I would sometimes stop mid-course to look around. To find myself equidistant between two points gave me the funniest feeling. To think that back on dry land people were going about business as usual was pretty peculiar too. Unsettling, that society could go on perfectly well without me.

I sat there for fifteen minutes before ambling back to the house. I sat down on the living-room sofa and continued reading my *Sherlock Holmes*.

At two o'clock, the Sheep Man came.

35

The Sheep Man Cometh

As the clock struck two, there came a knocking on the door. Two times at first, a two-breath pause, then three times.

It took me a while to recognize it as knocking. That anyone should knock on the door hadn't occurred to me. The Rat wouldn't knock, it was his house. The caretaker might knock, but he certainly wouldn't wait for a reply before walking in. Maybe my girlfriend—no, more likely she'd steal in through the kitchen door and help herself to a cup of coffee. She wasn't the type to knock.

I opened the door, and standing there, two yards away, was the Sheep Man. Showing markedly little interest in either the open door or myself who opened it. Carefully inspecting the mailbox as if it were a rare, exotic specimen. The Sheep Man was barely taller than the mailbox. Four foot ten at most. Slouched over and bowlegged besides.

There were, moreover, six inches between the doorsill, where I stood, and ground level, where he stood, so it was as if I were looking down at him from a bus window. As if ignoring his decisive shortcomings, he continued his scrutiny of the mailbox.

"CanIcomein?" the Sheep Man said rapid-fire, facing sideways the whole while. His tone was angry.

"Please do," I said.

He crouched down and gingerly untied the laces of his mountaineering boots. They were caked with a sweet-roll-thick crust of mud. The Sheep Man picked up his boots with both hands and, with practiced technique, whacked them solidly together. A shower of hardened mud fell to the ground. Then demonstrating consummate knowledge of the lay of the house, he put slippers on and padded over to the sofa and sat down.

Just great, his face was saying.

The Sheep Man wore a full sheepskin pulled over his head. The arms and legs were fake and patched on, but his stocky body fit the costume perfectly. The hood was also fake, but the two horns that curled from his crown were absolutely real. Two flat ears, probably wire-reinforced, stuck out level from either side of the hood. The leather mask that covered the upper half of his face, his matching gloves, and socks, all were black. There was a zipper from neck to crotch.

On his chest was a pocket, also zippered, from which he extracted his cigarettes and matches. The Sheep Man put a Seven Stars to his mouth, lit up, and let out a long sigh. I fetched the washed ashtray from the kitchen.

"Iwannadrink," said the Sheep Man. I duly went into the kitchen and got a half-bottle of Four Roses and two glasses with ice.

He poured whiskey over the ice, I did the same, we drank without a toast. As he drank, the Sheep Man mumbled to himself. His pug nose was big for his body, and with each breath he took, his nostrils flared dramatically. The two eyes that peered through the mask darted restlessly around the room.

hal.

When the Sheep Man finished his whiskey, he seemed more at ease. He put out his cigarette and with both hands rubbed his eyes under his mask.

"Woolgetsinmyeyes," said the Sheep Man.

I didn't know how to respond and said nothing.

"Youcamehereyesterdayafternooneh?" said the Sheep Man, rubbing his eyes some more. "Beenwatchingyouthewholetime."

The Sheep Man stopped to pour a slug of whiskey over the half-melted ice and downed it in one gulp.

"Andthewomanleftalonethisafternoon."

"You watched that too, did you?"

"Watchedher?Wedroveheraway."

"Drove her away?"

"Surestuckourheadthroughthekitchendoorsaidyoubettergohome."

"Why?"

That threw the Sheep Man into a pout. "Why?" was obviously not the way to phrase a question to him, but before I could say anything else, his eyes slowly took on a different gleam.

"ShewentbacktotheDolphinHotel," said the Sheep Man.

"Did she say so?

"Didn'tsaynothing.ButwheresheisistheDolphinHotel."

"How do you know that?"

Again the Sheep Man refused to speak. He put both hands on his knees and glared at the glass on the table.

"But she did go back to the Dolphin Hotel?" I said.

"UhhuhtheDolphinHotel'sanicehotel.Smellslikesheep," said the Sheep Man.

Silence again.

On closer inspection, I could see that the Sheep Man's fleece was filthy, the wool stiff with oil.

"Did she say anything by way of a message when she left?"

"Nope," the Sheep Man said, shaking his head. "Shedidn't sayanythingandwedidn'task."

"When you told her she'd better leave, she up and left without a word?"

"Right. Wetoldhershe'dbetterleavebecauseshewaswantingtoleave."

"She came up here because she wanted to."

"Wrong!" screamed the Sheep Man. "Shewantedtogetoutbutshe herselfwasconfused.That'swhywechasedherhome.Youconfusedher." The Sheep Man stood up and slammed his right hand down flat on the table. His whiskey glass slid two inches.

The Sheep Man froze in that pose until gradually his eyes lost their zeal and he collapsed back into the sofa, out of steam.

"Youconfusedthatwoman," the Sheep Man said, this time more calmly. "Notaverynicethingatall.Youdon'tknowathing.Allyou thinkaboutisyourself."

"You're telling me she shouldn't have come here?"

"That'sright.Shewasn'tmeanttocomehere.Youdon'tthinkabout anythingbutyourself."

I sat there speechless, lapping my whiskey.

"Butstillwhat'sdoneisdone.Anywayit'soverforher."

"Over?"

"You'llneverseethatwomanagain."

"Because I only thought about myself?"

"That'sright.Becauseyouthoughtonlyaboutyourself.Justdeserts."

The Sheep Man stood up and went to a window, forced up the window frame with one hand, and took a breath of the fresh air. No mean show of strength.

"Gottaopenwindowsonnicedayslikethis," said the Sheep Man. Then the Sheep Man did a quick half-turn around the room and stopped before the bookcase, peering over the spines of the books with folded arms. Sprouting from the rear end of his costume was a tiny tail. In this position, he looked like a sheep standing up on its two hind legs.

"I'm looking for a friend of mine," I ventured.

"Areyou?" said the Sheep Man, back to me in total disinterest.

"He was living here. Up to a week ago."

"Wouldn'tknow."

The Sheep Man stood in front of the fireplace shuffling the cards from the mantel.

"I'm also looking for a sheep with a star mark on its back," I pressed on.

"Haven'tseenit," said the Sheep Man.

But it was obvious that the Sheep Man knew something about the Rat and the sheep. His lack of concern was too affected. The timing of his response too pat, his tone false.

I changed tactics. Pretending I'd given up, I yawned, taking up my book from the table and flipping through the pages. A slightly vexed Sheep Man returned to the sofa and quietly eyed me reading the book.

"Readingbooksfun?" asked the Sheep Man.

"Hmm," I responded.

The Sheep Man bided his time. I kept reading to spite him.

"Sorryforshouting," said the Sheep Man in a low voice. "Sometimesit'slikethesheepinmeandthehumaninmeareatoddssoIgetlikethat. Didn'tmeananythingbyit.Andbesidesyoucomeonsayingthingsto threatenus."

"That's okay," I said.

"Toobadyou'llneverseethatwomanagain.Butit'snotourfault."

"Hmm."

I took the three packs of Larks out of my backpack and gave them to the Sheep Man. The Sheep Man was taken aback.

"Thanks.Neverhadthisbrand.Butdon'tyou needthem?"

"I quit smoking," I said.

"Yesthat'swise," the Sheep Man nodded in all seriousness. "They'rereallybadforyou."

He filed the cigarette packs away carefully in a pocket on his arm. The fleece buckled out in a rectangular lump.

"I've absolutely got to see my friend. I've come a long, long way here to see him."

The Sheep Man nodded.

"The same goes for that sheep."

The Sheep Man nodded.

"But you don't know anything about them, I take it?"

The Sheep Man shook his head forlornly. His fake ears flapped up and down. This time his denial was much weaker than before.

"It'saniceplacehere," the Sheep Man changed the subject. "Beautifulscenerygoodcleanair.You'regonnalikeithere."

"Yeah, it's a nice place," I said.

"It'sevennicerinthewinter.Nothingbutsnowallaround,everything frozenup.Alltheanimalssleepingnohumanfolk."

"You stay here all winter?"

"Uhhuh."

I didn't ask anything else. The Sheep Man was just like an animal. Approach him and he'd retreat, move away and he'd come closer. As long as I wasn't going anywhere, there was no hurry. I could take my time.

With his left hand the Sheep Man pulled at the fingers of his black right glove, one after the other. After a number of tugs, the glove slipped off, revealing a flaking blackened hand. Small but fleshy, an old burn scar from the base of his thumb to midway around the back of his hand.

The Sheep Man stared at the back of his hand, then turned it over to look at the palm. Exactly the way the Rat used to do, that gesture. But no way was this Sheep Man the Rat. There was a difference in height of eight inches between them.

"Yougonnastayhere?" asked the Sheep Man.

"No, as soon as I find either my friend or the sheep, I'm leaving. That's all I came for."

"Winter'snicehere," repeated the Sheep Man. "Sparkling white.Everythingallfrozen."

The Sheep Man snickered to himself, flaring those enormous nostrils. Dingy teeth peered out from his mouth, the two front teeth missing. There was something uneven to the rhythm of the Sheep Man's thoughts, which seemed to have the whole room expanding and contracting.

"Gottabegoing," the Sheep Man said suddenly. "Thanksfor thesmokes."

I nodded.

"Hopeyoufindyourfriendandthatsheepbeforetoolong."

"Hmm," I said. "Let me know if you hear of anything."

The Sheep Man hemmed and hawed, ill at ease. "Umwellyes surething."

I fought back the urge to laugh. The Sheep Man was one lame liar.

He put his glove back on and stood up to go. "I'llbeback.Can't sayhowmanydaysfromnowbutI'llbeback." Then his eyes clouded. "Noimpositionisit?"

"You kidding?" I threw in a quick shake of the head. "By all means, I'd love to see you again."

"WellI'llbeback," said the Sheep Man, then slammed the door behind him. He almost caught his tail, but it slipped through safe and sound.

Through a space in the shutters, I watched the Sheep Man stand staring at that peeling whitewashed mailbox, exactly as he had when he first appeared. Then wriggling a bit to adjust the costume better to his body, he took off fleetfoot across the pasture toward the woods in the east. His level ears were like a diving board of a swimming pool. In the growing distance, the Sheep Man became a fuzzy white dot, finally merging into the white of the birches.

Even after the Sheep Man disappeared from view, I kept staring at the pasture and birch woods. Had the Sheep Man been an illusion?

Yet here were a bottle of whiskey and Seven Stars butts left on the table, and there on the sofa were a few strands of wool. I compared them with the wool from the backseat of the Land Cruiser. Identical.

As a way to focus my thoughts, I went into the kitchen to fix some Salisbury steak. I minced up an onion and browned it in the frying pan. Meanwhile, I defrosted a chunk of beef from the freezer, then ground it with a medium blade. The kitchen was what you might call compact, but even so it had more than your typical run of utensils and seasonings.

If they'd only pave the road here, you could open a mountain-chalet–style restaurant. Wouldn't be bad, windows wide open, a view of the flocks, blue sky. Families could let their kids play with the sheep, lovers could stroll in the birch woods. A success for sure.

The Rat could run it, I could cook. The Sheep Man could be good for something too. His costume would be perfect up here in the mountains. Then for a practical, down-to-earth touch, the caretaker could join us; you need one practical person. The dog too. Even the Sheep Professor could drop in.

While browning the onions with a wooden spatula, I tossed these ideas around in my head.

But my beautiful-eared girlfriend—was she lost to me forever? The thought depressed me, though what the Sheep Man said was probably right. I should have come here on my own. I should not have . . . I shook my head. Then I took up where I'd left off with the restaurant.

Now, if we could get J to come up here, I'm sure things would work out fine. Everything should revolve around him, with forgiveness, compassion, and acceptance at the center.

While waiting for the onions to cool, I sat down by the window and gazed back out at the pasture.

36

The Winds' Own Private Thoroughfare

Three uneventful days passed. Not one thing happened. The Sheep Man didn't show. I fixed meals, ate them, read my book, and when the sun went down, I drank whiskey and went to sleep.

The morning air of the pasture turned steadily cooler. Day by day, the bright golden leaves of the birches turned more spotted as the first winds of winter slipped between the withered branches and across the highlands toward the southeast. Stopping in the center of the pasture, I could hear the winds clearly. No turning back, they pronounced. The brief autumn was gone.

Without exercise and without smoking, I had quickly gained six pounds. So I started to get up at six and jog a crescent halfway around the pasture. That took off a couple of pounds. It was tough not smoking, but with no store around for twenty miles, what was one to do? Each time I felt like smoking, I thought about her and her ears. Compared to everything I'd lost this far, losing smoking was trivial. And indeed it was.

With all this free time, I cooked up a storm. I made a roast beef. I defrosted a salmon and marinated it. I searched the pasture for edible vegetables and simmered my findings with bonito flakes and soy sauce. I made simple cabbage pickles. I prepared a number of snacks in case the Sheep Man showed up for a drink. The Sheep Man, however, never came.

Most of the afternoons I would pass looking out at the pasture. I soon began seeing things. A figure emerging from the birch woods and running straight in my direction. Usually it was the Sheep Man, but sometimes it was the Rat, sometimes my girlfriend. Other times it was the sheep with the star on its back.

In the end, though, nobody ever materialized. Only the winds blowing across the pasture. It was as if the pasture were the winds' own private thoroughfare. The winds raced across the pasture, never looking back, on missions of utmost urgency.

On the seventh day after my arrival on the mountain, the first snow fell. The winds had been unusually calm from morning, the skies overcast with dense lead-gray clouds. After my morning run and shower, as I settled down to coffee and records, the snow started. A hard snow. It struck the windowpanes with a battery of dull thuds. The wind had picked up, driving the snow down at a thirty-degree angle. Rather like the slanting lines of some department-store wrapping-paper pattern. Soon the storm intensified and everything outside was awash in white. The entire mountain range and woods were obscured. This was no pitiful snow as sometimes falls in Tokyo. This was the real thing, an honest-to-goodness north-country snow. A snow to blanket everything and freeze deep into the heart of the earth.

The snow was blinding. I drew the curtain and curled up to read by the heater. The record ended, the needle lifted, and all was silence. The sort of silence that follows in the wake of the death of all living things. I set down my book and for no particular reason felt the urge to walk through the house. From the living room into the kitchen, checking the storeroom, bath and cellar, upstairs to open the doors of each room. There was no one, of course. Only silence which rolled like oil into every corner. Only silence which changed ever so slightly from room to room.

I was all alone. Probably more alone than I'd been in all my life.

I'd been dying for a smoke the past two days, but as there were no cigarettes, I'd been drinking whiskey straight. One winter like this and I'd end up an alcoholic. Not that there was enough liquor around to do the trick, though. Three bottles of whiskey, one bottle of brandy, twelve cases of canned beer, and no more. Obviously, the same thought had occurred to the Rat.

Was my partner, my former partner, that is, still hitting the bottle? Had he managed to put the company in order, turn it back into a small translation firm, as I suggested? Maybe he'd done exactly that. But could he really make a go of it without me, as he worried? Our time together was up. Six years together, and now back to square one.

The snow let up by early afternoon. Abruptly, just as it had begun. The thick clouds tore off in places as grand columns of sunlight thrust down to play in the pasture. It was magnificent.

The hard snow lay sprinkled on the ground like candy. Solidified into pellets as if to defy melting away. Yet by the time the clock struck three, the snow had all but melted. The ground was thoroughly wet, the twilight sun enfolding the pasture in a soft light. The birds sang as if set free.

After dinner, I borrowed two books from the Rat's room, *Bread Baking* and the Conrad novel, then made myself comfortable on the living-room sofa. One-third of the way into the novel, I came across a four-inch-square newspaper clipping the Rat had been using for a bookmark. No date, but from the color of the paper it must have been recent. It was local news, a symposium on aging and society to be held at a Sapporo hotel, a rally at a train station near Asahikawa, a lecture on the Middle East crisis. Nothing to grab the Rat's interest, or mine. On the reverse, classified ads. I yawned, shut the book, went to heat up the leftover coffee.

I suddenly realized that this was the first time, in what now seemed like years, that I had seen a newspaper, and that I'd been left behind an entire week from the goings-on of the world. No radio or television, no newspapers, no magazines. A nuclear missile could have destroyed Tokyo, an epidemic could have swept the world, Martians could have occupied Australia, I wouldn't have known. Of course, the Land Cruiser in the garage had a radio, but I discovered that I had no pressing desire to go listen after all. If something could take place without my knowing, it was just as well. I had no real need to know. I, in any case, had plenty on my mind already.

Something gnawed at me. Something that had passed before my eyes but which I'd been too dense to notice. All the same, on an unconscious level, it had registered. I deposited my coffee cup in the sink and returned to the living room. I took another look at the newspaper clipping. There it was on the reverse:

> Attention: Rat
> Get in touch. Urgent!
> Dolphin Hotel, Room 406

I put the clipping back in the book and sank into the sofa.

So the Rat knew I was looking for him. Question: how had he found the item? By accident, when he'd come down off the mountain? Or maybe he'd been searching for something through several weeks' worth of papers?

And why didn't he contact me? Had I already checked out of the Dolphin Hotel by the time he came across it? Had his telephone line already gone dead?

No. The Rat could have gotten in touch if he wanted to, he just didn't want to. Because I was at the Dolphin Hotel, he figured I'd find my way up here, so that if he wanted to see me, he had only to wait, or at least leave me a note.

What it boiled down to was this: for some reason the Rat didn't want to face me. Even so, he wasn't rejecting me. If he didn't want me here, he could have shut me out any number of ways. It was his house, after all.

Grappling with these two propositions, I watched the second hand sweep slowly around the face of the clock. After one full circumgyration, my reasoning had made no progress. I couldn't figure out what lay at the center of all this.

The Sheep Man knew something. That much was certain. Someone who had monitored my arrival on the scene was sure to know about the Rat's living here for six months.

The more I thought about it, the more difficult I found it to escape the feeling that the Sheep Man's actions reflected the Rat's will. The Sheep Man had driven my girlfriend from the mountain and left me here alone. His showing up here was undoubtedly a harbinger of something. Something was progressing all around me. The area was being swept clean and purified. Something was about to happen.

I turned out the lights and went upstairs, climbed into bed, and looked out at the moon and pasture. Stars peeked through a tear in the clouds. I opened the window and smelled the night air. Among the rustling leaves I could hear a call in the distance. A strange cry, neither bird nor beast.

I woke and went for my run in the pasture, showered, and ate breakfast. A morning like the others. The sky was overcast like the day before, but the temperature had risen a bit. Not much chance of snow.

Into jeans and a sweater and a jacket over that, then tennis shoes, and I was off across the pasture. Heading for the woods to the east where I'd seen the Sheep Man disappear, I made my way into the thicket. There was no real path to speak of, no sign of human life. Occasionally, there'd be an old birch toppled over.

The forest floor was flat, except for a long, yard-wide trough, like a dried-up streambed or an abandoned trench. The trough wound its way through the woods for miles. Sometimes sunken deep, sometimes shallow, ankle-deep in dead leaves.

The ditch gave on to a ridge trail, both sides of which sloped down to dry hollows. Plump birds shuffled across the path through the leaves, losing themselves in the undergrowth. Here and there, brush azaleas blazed bright red.

I walked around for an hour and lost all sense of direction. At this rate, I was hardly going to find the Sheep Man. I roamed the bottom of one dry hollow until I heard the sound of water. I sought out the river, then followed it downstream. If my memory served me correctly, there had to be a waterfall and near it, the road we'd walked up.

After another ten minutes, I came across the waterfall. Splashing as it struck the rocks in the gorge below, lapping into frozen pools. There was no sign of fish, though a few fallen leaves traced slow circles on the surface of the pools. I crossed from rock to rock, made my way down below the falls, then crawled up the slippery opposite bank. I had reached the road.

Seated on the edge of a bridge, watching me, was the Sheep Man. A big sailcloth bag of firewood was slung over his shoulder.

"Wanderaroundtoomuchyou'llbebearbait," said the Sheep Man. "There'sboundtobeoneaboutinthesepartsyouknow.Yesterdayafter noonIfoundtraces.Ifyouhavetowalkaroundyououghttoputabellon yourhiplikeus."

The Sheep Man shook a little bell fastened to his hip with a safety pin.

"I've been looking for you," I said after catching my breath.

"Iknow," said the Sheep Man. "I'veseenyousearching."

"Well then, why didn't you call out?"

"You'retheonewhowantedtosearchmeout. So I held back."

The Sheep Man took a cigarette out of his pocket and smoked it with great pleasure. I sat down next to him.

"You live around here?"

"Hmm," said the Sheep Man. "Butdon'ttellanybody.Nobody knows."

"But my friend knows all about you."

Silence.

"You know, it's a very important matter."

Silence.

"And if you're friends with my friend, that makes us friends, no?"

"Iguessso," said the Sheep Man cautiously. "Iguessitprobably does."

"And if you're my friend, you wouldn't lie to me, would you? Think about it."

"Errno," answered one perplexed Sheep Man. He licked his parched lips. "Ican'ttellyouI'mrealsorryIcan'ttellyouIcan't.I'mnot supposedto."

"Someone's put it to you to keep quiet?"

The Sheep Man clammed up. The wind whistled through the barren trees.

"Nobody's around to hear," I whispered.

The Sheep Man looked me in the eye. "Youdon'tknowathing aboutourwaysheredoyou?"

"No, I don't."

"Welllistenthisisnoordinaryplacewegothere.Thatmuchyoushould keepinmind."

"But just the other day you told me this was such nice country."

"Forusyes," said the Sheep Man. "Forusthisistheonlyplacetolive. Ifwewerechasedoutofherewe'dhavenoplacetogo."

At that, the Sheep Man shut up. He would not say another word on the subject. I looked at his sailcloth bag filled with firewood.

"That your heating for the winter?"

The Sheep Man nodded silently.

"But I didn't see any smoke."

"Nofireyet.Nottillthesnowsetsin.Butevenafteritsnowsyouwouldn't beabletoseethesmokefromourfire.Wegotaspecialwayofbuildingfires." He grinned, self-satisfied.

"So when will the snow begin to pile up around here?"

The Sheep Man looked up at the sky, then looked at me. "The snow'llcomeearlythisyear.Maybeanothertendays."

"In another ten days the road will freeze over?"

"Probably.Nobodycomingupandnobodygoingdown.Wonderful timeofyear."

"And you've been living here how long?"

"Longtime," said the Sheep Man. "Reallongtime."

"What do you eat?"

"TubersshootsnutsbirdswhateverlittlefishandcrabsIcancatch."

"Don't you get cold?"

"Winter'ssupposedtobecold."

"If you need something, I'd be glad to share whatever I've got."

"ThanksbutI'mfinejustnow."

The Sheep Man suddenly stood up and started walking off in the direction of the pasture. So I got up to follow him.

"Why'd you take to hiding out up here?"

"You'dlaughifItoldyou," said the Sheep Man.

"No, I wouldn't laugh, I swear," I said. I couldn't imagine what there'd be to laugh about.

"Youwon'ttellanyone?"

"I won't tell anyone."

"Ididn'twanttogoofftowar."

For the next few minutes, we walked on without a word between us.

"War with whom?" I asked.

"Dunno," coughed out the Sheep Man. "ButIdidn'twanttogo. Anywaythat'swhyI'masheep.Asheepwhostayswherehebelongsup here."

"You from Junitaki-cho?"

"Uhhuhbutdon'ttellanyone."

"I won't," I said. "You don't like the town?"

"Thetowndownthere?"

"Yeah."

"Don'tlikeitatall.Toofullofsoldiers," the Sheep Man coughed again. "Whereyoufrom?"

"Tokyo."

"Heardaboutthewar?"

"Nope."

At that the Sheep Man seemed to lose all interest in me. He remained silent until we reached the entrance to the pasture.

"Care to stop by the house?" I asked the Sheep Man.

"Gottalayinwintersupplies," he said. "Realbusy.Maybenext time."

"I'd like to see my friend," I said. "I've got something I have to see him about next week."

The Sheep Man shook his head forlornly. His ears flapped. "Sorry butlikeIsaidbeforeit'snotuptous."

"Well, then, pass the word on if you can."

"Hmm," said the Sheep Man.

"Thanks a lot," I said. I turned to leave.

"Ifyougooutwalking," the Sheep Man called out as he departed, "makesureyoudon'tforgetthebell."

I headed straight back for the house as the Sheep Man disappeared into the woods to the east, the same as before. A winter-dark wordless green pasture stretched between us.

That afternoon I baked bread. The Rat's *Bread Baking* proved to be a thoughtfully written cookbook. On the cover was written: "If you can read, then you can bake bread." It was no exaggeration. The smell of bread filled the house, making it warm all over. For a fledgling effort, it didn't taste too bad either. There was plenty of flour and yeast in the kitchen, enough for bread the whole winter long, if it turned out I had to stay. And more rice and spaghetti than I cared to think about.

That evening, I had bread and salad and ham and eggs, with canned peaches for dessert.

The next morning I cooked rice and made a pilaf of canned salmon and seaweed and mushrooms.

For lunch, it was cheesecake from the freezer and strong milk tea.

At snacktime, I treated myself to hazelnut ice cream topped with Cointreau.

In the evening, broiled chicken and a can of Campbell's soup.

I was putting on weight again.

Early in the afternoon of the ninth day, as I was looking through the bookcase, I noticed one volume that seemed like it may have been read recently. It was the only one without dust on it, its spine protruding a bit farther out than the rest.

I pulled it out and sat on the chaise longue to flip through it. *The Heritage of Pan-Asianism.* A wartime edition. The paper was cheap and gave off a stink when I turned the pages. The contents, as expected from a wartime publication, terribly one-sided. Real boring too; stuff to yawn over every three pages. On some pages, words had been crossed out. There was not a single line on the February 26th Incident.

Tucked into the book, toward the end, was a sheet of white notepaper. After the yellowing pages, that white sheet came as some kind of miracle. It marked, on the right page, an addendum to the book. A list of names, birthdates, and permanent residences of all the so-called Pan-Asianists famous and unknown. I scanned the list from top to bottom, and there around the middle was the Boss. The very same "sheeped" Boss in whose name I had been brought here. His permanent residence, Hokkaido—Junitaki-cho.

In a daze, I set the book down in my lap. Words did not even form in my head. It was as if someone, or something, had given me a solid whack from behind.

How could I not have figured it out? It should have occurred to me first thing. The moment I learned that the Boss was from a poor farming background in Hokkaido I should have checked up on it. No matter how skillfully the Boss had managed to rub out his past, there would have been some way to search out the facts. That black-suited secretary would surely have looked it up for me.

Well no, maybe not.

I shook my head.

No way he wouldn't have looked that up himself. The man was not so careless. He would have checked every possible angle, complicated or not. Just as he had done his homework on me.

So he already knew everything.

That was indisputable. And yet, he had gone to great lengths to convince me, or rather to blackmail me, in order to get me up here. Why? If it was something that needed doing, surely he was in a better position to do it and to do a crack job of it. And if I were for some reason to be a pawn, why wouldn't he have told me the name of the place from the beginning?

As I sorted through my confusion, I started to get mad. More and more, this had turned into one grotesque comedy of mishaps, and I didn't think it was funny. How much did the Rat know? And while we're at it, how much did the man in the black suit know? Here I was, smack in the center of everything without a clue. At every turn, I'd been way off base, way off the mark. Of course, you could probably say the same thing about my whole life. In that sense, I suppose I had no one to blame. All the same, what gave them the right to treat me like this? I'd been used, I'd been beaten, I'd been wrung dry.

I was ready to get the hell off the mountain, but somehow that offered no satisfaction. I had gotten in too deep. It would have been so easy if only I could have cried. But crying wasn't an option, because I felt that far ahead of me there was something really worth crying about.

I went into the kitchen and got the bottle of whiskey. I could think of nothing to do but drink.

37

Things the Mirror Shows, Things the Mirror Doesn't

The morning of the tenth day, I decided to forget everything. I had already lost what I was supposed to lose.

In the middle of my morning run, it began to snow again. This time an opaque snow, a sticky, wet sleet edging toward ice flakes. Unlike the first loose snow, this one was nasty. It stuck to the body. I cut short my run, returned to the house, and drew a bath. While the bath was coming to temperature, I plunked myself down in front of the heater, but still I couldn't get warm. A damp chill had seeped into me. I couldn't bend my fingers and my ears burned and felt brittle, as if they would drop off any second. All over, my skin felt like cheap pulp paper.

A thirty-minute soak in the tub and hot tea with brandy finally brought my body back to normal, although for the next two hours I suffered from intermittent chills. So this was winter on the mountain.

The snow kept falling straight through until evening, covering the entire pasture in white. The snow let up just as night cloaked the world in darkness, and once again a profound hush drifted in like mist. A hush I could do nothing to deny. I put the record player on automatic repeat and listened to *White Christmas* twenty-six times.

The snow did not stick for long. As the Sheep Man had predicted, the ground would not freeze for a while yet. The following day, my eleventh, was bright and clear. The prodigal sun bided its time, leaving the pasture a patchwork of snow, which gleamed in the sunlight. The snow that had collected on the roof's gables came sliding down in would-be icebergs that broke up on the ground with an unnerving thud. Melting snow dripped outside the windows. Everything sparkled. Each droplet clinging to each tip of every oak leaf shone.

I dug my hands into my pockets and stood by the window, gazing out. There things unfolded entirely apart from me. Unrelated to my existence—unrelated to anybody's existence—everything was flowing. The snow fell, the snow melted.

I decided to do some housecleaning, accompanied by the sounds of snow dripping and tumbling. Holed up as I was on account of the snow, my body needed to do something; besides, wasn't I a guest in someone else's house? I have never been one to object to cleaning and cooking.

Still, cleaning a large house proved a lot harder work than I had imagined. Jogging ten miles was easy in comparison. I dusted every nook and cranny, then went around with the large vacuum cleaner to suck up the dust. I damp-mopped the wood floors, then got down on my hands and knees to wax them. It left me half out of breath, but thanks to having quit smoking, the other half of my breath managed to hold its own. None of that terrible rasping and catching in my throat.

I went into the kitchen for a glass of cold grape juice and finished straightening up what remained in one bout of cleaning before noon. I threw open the shutters, and the newly waxed floors glittered. There was a wonderful, nostalgic melding of the rich earthy scent of the country and the smell of the wax.

I washed out the rags I'd used to wax the floors, then put a pot of water on to boil. For the spaghetti, into which I mixed cod roe, plenty of butter, white wine, and soy sauce. A great lunch, complete with a woodpecker calling from the nearby woods.

I made short work of the spaghetti, washed up the dishes, then returned to the chores. I scrubbed the bathtub and washbasin, cleaned the toilet, polished the furniture. Thanks to the Rat, nothing was very dirty to begin with; a spray of furniture polish was about all that was needed. Next I pulled out a long hose and rinsed down the windows and shutters. With that, the whole house freshened up. After I washed the windows, my cleaning was done. I spent the remaining two hours before evening listening to records.

As I headed up to the Rat's room to borrow another book, I noticed the full-length mirror at the foot of the stairs. I'd overlooked it, and it was filthy. I wiped it down with a cloth, but no amount of wiping or glass cleaner would do the trick. I couldn't understand why the Rat would let this one mirror stay so dirty. I hauled over a bucket of warm water and worked on the mirror with a nylon scrub, cutting through the hardened grease. There was enough grime on the mirror to turn the bucket water black.

The crafted wooden frame told me it was an antique, probably worth a pretty sum, so I was careful not to work too enthusiastically.

The mirror reflected my image from head to toe, without warping, almost pristinely. I stood there and looked at myself. Nothing new. I was me, with my usual nothing-special expression. My image was unnecessarily sharp, however. I wasn't seeing my mirror-flat mirror-image. It wasn't myself I was seeing; on the contrary, it was as if I were the reflection of the mirror and this flat-me-of-an-image were seeing the real me. I brought my right hand up in front of my face and wiped my mouth. The me through the looking glass went through the same motions. But maybe it was only me copying what the me in the mirror had done. I couldn't be certain I'd wiped my mouth out of my own free will.

I filed the word "free will" away in my head and pinched my ear with my left hand. The me in the mirror did exactly the same. Apparently he had filed the word "free will" away in his head the same as I had.

I gave up and left the mirror. He also left the mirror.

On the twelfth day, snow fell for the third time. It was snowing before I woke up. An awfully silent snow, this one neither hard nor sticky wet. Pirouetting down slowly from the sky, melting before it amounted to anything. The kind of tranquil snow that makes you close your eyes, gently.

I pulled the old guitar out of the trunk room and, after tuning it with great difficulty, tried my hand at some old tunes. I practiced along with Benny Goodman's "Air Mail Special," and soon it was noontime. I made a sandwich of thick slices of ham on my home-made, already rock-hard bread, and opened a can of beer. After thirty minutes more of guitar practice, who should show up but the Sheep Man.

"IfIbotheryouI'llleave," said the Sheep Man through the open front door.

"No, not at all. I was getting kind of bored anyway," I said, setting the guitar on the floor.

The Sheep Man whacked the mud off his boots the same as

before, then came in. His body seemed to have filled out his thick sheep costume. He sat on the sofa opposite me, hand on the armrest and snuggled into position.

"It's not going to stick yet?" I asked.

"Notyet," answered the Sheep Man. "There'ssnowthatsticksand snowthatdoesn't.Thisisnonsticksnow."

"Hmm."

"Thestickingsnowcomesnextweek."

"Care for a beer?"

"Thanks.ButI'dreallyratherhaveabrandy."

I went to the kitchen, got him his brandy and me a beer, and carried it all back into the living room together with a cheese sandwich.

"Youwereplayingguitar," said the Sheep Man with interest. "Welikemusictoo.Can'tplayanyinstrumentthough."

"Neither can I. Haven't played in close to ten years."

"That'sokayawplaysomethingforme."

I didn't want to dampen the Sheep Man's spirits, so I played through the melody of "Air Mail Special," tacked on one chorus and an ad lib, then lost count of the bars and threw in the towel.

"You'regood," said the Sheep Man in all seriousness. "Proba blyloadsoffuntoplayaninstrumenteh?"

"If you're good. But if you want to get good, you have to train your ears. And when you've trained your ears, you get depressed at your own playing."

"Nahc'monreally?" said the Sheep Man.

The Sheep Man took dainty little sips from his brandy snifter, while I drank my beer from the can.

"Iwasn'tabletopassonyourmessage," said the Sheep Man.

I nodded.

"That'sallIcametosay."

I glanced over at the calendar on the wall. Only three more days until the time limit, the date marked in red. But what did that mean anymore?

"Things have changed," I spoke up. "I'm very, very angry. Never in my entire life have I been angry like this."

The Sheep Man sat there, snifter in hand, and said nothing.

I picked up the guitar by the neck and smashed it back against the bricks of the fireplace. With the crash came a loud, cacophonous twang of strings. The Sheep Man flew out of the sofa, his ears trembling.

"I've got a right to be angry," I said, addressing this fact rather to my own attention. Well, I did have the right to be angry.

"IfeelbadthatIcouldn'tcomeacrossforyou.Butyoumustunderstand. Wereallydolikeyou."

The two of us stood there. We looked at the snow. The snow was fluffy, like stuffing spilling out of a torn cloud.

I went into the kitchen for another beer. Each time I walked past the stairs, there was the mirror. The other me had apparently gone for another beer too. We looked each other in the face and sighed. Living in two separate worlds, we still thought about the same things. Just like Groucho and Harpo in *Duck Soup*.

Behind me the living room was reflected in the mirror. Or else it was his living room behind him. The living room behind me and the living room behind him were the same living room. Same sofa, same carpet, same clock and painting and bookcase, every last thing the same. Not particularly uncomfortable as living rooms go, if not in the finest taste. Yet something was different. Or maybe it was simply that I felt that something was different.

I grabbed another blue Löwenbrau and on the way back to the

living room, can in hand, I looked once more at the living room in the mirror, then looked over at the living room. The Sheep Man was on the sofa, lazily gazing out at the snow.

I checked the Sheep Man in the mirror. But there wasn't any Sheep Man in the mirror! There was nobody in the living room at all, only an empty sofa. In the mirror world, I was alone. Terror shot through my spine.

"Youlookpale," said the Sheep Man.

I plopped down on the sofa and, saying nothing, pulled the ring off the beer can and took a sip.

"Probablycaughtcold.Winterinthesepartscangettoyouifyou're notusedtoit.Air'sdamptoo.Youshouldgettobedearlytoday."

"Nope," I said. "Today I'm not going to sleep. I'm going to wait up for my friend here."

"Youknowhe'scomingtoday?"

"I know," I said. "He'll be here tonight at ten o'clock."

The Sheep Man looked up at me. The eyes peering through his mask had literally no expression.

"Tonight I'll pack, tomorrow I'll be gone. If you see him, tell him that. I don't think it'll be necessary, though."

The Sheep Man nodded comprehendingly. "Surewillbelonely whenyougo.Can'tbehelpedthoughIguess.BythewaycanIhavethat cheesesandwich?"

"Sure."

The Sheep Man wrapped the sandwich in a paper napkin, slipped it into his pocket, then put on his gloves.

"Hopewemeetagain," said the Sheep Man as he was leaving.

"We will," I said.

The Sheep Man left across the pasture to the east. Eventually, the veil of snow took him in. Afterward all was silent.

I poured an inch of brandy into the Sheep Man's snifter and downed it in one swallow. My throat burned, and gradually my stomach burned, but after thirty seconds my body stopped trembling. Only the ticking of the grandfather clock pounding inside my head.

Probably I did need to get some sleep.

I fetched a blanket from upstairs and slept on the sofa. I felt totally exhausted, like a child who'd been wandering around in the woods for three days. I closed my eyes and the next instant I was asleep.

I had a terrifying dream. A dream too terrifying to recall.

38

And So Time Passes

Darkness crept in through my ear like oil. Someone was trying to break up the frozen globe of the earth with a massive hammer. The hammer struck the earth precisely eight times. But the earth failed to break up. It only cracked a little.

Eight o'clock, eight at night.

I woke with a shake of the head. My body was numb, my head ached. Had someone put me in a cocktail shaker with cracked ice and like a madman shaken me up?

There's nothing worse than waking up in total darkness. It's like having to go back and live life all over from the beginning. When I first opened my eyes, it was as if I were living someone else's life. After an extremely long time, this began to match up with my own life. A curious overlap this, my own life as someone else's. It was improbable that such a person as myself could even be living.

I went to the kitchen sink and splashed water on my face, then drank down a couple of glasses quickly. The water was as cold as ice, but still my face was burning hot. I sat back down on the sofa amid the darkness and silence and began gradually to gather up the pieces of my life. I couldn't manage to grasp too much, but at least it was my life. Slowly I returned to myself. It's hard to explain what it is to get there, and it'd undoubtedly try your interest.

I had the feeling that someone was watching me, but I didn't pay it any mind. It's a feeling you get when you're all alone in a big room.

I thought about cells. Like my ex-wife had said, ultimately every last cell of you is lost. Lost even to yourself. I pressed the palm of my hand against my cheek. The face my hand felt in the dark wasn't my own, I didn't think. It was the face of another that had taken the shape of my face. But I couldn't remember the details. Everything—names, sensations, places—dissolved and was swallowed into the darkness.

In the dark the clock struck eight-thirty. The snow had stopped, but thick clouds still covered the sky. No light anywhere. For a long time, I lay buried in the sofa, fingers in my mouth. I couldn't see my hand. The heater was off, so the room was cold. Curled up under the blanket, I stared blankly out. I was crouching in the bottom of a deep well.

Time. Particles of darkness configured mysterious patterns on my retina. Patterns that degenerated without a sound, only to be replaced by new patterns. Darkness but darkness alone was shifting, like mercury in motionless space.

I put a stop to my thoughts and let time pass. Let time carry me along. Carry me to where a new darkness was configuring yet newer patterns.

The clock struck nine. As the ninth chime faded away, silence slipped in to fill its place.

"May I say my piece?" said the Rat.

"Fine by me," said I.

39

Dwellers in Darkness

"Fine by me," said I.

"I came an hour earlier than the appointed time," said the Rat apologetically.

"That's okay. As you can see, I wasn't doing anything."

The Rat laughed quietly. He was behind me. Almost as if we were back-to-back.

"Seems like the old days," said the Rat.

"I guess we can never get down to a good honest talk unless we've got time on our hands," I said.

"It sure seems that way." The Rat smiled.

Even in absolute lacquer-black darkness, seated back-to-back, I could tell he was smiling. You can tell a lot just by the tiniest change in the air. We used to be friends. So long ago, though I could hardly remember when.

"Didn't someone once say, 'A friend to kill time is a friend sublime'?"

"That was you who said that, no?"

"Sixth sense, sharp as ever. Right you are."

I sighed. "But this time around, with all this happening, my sixth sense has been way off. So far off it's embarrassing. And despite the number of hints you all have been giving me."

"Can't be helped. You did better than most."

We fell silent. The Rat seemed to be looking at his hand.

"I really made you go through a lot, didn't I?" said the Rat. "I was a real pain. But it was the only way. There wasn't another soul I could depend on. Like I wrote in those letters."

"That's what I want to ask you about. Because I can't accept everything just like that."

"Of course not," said the Rat, "not without my setting the record straight. But before that, let's have a beer."

The Rat stopped me before I could stand up.

"I'll get it," said the Rat. "This is my house, after all."

I heard the Rat walk his regular path to the kitchen in total darkness and take an armful of beer out of the refrigerator, me opening and closing my eyes the whole while. The darkness of the room was only a bit different in hue from the darkness of my eyes shut.

The Rat returned with his beer, which he set on the table. I felt around for a can, removed the pull ring, and drank half.

"It hardly seems like beer if you can't see it," I said.

"You have to forgive me, but it has to be dark."

We said nothing while we drank.

"Well then," said the Rat, clearing his throat. I set my empty back on the table and kept still, wrapped in my blanket. I waited for him to start talking, but no words followed. All I could hear was the Rat shaking his can to check how much was left. Old habit of his.

"Well then," said the Rat a second time. Then downing the last of his beer in one chug, he set the can back on the table with a dry clank. "First of all, let's begin with why I came here. Is that all right?"

I didn't answer. The Rat continued to speak.

"My father bought this place when I was five. Just why he went out of his way to buy property up here I don't know. Probably he got a good deal through some American military route. As you can see, the place is terribly inconvenient to get to and, aside from summer, the road is useless once the snow sets in. The Occupation Forces had planned on improving the road and using the place for a radar station or something, but the time and expense involved apparently changed their mind. And with the town being so poor, they can't afford to do anything about the road. It wouldn't help them to upgrade the road either. Which all makes this property a losing proposition, long since forgotten."

"How about the Sheep Professor? Wouldn't he be thinking to come back home here?"

"The Sheep Professor is living in his memories. He's got nowhere to go home to."

"Maybe not."

"Have some more beer," said the Rat.

"Fine for now," I said. With the heater off, I was nearly frozen through. The Rat opened another can and drank by himself.

"My father took a liking to this property, carried out some road improvements on his own, fixed up the house. He put a lot of money into it, I believe. Thanks to which, if you had a car, you could lead a fairly good life here, at least during the summer. Heat, flush toilet, shower, telephone, emergency electrical generator. How on earth the Sheep Professor lived here before that, I don't know."

The Rat made a noise that was neither belch nor sigh.

"Until I was fifteen, we came here every summer. My folks, my sister and me, and the maid who did the chores. When I think of it, those were probably the best years of my life. We leased the pasture to the town—still do, in fact—so when summer rolled around, the place was full of the town's sheep. Sheep up to your ears. That's why my memories of summer are always tied up with sheep.

"After that, the family almost never came up here. We got another vacation house closer to home for one thing, and my sister got married for another. I wasn't counting myself in the family much anymore, my father's company was going through hard times, and well, all sorts of things were going on. Whatever, the property was abandoned. The last time I came up here was eleven years ago. And that time I came alone. By myself for a month."

The Rat lingered for a second, as if he were remembering.

"Were you lonely?" I asked.

"Me, lonely? You got to be kidding. If it was possible, I would have stayed on up here. But no way that could have happened. It's my father's house, after all. You wouldn't have caught me doing my old man the service."

"But what about now?"

"The same goes," said the Rat. "I got to say that this was the last place I wanted to come back to. Yet when I came across the photograph of this place in the Dolphin Hotel, I wanted to see it one more time. For sentimental reasons. Even you get that way at times, don't you?"

"Yeah," I said. There was my shoreline that got filled in.

"That's when I heard the Sheep Professor's story. About the dream sheep with a star on its back. You know about that, I take it?"

"Indeed I do."

"So to put it simply," said the Rat, "I heard that story and hurried up here wanting to spend the whole winter. I couldn't shake the urge. Father or not, it didn't matter to me anymore. I pulled together my kit and came up. Like I was being drawn up here."

"That's when you ran into the sheep?"

"That's right," said the Rat.

"What happened after that is difficult to talk about," said the Rat.

The Rat took his second empty can and squeezed a dent into it.

"Maybe you could ask me questions? You already know pretty much what there is to know, right?"

"Okay, but if it makes no difference to you, let's not start at the beginning."

"Fire away."

"You're already dead, aren't you?"

I don't know how long it took the Rat to reply. Could have been a few seconds, could have been . . . It was a long silence. My mouth was all dry inside.

"That's right," said the Rat finally. "I'm dead."

40

The Rat Who Wound the Clock

"I hanged myself from a beam in the kitchen," said the Rat. "The Sheep Man buried me next to the garage. Dying itself wasn't all that painful, if you worry about that sort of thing. But really, that hardly matters."

"When?"

"A week before you got here."

"You wound the clock then, didn't you?"

The Rat laughed. "Damn, if that's not a mystery. I mean the very, very last thing I did in my thirty-year life was to wind a clock. Now why should anyone who's about to die wind a clock? Makes no sense."

The Rat stopped speaking, and everything was still, except for the ticking of the clock. The snow absorbed all other sound. We were like two castaways in outer space.

"What if . . ."

"Stop it," the Rat cut me short. "There are no more ifs. You know that, right?"

I shook my head. No, I didn't.

"If you had come here a week earlier, I still would have died. Maybe we could've met under warmer, brighter circumstances. But it's all the same. I would have had to die. Otherwise things would have only gotten harder. And I guess I didn't want to bear that kind of hardship."

"So why did you have to die?"

There was the sound of his rubbing the palms of his hands together.

"I don't want to talk too much about that. It would only turn into a self-acquittal. And there's nothing more inappropriate than a dead man coming to his own defense, don't you think?"

"But if you don't tell me, I'll never know."

"Have some more beer."

"I'm cold," I said.

"It's not that cold."

With trembling hands, I opened another beer and drank a sip. And with the drink in me, it really didn't seem as cold.

"Okay, if you promise not to tell this to anyone."

"Even if I did tell someone, who'd believe me?"

"You got me there," said the Rat with a chuckle. "I doubt anyone would believe it. It's so crazy."

The clock struck nine-thirty.

"Mind if I stop the clock?" asked the Rat. "It makes such a racket."

"Help yourself. It's your clock."

The Rat stood up, opened the door to the grandfather clock, and grabbed the pendulum. All sound, all time, vanished.

"What happened was this," said the Rat. "I died with the sheep in me. I waited until the sheep was fast asleep, then I tied a rope over the beam in the kitchen and hanged myself. There wasn't enough time for the sucker to escape."

"Did you have to go that far?"

"Yes, I had to go that far. If I waited, the sheep would have controlled me absolutely. It was my last chance."

The Rat rubbed his palms together again. "I wanted to meet you when I was myself, with everything squared away. My own self with my own memories and my own weaknesses. That's why I sent you that photograph as a kind of code. If by some accident it steered you this way, I thought I would be saved in the end."

"And have you been saved?"

"Yeah, I've been saved all right," said the Rat, quietly.

"The key point here is weakness," said the Rat. "Everything begins from there. Can you understand what I'm getting at?"

"People are weak."

"As a general rule," said the Rat, snapping his fingers a couple of times. "But line up all the generalities you like and you still won't get anywhere. What I'm talking about now is a very individual thing. Weakness is something that rots in the body. Like gangrene. I've felt that ever since I was a teenager. That's why I was always on edge. There's this something inside you that's rotting away and you feel it all along. Can you understand what that's like?"

I sat silent, wrapped up in the blanket.

"Probably not," the Rat continued. "There isn't that side to you. But, well, anyway, that's weakness. It's the same as a hereditary disease, weakness. No matter how much you understand it, there's nothing you can do to cure yourself. It's not going to go away with a clap of the hand. It just keeps getting worse and worse."

"Weakness toward what?"

"Everything. Moral weakness, weakness of consciousness, then there's the weakness of existence itself."

I laughed. This time the laugh came off. "You start talking like that and there's not a human alive who isn't weak."

"Enough generalities. Like I said before. Of course, it goes without saying that everybody has his weaknesses. But real weakness is as rare as real strength. You don't know the weakness that is ceaselessly dragging you under into darkness. You don't know that such a thing actually exists in the world. Your generalities don't cover everything, you know."

I could say nothing.

"That's why I left town. I didn't want others to see me sinking any lower. Traveling around alone in unknown territory, at least I wouldn't cause problems for anyone. And ultimately . . . ," the Rat trailed off for a bit.

"Ultimately, because of this weakness, I couldn't escape the specter of the sheep. There was nothing I myself could do about it. Probably even if you had shown up at the time, I wouldn't have been able to do anything about it. Even if I'd made up my mind to go down from the mountain, it would have been the same. I probably still would have come back up in the end. That's what weakness is."

"What did the sheep want of you?"

"Everything. The whole lock, stock, and barrel. My body, my memory, my weakness, my contradictions . . . That's the sort of stuff the sheep really goes for. The bastard's got all sorts of feelers. It sticks them down your ears and nose like straws and sucks you dry. Gives me the creeps even now."

"And for what in return?"

"Things far too good for the likes of me. Not that the sheep got around to showing me anything in real form. All I ever saw was one tiny slice of the pie. And . . ."

The Rat trailed off again.

"And it was enough to draw me in. More than I'd care to confess. It's not something I can explain in words. It's like, well, like a blast furnace that smelts down everything it touches. A thing of such beauty, it drives you out of your mind. But it's hair-raising evil. Give your body over to it and everything goes. Consciousness, values, emotions, pain, everything. Gone. What it comes closest to is a dynamo manifesting the vital force at the root of all life in one solitary point of the universe."

"Yet you were able to reject it."

"Yes. Everything was buried along with my body. There remains only one last thing to do in order to see it buried forever."

"One last thing?"

"One last thing. And that I have to ask you to do. But let's not talk about it now."

We both took sips of beer. I was warming up.

"The blood cyst works kind of like a whip, doesn't it?" I asked. "For the sheep to manipulate the host."

"Exactly. Once that forms, there's no escaping the sheep."

"So what on earth was the Boss after, doing what he was doing?"

"He went mad. He probably couldn't take the heat of that blast furnace. The sheep used him to build up a supreme power base. That's why the sheep entered him. He was, in a word, disposable. The man was zero as a thinker, after all."

"So when the Boss died, you were earmarked to take over that power base."

"I'm afraid so."

"And what lay ahead after that?"

"A realm of total conceptual anarchy. A scheme in which all opposites would be resolved into unity. With me and the sheep at the center."

"So why did you reject it?"

Time trailed off into death. And over this dead time, a silent snow was falling.

"I guess I felt attached to my weakness. My pain and suffering too. Summer light, the smell of a breeze, the sound of cicadas—if I like these things, why should I apologize. The same with having a beer with you . . ." The Rat swallowed his words. "I don't know why."

What could I say.

"Somehow or other, we have created two completely different entities out of the same ingredients," said the Rat. "Do you believe the world is getting better?"

"Better or worse, who can tell?"

The Rat laughed. "I swear, in the kingdom of generalities, you could be *imperius rex*."

"Sheeplessly."

"You bet, sheeplessly." The Rat threw back his third beer in one chug, then clunked the empty can down on the floor.

"You'd better be heading down the mountain as soon as you can. Before you get snowed in. You don't want to spend the whole winter here. Another four, maybe five days, the snow'll start to collect, and listen, it's a real trick traveling down frozen mountain roads."

"And what will you do from now on?"

The Rat let go a good, jolly laugh from off in the dark. "For me there is no 'from now on.' I just fade away over the winter. How long it takes depends on how long this one winter is. I don't know. But one winter is one winter. I'm glad I got to see you. A brighter, warmer place would have been nicer, of course."

"J sends his regards."

"Give him my regards, too, would you?"

"I also saw her."

"How was she?"

"All right. Still working for the same firm."

"Then she's not married?"

"No. She wanted to hear directly from you whether it was over or not."

"It's over," said the Rat, "as you know. Even if I was unable to end it on my own, the fact is it's over. My life had no meaning. Of course, to borrow upon your venerable generalities, this is to say that everyone's life has no meaning. Am I right?"

"So be it," I said. "Just two last questions."

"Okay."

"First, about our Sheep Man."

"The Sheep Man's a good guy."

"But the Sheep Man, the one who came visiting here, was you, right?"

The Rat rolled his neck around to crack it a couple of times. "Right. I took his form. So you could tell, could you?"

"Midway on," I said. "Up until then, though, I had no idea."

"To be absolutely honest, you surprised me, breaking the guitar. It was the first time I'd seen you so angry, and what's more, that was the first guitar I ever bought. A cheapie, but still . . ."

"Sorry about that. I was only trying to shake you up enough to show yourself."

"That's all right. Come tomorrow, everything'll be gone anyway," said the Rat dryly. "So now your other question is about your girlfriend, right?"

"Right."

The Rat said nothing for a long while. I could hear him rub his palms together and sigh. "I didn't want to deal with her. She was an extra factor I hadn't counted on."

"An extra factor?"

"Uh-huh. I meant this to be an in-group party. But she stumbled into the middle of it. We should never have allowed her to get mixed up in this. As you know very well, the girl's got amazing powers. Still, she wasn't meant to come here. The place is far beyond even her powers."

"What happened to her?"

"She's okay. Perfectly well," said the Rat. "Only there's nothing that you'd find attractive in her anymore. Sad, but that's how it is."

"How's that?"

"It's gone. Evaporated. Whatever it was she had, it's not there anymore."

I couldn't bring myself to say anything.

"I know how you must feel," continued the Rat. "But sooner or later, it was bound to disappear. Me and you, these girls with their certain somethings, we've all got to go sometime."

I thought about his words.

"I better be going," said the Rat. "It's getting on time. But we'll meet again, I just know it."

"Sure thing," I said.

"Preferably somewhere brighter, maybe in summer," said the Rat. "But for now, one last request. Tomorrow morning at nine, I want you to set the grandfather clock, then connect the cords behind the clock. Connect the green cord to the green cord and the red cord to the red cord. Then at nine-thirty I want you to get the hell out of here and go down the mountain. I've got a rendezvous with a fellow at twelve o'clock sharp. Got it?"

"Good as done."

"Glad I got to see you."

A moment's pause came between us.

"Goodbye," said the Rat.

"See you," said I.

Still snug in the blanket, I closed my eyes and listened. The Rat's shoes scuffed across the floor, the door opened. Freezing cold air entered the room. Not a breeze, but a slow-spreading, sinking chill.

The Rat stood in the open doorway for a moment. He seemed to be staring at something, not the scenery outside, not the room interior, not me, some completely other thing. The doorknob or the tip of his shoe, something. Then, as if closing the door of time, the door swung shut with a click.

Afterward all was silent. There was nothing else left but silence.

41

Green Cords and Red Cords; Frozen Seagulls

After the Rat disappeared, an unbearable cold spread throughout the house. I tried to throw up, but nothing would come, only gasps of stale breath.

I went upstairs, took off my sweater, and burrowed under the covers. I was swept by alternating waves of chills and fever. With each wave the room would swell and contract. My blanket and underwear were soaked in sweat, which congealed into a cold, constricting skin.

"Wind the clock at nine," someone whispers in my ear. "Green cord to green cord . . . red cord to red cord . . . get the hell out by nine-thirty."

"Don'tworry," says the Sheep Man. "It'llgofine."

"The cells replace themselves," says my ex-wife. She is holding a white lace slip in her right hand.

My head rocks.

Red cord to red cord . . . green cord to green cord . . .

"You don't understand a thing, do you?" accuses my girlfriend.

No, I don't understand a thing.

There comes the sound of waves. Heavy winter waves. A lead-gray sea specked with whitecaps. Frozen seagulls.

I am in the airtight exhibition room of the aquarium. Row upon row of whales' penises on display. It's hot and stuffy. Someone better open a window.

Someone opens a window. Shivering cold. Seagull cries, sharp piercing voices ripping at my flesh.

"Remember the name of your cat?"

"Kipper," I reply.

"No, it's not Kipper," the chauffeur says. "The name's already changed. Names change all the time. I bet you can't even remember your own name."

Shivering cold. And seagulls, far too many seagulls.

"Mediocrity walks a long, hard path," says the man in the black suit. "Green cord via red cord, red cord via green cord."

"Heardanythingaboutthewar?" asks the Sheep Man.

The Benny Goodman Orchestra strikes up "Air Mail Special." Charlie Christian takes a long solo. He is wearing a soft cream-colored hat.

42

Return Visit to the Unlucky Bend

Birds were singing.

Sunlight spilled in stripes across the bed from between the shutter slats. My watch lying on the floor read 7:35. My blanket and shirt were as wet as if they'd been soaked in a bucket of water.

My head was still fuzzy, but the fever had gone. Outside, the world was a snowswept landscape. The pasture gleamed positively silver in the new morning light. I went downstairs and took a hot shower. My face was pale, my cheeks stripped of their flesh overnight. I coated my entire face with three times the necessary amount of shaving cream, and I proceeded to shave methodically. Then I went and pissed so much I could hardly believe it myself.

I was so exhausted from the piss that I collapsed on the chaise longue for fifteen minutes. The birds kept on singing. The snow had begun to melt and drip from the eaves. Occasionally in the background there'd be a sharp creaking.

It was almost on eight-thirty by the time I got up. I drank two glasses of grape juice, ate a whole apple. Then I picked out a bottle of wine, a large Hershey bar, and two more apples from the cellar.

I packed my things. The room took on a forlorn air. Everything was coming to an end.

Checking with my watch, at nine o'clock I wound up the three weights of the grandfather clock. Then I slid the heavy timepiece around and connected the four cords behind. Green cord to green cord, red cord to red cord.

The cords came out of four holes drilled in the back. One pair above, one pair below. The cords were secured with twists of the same wire I'd seen in the jeep. I pushed the grandfather clock back in place, then went to the mirror and bid farewell to myself.

"Hope all goes well," I said.

"Hope all goes well," the other I said.

I crossed the middle of the pasture the same way as I had come. The snow crunched beneath my feet. The pasture looked like a silver volcanic lake. Not a footprint anywhere. Only mine which, when I turned around, led back in a trail to the house. My tracks meandered all over the place. It's not easy to walk in a straight line.

From this far off, the house looked almost like a living thing. Cramped and hunched over, it twisted to shake the snow down from its gabled roof. A block of snow slid off the roof and dashed to the ground with a thud.

I kept walking across the pasture. On through the endless birch woods, across the bridge, around the base of the conical peak, onto the unlucky bend in the road.

Miraculously, the snow on the curve had not frozen to the road. No matter, I was sure that as carefully as I stepped, I would get dragged to the bottom of that sheer drop. It was an effort just to keep walking until I cleared that curved ledge clinging to the crumbling cliff face. My armpits were soaked with sweat. A regular childhood nightmare.

Off to the right were the flatlands. They too were covered in snow, the Junitaki River glistening right down the middle. I thought I could hear a steam whistle in the distance. It was marvelous, actually.

I took a breath and hitched up my backpack, then set off down the gentle slope. At the next bend was a brand-new jeep. In front of the jeep, the Boss's black-suited secretary.

43

The Twelve-O'clock Rendezvous

"I have been waiting for you," said the man in the black suit. "Albeit only for twenty minutes."

"How'd you know?"

"The place? Or the time?"

"The time," I said, setting down my backpack.

"How do you think I got to be the Boss's secretary? Diligence? IQ? Tact? No. I am the Boss's secretary because of my special capacities. Sixth sense. I believe that's what you would call it."

He was wearing a beige down jacket over ski pants and green Ray-Ban glasses.

"We used to have many things in common, the Boss and I. Things that reached beyond rationality and logic and morality."

"Used to?"

"The Boss died a week ago. We had a beautiful funeral. All Tokyo is turned upside down now, trying to decide a successor. The whole mediocre lot of them running around like fools."

I sighed. The man took a silver cigarette case out of his jacket pocket, removed a plain-cut cigarette, and lit up.

"Smoke?"

"No thanks," I said.

"But I must say you did your stuff. Much more than I expected. Honestly, you surprised me. At first, I thought I might have to help you along and give you hints when you got stuck. Which makes your coming across the Sheep Professor an even greater stroke of genius. I almost wish you would consider working for me."

"So I take it you knew about this place here from the very beginning?"

"Naturally. Come now, who do you think I am?"

"May I ask you something, then?"

"Certainly," said the man, in top spirits. "But keep it short."

"Why didn't you tell me right from the start?"

"I wanted you to come all this way spontaneously of your own free will. And I wanted you to lure him out of his lair."

"Lair?"

"His mental lair. When a person becomes sheeped, he is temporarily dazed out of his mind and goes into retreat. As with, say, shell shock. It was your role to coax him out of that state. Yet in order for him to trust you, you had to be a blank slate, as it were. Simple enough, is it not?"

"Quite."

"Lay out the seeds and everything is simple. Constructing the program was the hard part. Computers can't account for human error, after all. So much for handiwork. Ah, but it is a pleasure second to none, seeing one's painstakingly constructed program move along exactly according to plan."

I shrugged.

"Well then," the man continued, "our wild sheep chase is drawing to a close. Thanks to my calculations and your innocence. I've got him right where I want him. True?"

"So it would seem," I said. "He's waiting for you up there. Says you've got a rendezvous at twelve o'clock sharp."

The man and I glanced at our watches simultaneously. Ten-forty.

"I had better be going," the man said. "Must not keep him waiting. You may ride down in the jeep, if you wish. Oh yes, here is your recompense."

The man reached into his pocket and handed me a check. I pocketed it without looking at it.

"Should you not examine it?"

"I don't believe there's any need."

The man laughed, visibly amused. "It has been a pleasure to do business with you. And by the way, your partner closed down your company. Regrettable. It had such promise too. There is a bright future for the advertising industry. You should go into it on your own."

"You must be crazy," I said.

"We shall meet again, I expect," said the man. And he set off on foot around the curve toward the highlands.

"Kipper's doing fine," said the chauffeur, as he drove the jeep down. "Gotten nice and fat."

I took the seat next to the chauffeur. He was a different person than the man who drove that monster of a limo. He told me in considerable detail about the Boss's funeral and about his Kipper-sitting, but I hardly heard a word.

It was eleven-thirty when the jeep pulled up in front of the station. The town was dead still. Except for an old man shoveling away the snow from the rotary and a gangly dog sitting nearby wagging its tail.

"Thanks," I told the chauffeur.

"Don't mention it," he said. "By the way, have you tried God's telephone number?"

"No, I haven't had time."

"Since the Boss died, I can't get through. What do you suppose happened?"

"Probably just busy," I suggested.

"Maybe so," said the chauffeur. "Well now, take care."

"Goodbye," I said.

There was a train leaving at twelve o'clock sharp. Not a soul on the platform. On board only four passengers, including myself. Even so, it was a relief to see people after so long. One way or another, I'd made it back to the land of the living. No matter how boring or mediocre it might be, this was my world.

The departure bell sounded as I chewed on my chocolate bar. Then, as the ringing stopped and the train clanked into readiness, there came the sound of a distant explosion. I lifted the window all the way open and stuck my head out. Ten seconds later there was a second explosion. The train started moving. After three minutes, in the direction of the conical peak, a column of black smoke was slowly rising.

I stared at it until the train cut a curve to the right and the smoke was out of sight.

Epilogue

"It's all over," said the Sheep Professor, "all over."

"Over and done."

"I suppose I should thank you."

"Now that I've lost practically everything."

"No, you haven't," the Sheep Professor shook his head. "You've got your life."

"As you say," I said.

The Sheep Professor threw himself facedown on his desk, sobbing, as I left the room. I had robbed him of his obsession, woeful though it had been, and whether I was right to have done it, I was never more unsure.

"She departed for somewhere," said the proprietor of the Dolphin Hotel. "She made no mention of any destination. She seemed kind of sick."

"Never mind," I said.

I picked up the bags and checked into the same room as before. With the same view of the same unfathomable company. The woman with the big breasts was nowhere to be seen. Two young male employees worked at their desks, smoking. One was reading lists of figures, one was drawing a broken-line graph with a ruler on a huge sheet of paper. Maybe it was because the big-breasted woman wasn't there, but the office seemed like a wholly different place. Only the fact that I couldn't figure out what kind of company it was remained the same. At six o'clock, all employees exited, and the building grew dark.

I turned on the television and watched the news. There was no report of any explosion on any mountain. But wait, did that explosion happen yesterday? What on earth had I done for one whole day? Where had I been? My brain throbbed.

Well, one day had passed in any case.

In just this way, one day at a time, I learned to distance myself from "memory." Until that day in the uncertain future when a distant voice calls from out of the lacquer blackness.

I switched off the television and toppled over onto the bed with my shoes still on. All alone, I stared up at the stain-blotched ceiling. Reminders of persons long dead and forgotten.

The room changed colors to the pulse of neon lights. My watch ticked away by my ear. I undid the band and tossed it onto the floor. Traffic sounds came in soft chorus, layer upon layer. I tried to sleep, but without success. Who can sleep with such inexpressibleness?

I donned a sweater and headed out to town, stepping into the first discotheque I happened upon. I had three whiskeys-on-the-rocks while taking in the non-stop soul music. That helped give me a sense of the normal. And getting back to normal was everything. Everybody was counting on me to be normal.

Returning to the Dolphin Hotel, I found the three-fingered proprietor sitting on the chaise longue, watching the late night news.

"I'll be leaving tomorrow morning at nine," I said.

"Back to Tokyo, is it?"

"No," I said. "I have one place to stop off before that. Wake me at eight, please."

"Okay," he said.

"Thanks for everything."

"Don't mention it." Then the proprietor let out a sigh. "Father refuses to eat. At this rate, he'll die."

"He took a great blow."

"I know," said the proprietor sadly. "Not that my father ever tells me anything."

"Give it time."

The following day I took a plane to Tokyo-Haneda, then flew off again. The sea was shining when I arrived at my destination.

J was peeling potatoes the same as ever. A young female part-timer was filling flower vases and wiping off the tables. Hokkaido had lost its autumn, but autumn still held on here. Through the windows of J's Bar, the hills were in beautiful color.

I sat at the counter and had a beer before the bar opened. Cracking peanuts with one hand.

"It's hard to come by peanuts that crack so nice and crisp," said J.

"Oh?" I said, nibbling away.

"So tell me, no vacation still?"

"I quit."

"Quit?"

"It's a long story."

J finished peeling the potatoes, then dumped them into a large colander to rinse. "What will you do from here on?"

"Don't know. I've got some severance money coming, plus my

half of the sale of the business. Not much really. And then there's this."

I pulled the check out of my pocket and passed it over to J, amount unseen. J looked at it and shook his head.

"This is unbelievable money, unbelievable."

"You said it."

"But it's a long story, right?"

I laughed. "Let me leave it with you. Put it in the shop safe."

"Where would I have a safe here?"

"How about the cash register?"

"I'll put it in my safe-deposit box at the bank," said J worriedly. "But what do you plan to do with it?"

"Say, J, it took a lot of money to move to this new location, didn't it?"

"That it did."

"Loans?"

"Real big ones."

"Will that check pay off those loans?"

"With change to spare. But . . ."

"How about it? What say you take on the Rat and me as copartners? No worry about dividends or interest. A partnership in name is fine."

"But I couldn't do that."

"Sure you could. All you got to do in return is take in the Rat and me whenever one of us gets into a fix."

"That's no different than what I've done all along."

Beer glass in hand, I looked J in the face. "I know. But that's how I want it."

J laughed and shoved the check into his pocket. "I still remember the very first time you got drunk. How many years ago was that now?"

"Thirteen."

"Already?"

J talked about old times the next half hour, something he rarely did. Customers began to filter in, and I got up to leave.

"But you only just got here," said J.

"The well-mannered child doesn't overstay," said I.

"Did you see the Rat?"

I took a deep breath, both hands on the counter. "I saw him all right."

"That a long story too?"

"A longer story than you've ever heard in your whole life."

"Can't you give me the highlights?"

"Highlights wouldn't mean anything."

"Was he well?"

"Fine. He wished he could see you."

"Do you suppose I'll get to see him sometime?"

"You'll get to see him. He's a co-partner, after all. That's money the Rat and I earned."

"Well then, I'm glad."

I stepped down from the barstool and took a whiff of the old place.

"Oh, and as I'm a co-partner, how about a pinball machine and jukebox?"

"I'll have them here by your next visit," said J.

I walked along the river to its mouth. I sat down on the last fifty yards of beach, and I cried. I never cried so much in my life.

I brushed the sand from my trousers and got up, as if I had somewhere to go.

The day had all but ended. I could hear the sound of waves as I started to walk.

ALSO BY HARUKI MURAKAMI

BLIND WILLOW, SLEEPING WOMAN

This superb collection of stories generously express Murakami's mastery of the form. Here are animated crows, a criminal monkey, and an ice man, as well as the dreams that shape us and the things we might wish for. Whether during a chance reunion in Italy, a romantic exile in Greece, or in the grip of everyday life, Murakami's characters confront grievous loss, or sexuality, or the glow of a firefly, or the impossible distances between those who ought to be closest of all.

Fiction/Short Stories/978-1-4000-9608-4

KAFKA ON THE SHORE

This book is powered by two remarkable characters: a teenage boy, Kafka Tamura, who runs away from home—either to escape a gruesome oedipal prophecy or to search for his long-missing mother and sister—and an aging simpleton called Nakata, who never recovered from a wartime affliction and now is drawn toward Kafka for reasons that he cannot fathom. As their paths converge, Murakami enfolds readers in a world where cats talk, fish fall from the sky, and spirits slip out of their bodies to make love or commit murder.

Fiction/Literature/978-1-4000-7927-8

ALSO AVAILABLE

After the Quake, 978-0-375-71327-9

Dance Dance Dance, 978-0-679-75379-7

The Elephant Vanishes, 978-0-679-75053-6

Hard-Boiled Wonderland and the End of the World, 978-0-679-74346-0

Norwegian Wood, 978-0-375-70402-4

Sputnik Sweetheart, 978-0-375-72605-7

Underground, 978-0-375-72580-7

The Wind-Up Bird Chronicle, 978-0-679-77543-0

South of the Border, West of the Sun, 978-0-679-76739-8

Vintage Murakami, 978-1-4000-3396-6

VINTAGE INTERNATIONAL
Available at your local bookstore, or
visit www.randomhouse.com